SATAN'S LAST
FRAY

SEALIE WEST

ISBN
978-1-963254-66-2 (Paperback)
978-1-963254-67-9 (eBook)
978-1-963254-68-6 (Hardcover)

TABLE OF CONTENTS

As the thousand-year reign of peace comes to an end, evil is unleashed upon the world. Satan, long imprisoned, is released to deceive the nations, drawing them into a massive battle that threatens to destroy everything. The nations of Gog and Magog march across the earth like a vast tide, their numbers like sand on the seashore. They surround the city of God's people, intent on destruction.

But amidst this chaos, a hero emerges. A lone warrior, known only as "the Defender," stands against the armies of darkness. Clad in armor of shining silver and wielding a sword of pure light, he faces impossible odds with unshakable faith. As the enemy closes in, he fights with all his might, calling upon the power of heaven to aid him.

The battle rages on for days, with no clear victor in sight. The Defender fights with fierce determination, cutting down wave after wave of demonic foes. But as the sun sets on the final day of battle, it seems that all is lost. The enemy has breached the city walls, and the defenders are outnumbered and outmatched.

But then, just as all hope seems lost, fire rains down from heaven. The armies of darkness are consumed in a blaze of holy fire, leaving nothing but ash in their wake. And standing amidst the flames is the Defender, victorious at last.

As the smoke clears and the sun rises on a new day, the Defender stands alone amidst the ruins of the battlefield. His mission complete, he sheaths his sword and turns to face the rising sun. In that moment, he knows that his work is done, and he can rest easy knowing that evil has been vanquished.

And so it is that Satan is thrown into the lake of burning sulfur, where he will be tormented day and night for all eternity. The world is safe once more, thanks to the bravery and faith of one hero.

THE LUSH GARDEN
AND THE FORBIDDING TREE

In a lush garden, the serpent, the most cunning beast of the field, approaches a woman and questions her about God's commands. The woman responds that they may eat of any tree except the one in the middle of the garden, lest they die. The serpent manipulates the woman into eating the fruit from the forbidden tree by saying that she will become like God by doing so. She eats and shares the fruit with her husband, and suddenly they realize their nakedness and cover themselves with fig leaves.

As they hear the sound of the Lord God walking in the garden, they hide themselves among the trees. When God calls out to them, they admit to eating the forbidden fruit and are punished accordingly. The serpent is cursed to crawl on its belly and eat dust for all of its days. The woman is cursed with pain in childbirth and a desire to be contrary to her husband, who will nonetheless rule over her. The man is cursed with the need to labor hard for his food, as the ground is now cursed because of his disobedience.

God expels them from the garden of Eden, and they must work the ground from which they were taken for the rest of their lives. However, God shows mercy by clothing them in garments made of skins. Adam names his wife Eve, as she is the mother of all living.

The lush garden shimmered beneath the celestial light, a radiant masterpiece of creation. A rich tapestry of vibrant hues melded together, painting a breathtaking scene of verdant foliage and blossoming flora. The air was perfumed with the sweet scent of jasmine and honeysuckle, while melodious birdsong interwoven with the gentle rustling of leaves, composing a symphony that serenaded the heavens.

Amidst this serene oasis stood Eve, her long auburn hair cascading down her back like a silken waterfall, her hazel eyes reflecting the innocence and wonder of this divine sanctuary. Her every movement, graceful and fluid, seemed to be in perfect harmony with the garden's heartbeat.

"Adam," she called, her voice like the soft song of a lark, "I've found the most exquisite rosebush over here!"

Adam strode towards her, his tall, broad-shouldered frame exuding strength and determination. His dark brown hair framed his rugged visage, a testament to his role as protector and guardian of both Eve and their cherished garden.

"Show it to me, my love," he replied, a warmth glowing in his eyes as they met hers. Together, they marveled at the beauty of the rosebush, its resplendent petals appearing as if kissed by the sun itself.

As they tended to the garden, their devotion to each other and their shared labor of love were evident in every tender touch and affectionate glance exchanged between them. The weight of responsibility Adam bore in his heart was alleviated by the joy and tranquility they found within this haven, nurturing its fragile balance as one.

"Sometimes I feel as though my purpose extends beyond this garden," Eve whispered, her thoughts mingling with the caressing breeze as they rested under the shade of an ancient tree. "Do you ever ponder what lies outside these borders?"

"Indeed, I do," Adam replied, his voice tinged with a mix of curiosity and apprehension. "But our duty is here, tending to this paradise that God has entrusted to us."

"Of course," she agreed, her gaze wandering towards the horizon, where the boundaries of their world seemed to blend into the vast unknown.

"I am grateful for all that we have, and for the love we share in this divine sanctuary."

As they sat amidst the verdant splendor, basking in each other's presence, Eve and Adam were enveloped by the tranquil atmosphere of the garden. Their connection to this sacred realm was profound, as was their love for one another. And although the whispers of curiosity beckoned from beyond the garden's edge, they remained steadfast in their devotion, cherishing the serenity that bloomed within their hearts.

The sun cast golden rays upon the vibrant foliage of the garden, bathing it in heavenly light as Adam and Eve embarked on their daily tasks. They moved with grace, their hands working in tandem to cultivate the verdant Eden that had been entrusted to them. With every sweep of their fingers through the soil or gentle caress of a flower's petal, their love for this sacred realm was evident.

"Look, Adam," Eve said, her hazel eyes dancing with delight as she held up a plump, crimson strawberry. "This is the sweetest one yet! A gift from God, surely."

"Indeed," Adam replied, his broad shoulders shaking with laughter. "We are truly blessed to have such abundance at our fingertips."

As they worked side by side, their bodies entwined in a harmonious dance, the garden thrived under their tender ministrations. The air was filled with the heady scent of ripe fruits, mingling with the delicate perfume of blossoming flowers. Every corner of this lush haven was brimming with life, from the graceful gazelles that grazed on tender shoots to the vibrant plumage of birds that flitted among the branches overhead.

"Adam, do you ever marvel at the sheer diversity of creation?" Eve asked, her voice soft but filled with wonder as she gazed upon a flock of butterflies, their wings aglow in the warm sunlight.

"Every day, my love," he answered, his dark brown eyes reflecting the same awe that filled her heart. "And each time I am reminded of the power and wisdom of our Creator."

As they continued tending to the garden, their hands moving in perfect synchronicity, the couple reveled in the joy and contentment that filled their souls. Each new discovery– be it a cluster of fragrant roses or a hidden grove of fruit-laden trees– served as a testament to the boundless generosity of their divine benefactor.

"Adam," Eve whispered, her fingers tracing the delicate curve of a lily's petals. "I cannot fathom how we could ever repay God for this paradise He has bestowed upon us."

"Nor can I," Adam admitted, his voice tinged with humility. "Yet we must strive to be worthy of His trust, by nurturing and protecting this garden with all our might."

As they spoke, the air around them seemed to hum with a subtle energy, a reminder of the divine presence that watched over their every action. In that moment, Eve and Adam were united not only in their love for one another but in their unwavering commitment to fulfilling their sacred duty.

"Let us continue our work, then," Eve declared, her eyes shining with determination as she picked up her gardening tools. "Together, we shall ensure that this paradise remains an eternal testament to the glory of God."

And so, in the twilight of the thousand years of Satan's captivity, Adam and Eve worked tirelessly, hand in hand, within the bountiful garden. They knew not what awaited them beyond its borders, nor did they seek to defy the divine will that guided their every step. For theirs was a life of joy and contentment, cradled within the loving embrace of their Creator.

With the sun setting over the horizon, casting a warm golden glow on the garden, Eve and Adam paused in their work to marvel at the sight. The vibrant hues of the sky seemed to infuse the foliage around them with an ethereal beauty, creating a tableau that was both breathtaking and humbling.

"Look, my love," Eve whispered, her voice filled with awe as she pointed to a flock of birds soaring overhead, their wings catching the sunlight as they danced gracefully through the air. "Even the creatures of the sky rejoice in this divine gift."

Adam watched as his wife's face lit up in wonderment, her hazel eyes reflecting the tranquility and peace of the moment. He knew that there was no greater blessing than sharing this connection with her– a bond that went beyond mere physical touch, transcending into a spiritual union that resonated in harmony with the very rhythm of creation.

"Indeed," he replied softly, his hand reaching out to entwine with hers. "There is a serenity here that can only be found within the embrace of God's love."

As they stood together, basking in the hallowed silence of dusk, the air around them pulsed with the gentle heartbeat of life itself. A soft breeze rustled the leaves, whispering sacred secrets known only to the Creator and His beloved creations.

"Adam," Eve murmured, her thoughts turning to the commands handed down to them by their Heavenly Father. "I know that we are meant to obey God's word without question, but sometimes I cannot help but wonder what lies beyond our understanding."

"Trust in Him, my dearest one," Adam reassured her, his voice steady and filled with conviction. "He has given us this paradise to tend and cherish, and in return, we need only have faith in His wisdom and guidance."

"Of course," Eve nodded, her heart swelling with love for the man who stood by her side, steadfast in his devotion to both her and their divine purpose. "Together, we shall walk the path laid before us, hand in hand and with unwavering trust in our Creator."

"Indeed," Adam agreed, his own resolve strengthened by the depth of his wife's faith. "For it is through our obedience that we demonstrate our love for Him, and it is through His grace that we are granted a life of peace and joy within this sacred garden."

As the last rays of the sun dipped below the horizon, bathing the world in twilight, Eve and Adam turned back to their work, their hearts filled with the serenity that came from knowing they were fulfilling their divine duty.

"Let us continue our task, my love," Adam said as he picked up his tools once more. "For it is in our service to God that we find our true purpose."

And so, as the thousand years of Satan's captivity drew to a close, Eve and Adam pressed on, forging a legacy of unwavering trust and obedience to their Heavenly Father. Hand in hand, they walked the path laid before them, guided by the light of divine love and the promise of eternal peace.

With every tender touch, Eve and Adam nurtured the garden that had been entrusted to them. Their hands, though calloused from their labor, moved with delicate precision as they sowed seeds into the rich, fertile soil. The warmth of the sun kissed their skin as beads of perspiration formed, a testament to their diligent efforts.

"Adam, my love, can you bring me more water for these saplings?" Eve called out, her voice lilting like a melody carried on the breeze.

"Of course, my dear," he replied, his voice strong yet gentle, as he fetched a clay jug filled with cool, crystal-clear water. He strode across the lush grass, careful not to disturb the vibrant blooms that adorned their path.

As the water flowed from the mouth of the jug, soaking into the earth and quenching the thirst of the newly planted trees, Eve couldn't help but smile at the harmony they shared. Together, they were the caretakers of this magnificent haven, where life flourished under their attentive gaze.

"Look, Eve," Adam said softly, his eyes alight with wonder. "The pomegranate tree is laden with ripe fruit, ready to be picked."

"Indeed," she replied in awe, her hazel eyes shining with excitement. "Let us gather them and thank our Creator for this bountiful harvest."

As they plucked the ruby-red orbs, their fingers brushing against the velvety skin of the fruit, the garden seemed to come alive around them. Birds sang sweet symphonies amidst the foliage, their melodies interwoven with the gentle rustling of leaves and the distant murmur of flowing water. The air was perfumed with the heady fragrance of blossoming flowers, mingling with the earthy scent of damp soil and the tangy aroma of ripe fruit.

"Adam," Eve whispered, pausing for a moment to inhale deeply, her chest swelling with the life-giving breath. "Do you feel it? The very essence of the garden coursing through our veins, connecting us to everything around us?"

He looked at her, his dark brown eyes reflecting her wonderment, and nodded. "Yes, my love. Our Creator has blessed us with this paradise, and we are forever entwined with its beauty and splendor."

In that moment, as they stood surrounded by the lush abundance of their Eden, Eve and Adam knew they were fulfilling their divine purpose—to tend to this sacred space with unwavering devotion and love. And so, with every seed sown and fruit gathered, they offered silent prayers of gratitude, their hearts brimming with reverence for their Heavenly Father.

"Let us never forget the gift we have been given, nor the responsibility that comes with it," Eve murmured, her voice barely audible above the symphony of nature.

"Never," Adam vowed, his hand gripping hers with steadfast determination. "Together, we shall continue to care for this garden, honoring our Creator and the life He has entrusted to our keeping."

And so, beneath the watchful gaze of Heaven, Eve and Adam carried on, tending to the garden that was both their sanctuary and their divine duty, even as the shadows of prophecy began to stretch across the land.

The sun began its descent, casting golden rays through the verdant canopy above. Eve and Adam paused in their labor, sensing the shift in the day's rhythm. They sought respite beneath a towering tree whose branches drooped with the weight of ripe fruits. The air around them hummed with the gentle rustling of leaves, the soft chirping of birds, and the faint murmurs of a nearby stream.

"Come, my love," said Eve, her hazel eyes twinkling with mischief. "Let us rest and find joy in each other's company."

Adam, his face lined with sweat and dirt from the day's work, smiled at his wife's invitation. With a nod, he followed her to the water's edge, where they settled on the cool grass.

As they reclined together, Eve plucked a blade of grass from the ground and held it aloft, watching as it danced in the breeze. A smile played upon her lips as she turned to Adam, her eyes alight with curiosity.

"Have you ever wondered," she asked, "if the wind carries secrets from faraway lands? Perhaps whispers of what lies beyond our garden?"

Adam considered her words, his dark brows furrowing in thought. "Perhaps," he replied, reaching out to take her hand. "But I believe the wind also sings the songs of the earth, telling tales of creation and the beauty that surrounds us."

Eve laughed, her voice like the tinkling of a crystal brook. "You always see the world through such beautiful lenses, my love." She leaned closer, resting her head against his chest and listening to the steady beat of his heart.

"Life is but a wondrous melody, dearest Eve," Adam whispered, his fingers tracing lazy patterns on her arm. "And we are blessed to be part of it."

As the sun dipped below the horizon, casting brilliant hues across the sky, Eve and Adam lay entwined in each other's arms, their laughter mingling with the melodies of the garden. And though shadows loomed on the fringes of prophecy, for now, they reveled in the solace and joy found within their Edenic sanctuary.

In the dawning light, tendrils of mist curled around the lush foliage as Eve and Adam rose to greet the new day. With every step they took, the dew-kissed grass bowed beneath their feet, leaving a trail of darkened green in their wake. The air was heavy with the scent of damp earth and the vibrant aroma of blossoming flowers, as if the garden itself breathed a silent hymn of praise.

"Adam," Eve whispered, her voice filled with reverence, "do you feel it? God's presence is unmistakable today."

He paused, his gaze drifting skyward as he allowed the divine essence to wash over him. "Yes, dearest. I sense His love in every corner of the garden– in the gentle caress of the breeze, the song of the birds, and the vibrant colors that paint our world."

Together, they moved through their daily tasks, the invisible hand of the Almighty guiding them as they tended to the life that flourished under their care. They felt both humbled and awestruck by the magnitude of their responsibility, knowing that their actions shaped the destiny of this sacred sanctuary.

"Look, Eve," Adam said, pointing to a delicate sapling that had recently sprouted from the ground. "It seems God has blessed us with a new addition to our garden."

Eve's hazel eyes sparkled with wonder as she knelt beside the young tree, her fingers tracing its tender leaves. "How remarkable," she marveled. "To think that from such small beginnings, great beauty can arise."

"Indeed," Adam agreed, his heart swelling with gratitude for the life they shared. "It is a testament to the power of creation and the boundless love of our Creator."

As the day wore on, the sun climbed higher in the sky, casting golden beams of light through the canopy of leaves above. In the quiet moments between their labor, Eve and Adam would pause to offer silent prayers of thanksgiving, acutely aware of the divine presence that infused every aspect of their existence.

"Adam," Eve murmured, her eyes taking in the vast expanse of their garden, "how fortunate we are to have been chosen for this task– to be the caretakers of such a paradise."

"Indeed," he replied, his voice heavy with emotion. "And let us never forget the source of our blessings, nor the love and guidance that sustains us."

As twilight descended upon the garden, painting the sky in hues of lavender and rose, Eve and Adam stood hand in hand, their hearts filled with reverence for their Creator. The world around them hummed with life, a symphony of harmony and peace that mirrored the tranquility within their souls.

"May we always remember this moment," Eve whispered, her fingers entwined with Adam's. "The love that binds us, and the grace that surrounds us."

"Forever, my love," Adam vowed, pressing a tender kiss to her brow In that sacred space, as darkness gave way to the brilliance of a thousand stars, the knowledge of God's love envelope them like a warm embrace, anchoring their hearts to the eternal truth that bound them together. And though unseen forces stirred in the shadows, awaiting the moment to strike, for now, Eve and Adam found solace in the serenity of their garden, trusting in the divine wisdom that guided their every step.

The thousand years is imminent, has Satan scape?!
A hero emerges out of the dust of war and chaos
To take on Satan as he roams the universe
Is humanity ready for the chaos and
Destruction against God's people
Against humanity, against civilization
Chaos! Chaos!
is about to be unleashed?!
Are you ready?!
You Haven't seen nothing yet!

II

THE KINGDOM OF ELYRIA

The kingdom of Elyria stretched out before Lucian Valarian like a verdant tapestry, its idyllic landscapes woven together by sunlight and shadow. Rolling hills undulated like gentle waves, their green crests adorned with patches of wildflowers that swayed in the breeze. Majestic forests stood tall and proud, their lush canopies creating dappled patterns on the forest floor below, while crystalline rivers meandered through the valleys, their melodious murmurs echoing throughout the land.

Amidst this serenity, the people of Elyria went about their daily lives, tending to crop and livestock, and exchanging pleasantries as they passed one another on the cobblestone streets. It was a simple, peaceful existence, untouched by the turmoil and strife that plagued the world beyond their borders.

As Lucian walked through the village square, he couldn't help but notice a hushed conversation between two villagers. Their furrowed brows and anxious glances piqued his curiosity, drawing him closer to eavesdrop.

"Have you heard the whispers?" the first villager asked, her voice barely audible above the rustling leaves.

"About the prophecy?" the second villager replied, his eyes darting around nervously. "Aye, I've heard them. They say darkness is coming, that it will consume everything in its path."

"An ancient battle, they say," the first villager added, her voice trembling with fear. "Between light and darkness, good and evil. And our peaceful kingdom is caught in the middle, helpless against the tide."

Lucian's heart raced at the mention of the prophecy, though he tried to keep his expression neutral. He had always been fascinated by tales of divine battles and heroic deeds, but these were just stories, mere fables meant to entertain and inspire. Surely, the Elyria were safe within their tranquil haven, far from the grasp of any malevolent force.

In the peaceful kingdom of Illyria, Lucian is a curious young man who has always been fascinated by tales of divine battles and heroic deeds. However, he never believed that these stories could be anything more than mere fables meant to entertain and inspire. That is until he hears the prophecy of an ancient battle between light and darkness, good and evil.

Lucian's heart races at the mention of the prophecy, but he tries to keep his expression neutral. He is convinced that the Illyrians are safe within their tranquil haven, far from the grasp of any malevolent force. However, as days pass, Lucian realizes that something is amiss. Strange occurrences begin to happen in the kingdom, and people start to act out of character.

As tensions rise, Lucian discovers that the prophecy was not just a tale after all. The kingdom is caught in the middle of a battle between light and darkness, and they are helpless against the tide. The inciting incident comes when Lucian is chosen by fate to lead the fight against the malevolent force that threatens to destroy everything he holds dear.

The conflict rises as Lucian struggles to come to terms with his new role as a leader. He must navigate treacherous waters as he tries to rally his people and prepare them for battle. The cause-and-effect of this conflict is strong, as every decision he makes has dire consequences for himself and those around him.

As the battle rages on, Lucian must confront his own fears and doubts if he hopes to emerge victorious. The climactic scenes are full of tension and drama as the fate of the kingdom hangs in the balance.

The peaceful kingdom of Illyria lay bathed in the golden light of the setting sun, painting its idyllic beauty and harmony with warm hues. Lush landscapes stretched as far as the eye could see- verdant meadows kissed by gentle breezes, sparkling rivers winding their way through the valleys, and thick forests standing proudly on the horizon. The air was filled with laughter and cheerful chatter of happy people going about their daily lives, their faces glowing with contentment.

In the midst of this utopian world stood Lord Lucian, a middle-aged man in his early 40s with short dark hair and piercing blue eyes that seemed to see right through people. Clad in simple yet elegant garments, he moved gracefully among the bustling crowds, observing the lively scene unfolding before him.

"Lucian!" a voice called out, drawing his attention momentarily away from the enchanting tableau.

"Ah, good day, Master Thomas," Lucian replied, greeting the elderly merchant with a warm smile as he approached. "How fares your trade?"

"Never been better, my boy," the old man beamed, patting Lucian's shoulder affectionately. "Your wise counsel has indeed brought prosperity to our humble market!"

As Lord Lucian exchanged pleasantries with the merchant, his sharp mind couldn't help but take note of the intricate details surrounding him. He observed the intertwining fingers of young lovers nearby, the carefree laughter of children chasing butterflies, and the satisfied sigh of a farmer who had just made a successful sale. Albeit overwhelmed by the symphony of life playing around him, Lucian's heart swelled with pride for his beloved kingdom.

"Always a pleasure, Master Thomas," Lucian said, parting ways with the merchant. As he continued his journey through the thriving marketplace, his thoughts turned inward, contemplating the significance of the tales he had been hearing lately– stories of divine battles and ancient prophecies involving the end of the thousand years of captivity of Satan. His curiosity piqued, Lucian wondered if there was any truth to these legends or if they were merely fanciful tales crafted for the entertainment of the masses.

"Can such things truly come to pass?" he mused quietly to himself, his piercing gaze scanning the faces of those around him. "Could this tranquil world ever be shaken by such darkness?"

As he pondered these questions, Lucian's eyes unconsciously flickered towards the heavens, searching for answers among the celestial bodies that decorated the sky. The sun dipped lower in the horizon, casting long shadows that seemed to stretch out like ominous fingers, foretelling the impending arrival of night.

"Perhaps," he whispered, "it is wise to remain vigilant, even in times of peace."

And with a determined glint in his sapphire eyes, Lucian Everbright continued on his way, his heart aching with both love and concern for the enchanting kingdom of Illyria, unaware of the strange occurrences that would soon disrupt its tranquility.

The fading sunlight cast a warm, golden glow over the cobbled streets of Illyria. A soft breeze rustled through the leaves of the ancient trees, their branches reaching out to one another like lovers entwined in a tender embrace. The laughter and chatter of townspeople filled the air, creating a symphony as harmonious as the songbirds that flitted amongst the fragrant blossoms.

It was within this idyllic setting that Lucian Everbright found himself, his lean figure leaning against the trunk of a majestic oak, its gnarled roots providing an impromptu seat for the young man. Friends and acquaintances gathered around him, their faces animated with excitement as they shared tales of divine battles and heroic deeds.

"…and so it was that the archangel descended upon the battlefield, his sword blazing with heavenly fire!" cried the storyteller, his voice captivating the rapt audience. Every word that flowed from his lips seemed to be imbued with passion and excitement, transporting them to the very heart of the epic struggles between good and evil.

"His wings spread wide, casting an otherworldly radiance across the war-torn land," he continued, his arms gesturing wildly as if attempting to encompass the magnitude of the celestial being's presence. "With a mighty cry, he smote the dark horde, banishing them back to the depths from whence they came!"

A hushed silence fell upon the assembly as the storyteller paused, allowing the vivid images he had painted to settle in their minds. Murmurs of admiration and disbelief rippled through the crowd, the tension palpable as all awaited the conclusion of the tale.

"Tell us more!" urged a young woman, her eyes wide with wonder. "What happened to the archangel after the battle?"

"Ah, that is a story for another time," the storyteller replied, a knowing smile playing upon his lips. "For now, let us revel in the triumph of good over evil, and remember that even in our darkest hour, there is always hope."

As the storyteller's words echoed in his mind, Lucian found himself torn between fascination and skepticism. The tales were undeniably enthralling, but he could not help but question their authenticity. Were these accounts of divine intervention truly prophetic, or merely cleverly crafted fables meant to entertain?

"Believe what you will," Lucian thought, his eyes narrowing as he studied the faces of those around him. "But it would be foolish to dismiss these legends without further investigation."

As the gathering slowly dispersed, leaving Lucian alone with his thoughts, a sudden chill swept through the air, carrying with it an ominous whisper that seemed to echo the young man's fears for the future.

"Be vigilant, Lucian Everbright," the wind seemed to murmur. "For dark days are indeed approaching, and only the steadfast heart can weather the storm."

The storyteller's voice swelled with the intensity of a gathering storm, evoking images of thundering hooves and clashing steel. "And there, upon the scorched battlefield, stood the Archangel Michael, his golden armor gleaming like the sun itself! In his right hand, he wielded a flaming sword, its blade forged from the very fires of Heaven!"

Lucian leaned forward, his piercing blue eyes locked onto the storyteller, absorbing every word as if they were precious gems. The tales of divine battles and heroic deeds had always stirred something deep within him– a restless longing for adventure and purpose beyond the peaceful borders of Illyria.

"Beside the Archangel stood the warriors of light, their radiant armor reflecting the brilliance of their leader," the storyteller continued. "Each one bore a weapon crafted by celestial hands– swords that could cleave through the darkest of shadows, spears that could pierce the heart of evil itself!"

The listeners' eyes widened in awe as the story unfolded before them, the vivid descriptions painting a breathtaking scene of grandeur and power. Lucian, too, was captivated by the imagery, but it was not mere wonder that held his attention; it was the spark of curiosity that danced in his mind, urging him to question, to analyze, to seek the truth behind the legends.

"Wave after wave of demonic hordes charged at the heavenly host, their twisted forms a stark contrast to the shining warriors," the storyteller intoned. "Yet, despite their monstrous visages and seemingly endless numbers, the forces of darkness could not withstand the righteous might of the Archangel and his celestial soldiers!"

Lucian's fingers drummed against his thigh as the battle raged on in the storyteller's words. His gaze never wavered from the animated figure before him, his entire being focused on the tale that seemed to resonate with his very soul. But as the story reached its climax, Lucian couldn't help but question the authenticity of these tales. Perhaps they were simply meant to inspire hope in the hearts of those who heard them.

"Finally, with one mighty swing of his flaming sword, the Archangel Michael banished the leader of the demonic horde back into the abyss!" The storyteller's voice rang out triumphantly, drawing gasps and murmurs of amazement from the enthralled audience. "And thus, the forces of good emerged victorious, casting the shadow of evil back into the depths from whence it came."

As the tale drew to a close, Lucian found himself caught between fascination and skepticism. Could such divine battles truly have taken place? Or were they nothing more than skillfully woven stories meant to entertain and inspire? For now, he chose to ponder these questions in silence, his heart racing at the mention of the prophecy, while his expression remained carefully neutral. Only time would tell if the answers he sought would be revealed.

The sun dipped low in the sky, casting a warm golden glow over the gathered crowd as the storyteller's words continued to enthrall them. The scent of freshly baked bread wafted through the air, mingling with the earthy aroma of the surrounding countryside. Lucian listened intently, his piercing blue eyes never leaving the animated face of the storyteller.

"...and as the final battle raged on, the heavens above seemed to crack open, pouring forth a torrential deluge that doused the fires of hell," the storyteller recounted passionately, his voice rising and falling with the rhythm of the tale.

As the story unfolded, Lucian found himself questioning the authenticity of these accounts. Were they real events or mere fabrications designed to entertain and inspire hope? He leaned in closer, arching a brow as he interjected, "These tales are truly fascinating, but have you ever considered the possibility that they are simply allegorical in nature? Perhaps intended to provide moral guidance rather than describe actual events?"

The storyteller paused, taken aback by Lucian's inquiry, then chuckled warmly. "Ah, young man, I can see that your mind is sharp and inquisitive. It is true that some may interpret these stories as symbolic, but many believe them to be genuine accounts of battles between good and evil."

Lucian nodded thoughtfully; his skepticism not entirely quashed but intrigued by the prospect of further analyzing the tales. As the storyteller resumed his narrative, Lucian's thoughts raced, searching for inconsistencies or logical explanations behind the supernatural events depicted in the stories.

"Then the Archangel Gabriel sounded his horn, and the very ground shook beneath the feet of the demonic hordes, swallowing them up into the abyss!" the storyteller declared, his voice resonating with authority.

"Could it not be possible that such an event was caused by a natural phenomenon, such as an earthquake?" Lucian mused quietly, more to himself than anyone else. "After all, our world is subject to various geological forces that could trigger such a cataclysm."

"Ah, but the timing of the event coincides perfectly with the prophecy," countered a woman standing nearby, her eyes wide with fervor. "Surely that cannot be mere coincidence?"

"Perhaps not," Lucian conceded, his thirst for knowledge and understanding driving him to explore every angle of the stories. His logical and rational nature demanded that he not accept these tales at face value, even as his heart ached for the possibility of something greater than the mundane world he knew.

As the crowd dispersed, shadows lengthening in the fading light, Lucian remained lost in thought, the seed of curiosity planted firmly within him. He could not have known that this day would mark the beginning of a journey that would change not only his life, but the fate of his beloved kingdom of Illyria as well. The end of days was approaching and, unbeknownst to him, Lucian Everbright would play a crucial role in the final battle between good and evil.

The warm glow of the setting sun cast long shadows across the courtyard as Lucian stood apart from the dispersing crowd, his thoughts a swirling maelstrom of intrigue and skepticism. His hands dug into the pockets of his simple tunic, fingers clenching and unclenching as he turned the tales over in his mind.

"Those stories… they couldn't possibly be true," Lucian whispered to himself, feeling the intensity of his heartbeat match the quickening pace of his thoughts. "But then again, there has always been something alluring about them…"

His piercing blue eyes darted around the now-empty courtyard, as if seeking some hidden truth among the stones beneath his feet. He could still hear the storyteller's fervent voice echoing through his mind, painting vivid images of divine battles and prophecies foretold. It was an intoxicating blend of wonder and fear that had captured the hearts of so many before him.

"Lucian!" called out a familiar voice, breaking through his reverie. It was his friend, Elias, who approached with a smile. "What's got you so deep in thought? You look like you've seen a ghost."

"Ah, it's nothing, really," Lucian replied, forcing a casual smile as he tried to shrug off his internal conflict. "Just pondering those stories we heard earlier. You know me, always trying to find the logic behind everything."

Elias laughed, playfully nudging his shoulder. "Well, don't think too hard. They're just stories, after all. Meant to entertain and keep us on our toes."

"Right, just stories," Lucian echoed, though he couldn't shake the nagging sensation that there was more to them than mere entertainment value.

As the two friends walked away from the courtyard, Lucian's heart continued to race, fueled by the mention of the prophecy- the end of days. Though his expression remained neutral, a storm brewed within him; a battle between logic and deep-rooted fascination.

"Remember," Elias said, seeing the distant look in Lucian's eyes, "there's no need to let those tales consume you. It's just as important to enjoy life and appreciate the beauty around us."

Lucian nodded, trying to heed his friend's advice and turn his attention to the peaceful kingdom that surrounded them. But as they walked through the idyllic streets of Illyria, the whisperings of prophecies and divine battles continued to haunt him, refusing to be silenced. And with each step he took, the shadows of doubt and curiosity grew longer, reaching out like tendrils to grasp hold of his restless heart.

As Lucian and Elias continued their stroll through the sun-kissed streets of Illyria, a sudden gust of wind swept across the kingdom, stirring the leaves on the ground and sending an inexplicable shiver down Lucian's spine. He glanced around, noticing how the once-vibrant colors of the landscape now seemed muted and shadowed, as if a thin veil had been drawn over reality.

"Did you feel that?" he asked Elias, trying to shake off the eerie sensation.

"Feel what?" Elias replied, his eyes scanning their surroundings with a puzzled expression. "The wind?"

"No," Lucian said, his voice lowering to a hushed tone. "Something... different. A sense of change in the air."

"Change?" Elias chuckled uneasily, attempting to dismiss his friend's concerns. "Lucian, you're letting those stories get to your head."

"Perhaps," Lucian conceded, but his piercing blue eyes remained locked on the horizon, where dark clouds began to gather like an ominous portent.

As they turned into the bustling marketplace, Lucian couldn't help but notice the uneasy glances exchanged between the townspeople, as if they too sensed the impending disruption to their peaceful lives. Though they carried on with their daily routines, there was a palpable tension that seemed to have settled over the entire kingdom.

"Come, let's find something to eat," Elias suggested, trying to lighten the mood. "Maybe a good meal will chase away those ominous thoughts."

"Maybe," Lucian agreed, but despite his attempts to focus on the present moment, his mind refused to let go of the nagging sense of foreboding that had taken root within him.

As they sat down at a small wooden table near the center of the marketplace, Lucian's gaze was drawn to a cloaked figure standing in the shadows, barely visible among the throngs of people. He felt an inexplicable pull toward the stranger, as though a secret truth lay hidden beneath the layers of concealing fabric.

"Lucian," Elias called out, trying to get his friend's attention. "Are you alright? You seem... distant."

"Sorry," Lucian muttered, forcing himself to look away from the mysterious figure. "I'm just not feeling like myself today."

"Let's enjoy this meal and then head home," Elias suggested, placing a comforting hand on Lucian's shoulder. "You could use some rest."

"Rest," Lucian murmured, but even as he picked up his fork, he knew that sleep would bring him no solace. The seeds of doubt had been planted, and his once-sturdy wall of skepticism had begun to crumble.

As they finished their meal and prepared to leave, Lucian couldn't resist one last glance at the spot where the cloaked figure had stood. To his surprise, the stranger was gone, vanished without a trace. In its place, a single black feather lay on the ground, gleaming ominously in the fading light.

"Strange…" Lucian whispered, his heart pounding with a mix of fear and anticipation. And as he turned to follow Elias back home, he knew that the tranquility of Illyria was about to be shattered– and there would be no turning back.

"Who will stand against this darkness?" the second villager asked, his voice barely more than a whisper. "Is there anyone brave enough to fight for the light?"

The first villager shook her head sadly. "I don't know. All I know is that our world is changing, and we must be prepared for whatever comes."

As Lucian continued on his way, the villagers' words resonated within him, filling his chest with an unfamiliar mixture of dread and determination. He could not ignore the sense of urgency that gripped his heart, nor could he shake the feeling that somehow, this prophecy was connected to him. The weight of destiny settled upon his broad shoulders, and in that moment, Lucian Valarian, the Defender, began his journey towards the battle between light and darkness.

As Lucian walked through the village, he noticed an uneasiness in the air that seemed to infect those around him. Mothers clutched their children a little tighter as they hurried past, and the usual friendly chatter among neighbors had been reduced to hushed whispers. The once vibrant marketplace now seemed a place of shadows, with merchants hurriedly packing up their wares as if expecting some unseen danger to descend upon them at any moment.

"Have you heard the news?" a woman asked her neighbor, her voice barely audible. "They say the prophecy is coming true."

"Surely it can't be," the other replied, his eyes darting nervously about. "We've lived in peace for so long… What could possibly threaten our tranquil lives?"

"Darkness, my friend," the woman whispered, her eyes filled with fear. "A darkness so deep and terrible that it threatens to swallow us all."

As Lucian continued down the path, he couldn't help but feel the weight of their words pressing down on him, like a heavy cloak that threatened to suffocate him. His thoughts raced, searching for answers or reassurance, but finding none.

That evening, a gathering of scholars and religious leaders was called at the Temple of Light, a magnificent structure that towered above the village, its golden spire reaching towards the heavens. The urgency in their voices echoed throughout the marble halls, betraying their concern.

"Brothers and sisters," began the high priest, his voice heavy with somber gravity. "We have convened here tonight to discuss a matter of utmost importance. The prophecy we have long studied and revered seems to be unfolding before our very eyes."

"Can it truly be?" questioned a scholar, his hands trembling as they held an ancient scroll. "After all these years of peace, are we truly destined for such darkness?"

"Unfortunately, it seems so," replied another, his voice strained. "The signs are all around us. The uneasy winds, the troubled skies—they all foretell of a great battle between light and darkness that is fast approaching."

"Then we must prepare," declared the high priest, determination etched upon his face. "We must find a way to protect our people from the encroaching evil and ensure the survival of our kingdom."

As Lucian stood in the shadows outside the temple, he could not help but be drawn in by their words. He felt a newfound sense of responsibility welling up within him, as if some guiding force was urging him forward. And though fear gnawed at the edges of his heart, it was overshadowed by a burning desire to defend Elyria and its people from the gathering storm.

"Let us pray for guidance," intoned the high priest, as the assembled scholars and religious leaders bowed their heads in solemn supplication. "May the gods grant us the wisdom to navigate this dark path and emerge victorious on the other side."

In the quiet of the temple, with the weight of prophecy hanging heavy in the air, Lucian Valorian knew that his life would never be the same.

An epic battle loomed on the horizon, and he had been chosen by fate to stand against the darkness.

The high priest unfurled an ancient scroll with trembling hands, its parchment yellowed and frayed at the edges. The scholars and religious leaders gathered around, their faces bathed in the dim glow of flickering candlelight. Lucian, hidden behind a pillar, strained to hear every word.

"Here," the high priest began, his voice barely above a whisper, "is the prophecy that foretells the rise of the Defender and the battle that shall determine the fate of our world." He read the words aloud, his tone grave as he traced the lines of faded ink:

"From the light a hero rises,
Bringer of hope in darkest times;
His sacred sword the darkness smites,
Defender of Elyria's light.
"Against him stands the Destroyer,
Fearsome leader of Gog and Magog;
Blood and fire mark his path,
His conquest fueled by boundless wrath.
"Two armies clash on hallowed ground,
Their cries of war a deafening sound;
The victor rules o'er all creation,
The vanquished fall to devastation."

As the last word echoed through the hushed chamber, the scholars and religious leaders exchanged uneasy glances. Hope and fear mingled in their eyes, as though they dared not believe the prophecy's promise of salvation, yet could not ignore its warning of destruction.

"Could it be true?" whispered a young acolyte, his face pale and drawn. "Is there really one among us who can stand against the Destroyer and his armies?"

"Perhaps," replied a wizened scholar, stroking his long gray beard. "But prophecies are fickle things, and we must not place all our faith in the coming of a savior. We must also prepare ourselves for the possibility of failure."

"Indeed," agreed another, her eyes narrowing in thought. "We should not be idle in the face of the impending darkness. We must strengthen our defenses and gather allies, even as we search for the one who will bear the title of Defender."

"Then it is settled," declared the high priest, his voice resolute. "We shall not cower in fear, nor shirk our responsibility to protect our people. We shall face the coming storm with courage and faith, for it is written that the light shall always triumph over the darkness."

Lucian's heart pounded in his chest as he listened, the prophecy's words resonating with a force that shook him to his core. He could not deny the sense of destiny that pulsed through his veins, calling him to embrace the mantle of the Defender.

And so, as the scholars and religious leaders dispersed to prepare for the battle ahead, Lucian Valorian stepped from the shadows, his eyes alight with determination and purpose. He knew that his time had come– and he would not shrink from the immense task set before him.

The sun hung low in the sky, casting an orange glow over the cobblestone streets of Elyria as Lucian Valorian made his way through the bustling marketplace. The scent of freshly baked bread and ripe fruit mingled with the murmur of haggling merchants and laughing children. Though the kingdom was preparing for a battle against darkness, life continued its usual course, and the people seemed determined to cling to normalcy.

Lucian could not help but feel a sense of unease as he passed by a group of scholars deep in animated conversation. He caught snippets of their discussion– whispers of prophecy, fate, and a coming storm that would shake the world to its very foundations.

"Come, Lucian," murmured an aged voice, beckoning him toward the entrance of a dimly-lit alleyway. The old sage, Orin, stood tall despite the weight of his years, his piercing green eyes filled with wisdom and understanding.

"Orin, what do you know of this prophecy?" Lucian asked, his curiosity piqued.

"Ah, my boy," the wise man replied, his voice heavy with the weight of knowledge. "I have studied it for many years, and I believe that we are on the cusp of its fulfillment."

"Tell me more," Lucian implored, his heart pounding in anticipation.

"Very well," Orin agreed, pausing for a moment before he began. "It speaks of a great battle between light and darkness, one that will test the mettle of all who dwell upon this earth. A champion will rise to vanquish evil, bearing the title of the Defender. But he must be found and prepared for the trials that await him."

"Can such a person truly exist?" Lucian wondered aloud, his mind racing with the implications of the prophecy.

"Indeed," Orin confirmed, his gaze locking onto Lucian's. "I believe that you, my boy, are destined to become the Defender."

"Me?" Lucian stammered, the weight of the revelation settling heavily upon him.

"Your heart has always been pure, and your skill in battle is unmatched," Orin continued, his voice filled with conviction. "You have the potential to become the light that drives back the shadows, but it will not be an easy path."

"Wh-what must I do?" Lucian asked, struggling to come to terms with the enormity of his newfound destiny.

"Trust in yourself, and in the power of good," Orin advised, placing a reassuring hand on Lucian's shoulder. "Embrace the mantle of the Defender, and let your light guide you through the darkness that lies ahead."

As Lucian looked into the old sage's eyes, he felt a sudden surge of determination. He would rise to the challenge, no matter how insurmountable it seemed, for the fate of Elyria– and the world– now rested upon his shoulders.

The sun dipped below the horizon, casting a warm golden glow over Elyria. Lucian stood alone atop a hill overlooking the peaceful kingdom, his mind consumed by the weight of his newfound destiny. In the distance, he could see the villagers returning to their homes, unaware of the darkness that loomed on the horizon. As the last rays of sunlight faded, an eerie calm enveloped the land– a deceptive tranquility that masked the gathering storm.

"Is it truly possible?" Lucian whispered to himself, his voice barely audible against the gentle rustle of leaves. "Can I be the one to stand against the darkness?"

"Only you can answer that question," came a familiar voice from behind him. Lucian turned to find Orin, who approached with slow, measured steps. The old sage's eyes held a mixture of hope and concern, reflecting the gravity of their situation.

"Then I must find the courage within myself," Lucian declared, his voice growing more resolute. "I cannot let fear dictate my path."

"Indeed," Orin agreed, nodding solemnly. "But remember, even the greatest heroes have moments of doubt. It is how they confront those doubts that defines them."

As the two men spoke, an unsettling chill crept through the air, making the hairs on the back of Lucian's neck stand on end. He glanced around, searching for the source of his unease. "Do you sense it as well?" he asked Orin, his voice tinged with apprehension.

"Something is coming," Orin confirmed, his gaze fixed on the darkening sky. "A storm like no other, born of malice and hatred."

"Valthor," Lucian muttered, his grip tightening on his sword hilt. Images of the fearsome warrior filled his mind– the ruthless leader of darkness who sought to conquer all in his path. If the prophecy was true, their fates were now inexorably linked.

"Face him you must, but not alone," Orin reassured. "There are others who will stand by your side in this battle."

"Then let us find them," Lucian urged, his voice steady and determined. "The time for preparation is over; we must act, or all is lost."

"Patience, my boy," Orin cautioned. "A great warrior knows when to strike, and when to wait."

"Waiting will not save Elyria," Lucian countered, a note of frustration seeping into his words. "Every day that passes brings us closer to the abyss."

"Indeed," Orin conceded. "But the path before you is treacherous and filled with unknown perils. You must be prepared, both in body and mind, for the trials that await."

As the two men stood on the hill, a sudden gust of wind whipped around them, carrying an ominous, guttural roar that echoed through the night. The tranquility of Elyria shattered in an instant, replaced by a palpable sense of dread.

"What was that?" Lucian gasped, his eyes widening with terror.

"An omen," Orin replied, his voice barely above a whisper. "The armies of darkness have begun their march, and soon they will be upon us."

Lucian's heart pounded in his chest as the reality of their situation came crashing down. The time for doubt had passed– he was the Defender, and the fate of the world now rested in his hands. As the shadows closed in around him, he steeled himself for the battle ahead, knowing that the road would be long and fraught with danger. But he could not– would not– let fear hold him back.

For Elyria. For the world. For the light.

With the sun's first light painting the horizon a brilliant gold, Lucian Valorian stood at the edge of a cliff overlooking the kingdom of Elyria. The land stretched before him like a tapestry woven from the finest silk, each thread a testament to the beauty and tranquility that defined this realm. Verdant fields rolled out in all directions, their lushness interrupted only by crystalline rivers that shimmered like liquid silver. Beyond them, the majestic mountains stood sentinel, their peaks crowned with snow that gleamed like living diamonds.

"Such splendor," Lucian murmured, his eyes taking in the scene below. A sense of calm washed over him, soothing the anxiety that had plagued him since the ominous roar had echoed through the night. For a fleeting moment, he could almost forget the darkness that threatened to consume this paradise.

"Enjoy it while you can," a voice spoke from behind him, shattering the illusion. Lucian turned to find Orin standing beside him, his wise old eyes tinged with sadness. "This peace may not last much longer."

As Lucian gazed upon the tranquil landscape, he could not help but feel the weight of responsibility settle upon his shoulders. He knew what lay ahead– a battle between light and darkness, the outcome of which would determine the fate of all. And he, Lucian Valorian, was the Defender, chosen to lead the charge against Valthor Malgath and his armies of Gog and Magog.

"Tell me, Orin," Lucian began, his voice steady despite the fear that gnawed at his heart, "how does one prepare for such a task? How can I, a mere mortal, hope to stand against the tide of darkness that threatens to drown our world?"

"By embracing your destiny," the sage replied with quiet conviction, "and trusting in the power of the light within you."

"Is that enough?" Lucian's voice trembled, his inner doubts clawing their way to the surface.

"Only time will tell," Orin said cryptically, his gaze fixed upon the horizon. "But you must believe in yourself, Lucian. It is our belief in the light that fuels its power."

As they stood together on the precipice, the once serene skies darkened with foreboding clouds that gathered like vultures circling their prey. A chill wind rustled the leaves of the nearby trees, whispering sinister secrets as it passed. The shadows grew long and deep, stretching out across the land like grasping fingers, reaching for the heart of Elyria.

"Can you feel it?" Orin asked, his voice barely audible above the howling wind. "The darkness approaches, and with it, the beginning of the end."

Lucian closed his eyes, searching within himself for the strength he would need to face the coming storm. The tranquility of Elyria was nothing but a fleeting memory now, replaced by a sense of urgency that set his every nerve alight. He knew what must be done– the battle between light and darkness was inevitable, and he was the only one who could stand against the encroaching shadows.

"Then let them come," Lucian declared, steeling himself for the trials ahead. "For I am the Defender, and I shall not falter in the face of darkness."

"May the light guide your path, Lucian Valorian," Orin intoned solemnly, his words carried away by the relentless wind. "For the fate of Elyria, and all the world, now rests upon your shoulders."

III

LUCIAN "THE DEFENDER"

The sun rose over the horizon, casting its golden light upon the outskirts of Elyria, where a small village lay nestled between rolling hills and lush forests. Amidst the humble wooden cottages, one man stood apart like a beacon of strength in uncertain times. Lucian Valoria, a seasoned warrior who had chosen a life of peace in this quaint corner of the world, towered over most men with his muscular build, his long, dark hair cascading over broad shoulders. His piercing blue eyes seemed to see through one's soul, yet beneath that stern gaze was a heart filled with kindness.

"Rise and shine, Caelum," Lucian called out, rousing the young apprentice from his slumber. The boy blinked sleepily, rubbing his eyes before scrambling to his feet, eager to please his mentor.

Lucian's days began before dawn, when he would rise to tend to the needs of the village. From helping repair a neighbor's broken fences to aiding in the harvest, his presence was welcomed by all. His once-bloodied hands, now calloused from labor and love, were a testament to the man he had become.

As the morning progressed, Lucian dedicated himself to training the village's young fighters. They gathered in a makeshift arena of trodden earth, their faces flushed with anticipation as they awaited instruction. The air hummed with the sound of clashing blades, grunts of exertion, and laughter, as the seasoned warrior shared his knowledge and wisdom.

"Remember, balance is key," Lucian instructed, demonstrating the proper stance as his students mimicked him. "You cannot hope to strike your enemy if you are easily toppled yourself."

"Thank you, Master Valoria!" a girl named Ellia exclaimed, her eyes shining with admiration. Lucian offered a nod and a rare smile, his stern countenance softening for a brief moment.

"Alright, take a break," he called out as the sun reached its zenith. The young fighters dispersed, leaving Lucian to share a quiet meal with Caelum. They sat side by side on a worn wooden bench, the boy eagerly devouring his food while listening intently to the older man's tales of battles past.

"Master Valoria, do you ever miss being in the thick of the fight, defending the realm?" Caelum asked between bites, his eyes wide with curiosity.

"Sometimes," Lucian admitted, his gaze distant. "But there is honor and purpose in what I do here, too. It is my duty to pass on my knowledge to the next generation, so that they may protect this land when I am no longer able."

As evening approached, Lucian bid farewell to his students and returned to the village, offering assistance where needed and sharing stories with the grateful townsfolk. He was a pillar of strength and wisdom in their community, and he knew that he had found his true home among them.

"Your dedication is an inspiration, Lucian," old Bria, the village healer, remarked as she watched him mend a child's toy. "We are fortunate to have you with us."

"Thank you, Bria, but it is I who am fortunate," Lucian replied with sincerity, handing the repaired toy back to the beaming child. "To live among such good people, in a place untouched by the darkness that plagues our world... I could ask for nothing more."

As night fell upon the village, Lucian retired to his modest cottage, reflecting on the day's events and the lives he had touched. He knew that his role in this peaceful hamlet was just as important as any battle he had fought, and he cherished the sense of purpose that his new life afforded him. But deep within his heart, a warrior's spirit still burned, ready to be called forth should the darkness ever threaten his home.

In the dawning light of a new day, Lucian Valoria stood at the edge of the village, gazing out over the verdant landscape that surrounded his adopted home. The rolling hills were blanketed in soft grasses and wildflowers, providing a serene backdrop for the modest houses nestled within their folds. Each structure was composed of wood and stone, their roofs adorned with thick layers of thatch– a testament to the resourcefulness of the villagers who had built them. It was a sight that never ceased to calm his troubled spirit, bringing solace to the weary warrior.

"Good morning, Lucian," a gentle voice called out, drawing his attention from the peaceful scene before him. He turned to see Mara Willow approaching, her long, wavy brown hair cascading down her back like a waterfall of rich silk. Her warm hazel eyes sparkled with kindness, a reflection of her nurturing soul. She carried a woven basket laden with vibrant herbs and plants; their medicinal properties known only to her skilled hands.

"Good morning, Mara," he replied with a smile, taking a moment to admire her natural beauty. "You're up early today."

"Indeed. I wanted to gather some fresh herbs for Bria before the morning dew evaporated," she explained, holding up her bountiful harvest. "It's the best time to collect them, you know."

Lucian nodded, appreciating her dedication to the well-being of the community. "Your knowledge and selflessness are gifts to us all, Mara. This village is truly blessed to have you."

"Thank you, Lucian," she said, her cheeks flushing with humbled pride. "But it is this village that has given me purpose and a place to call home. I am just as grateful for the people here, as they are for my help."

As they stood there, exchanging words of gratitude and admiration, the world around them seemed to stand still. The sweet songs of birds filled the air, accompanied by the gentle rustling of leaves in the soft breeze. The sun's rays crept over the horizon, casting golden light upon the village and its inhabitants as they awoke to face another day. It was a moment of tranquility that served as a balm for the scars etched upon their souls– a reminder of the sanctuary they had found within this haven.

"Lucian," Mara spoke up, her voice laced with concern, "I know that you carry a heavy burden in your heart. The darkness that plagues our world weighs on you, even here among these peaceful hills."

He sighed, acknowledging the truth in her words. "Yes, I cannot deny it. As much as I cherish this life and the people here, there is a part of me that still feels the call of my warrior's path… of the duty I once swore to uphold."

"Sometimes, Lucian," she said, placing a comforting hand on his arm, "our destinies are not written in stone, but rather forged in the fires of our hearts. Perhaps the time has come for you to embrace a new purpose, one that will bring light into the shadows of this world."

As he looked into her eyes, Lucian felt the stirrings of something deep within his soul. A resolve born from the love and compassion that surrounded him in this haven of peace. And with that resolve, he knew that he would do whatever it took to defend this home, and the world beyond its borders, from the encroaching darkness.

The sun had barely risen over the horizon, casting a warm orange glow across the tranquil village nestled amidst lush hills. Birds sang their morning melodies, and the air was filled with the scent of dew-soaked earth.

Lucian Valoria stood in the center of an open field, his muscular frame poised and ready for action. Beside him, Caelum Stormrider, a young warrior-in-training, mirrored his stance, his stormy blue eyes alight with anticipation.

"Remember, Caelum," Lucian instructed, his voice firm yet gentle, "the blade is an extension of your body, your mind, and your spirit. Feel its weight, its balance, and let it guide you."

Caelum nodded fervently, gripping the hilt of his sword as he prepared to strike. He lunged forward, his movements fluid and swift, but Lucian effortlessly parried the attack, his own blade gliding through the air like liquid silver.

"Excellent," Lucian praised, a hint of a smile tugging at the corners of his mouth. "Your form has improved greatly since we first began. However, you must not rely solely on strength or speed. It is the harmony of all three elements that will make you a true master of the blade."

Caelum's chest swelled with pride at the compliment, and he eagerly continued their training session, his enthusiasm seemingly boundless. As they sparred, Lucian marveled at the progress Caelum had made, his thoughts drifting to the prophetic vision that haunted his dreams.

"Is this my purpose?" he wondered, his inner turmoil threatening to overshadow the peaceful scene before him. "To train the next generation of warriors, and protect them from the darkness that looms ever nearer?"

With each clash of steel against steel, Lucian pondered Mara's words, and the weight of his responsibility settled upon his broad shoulders.

As the morning wore on, the sun climbed higher in the sky, and soon villagers began to emerge from their homes, going about their daily tasks. They greeted Lucian and Caelum with warm smiles and waves, their respect for the seasoned warrior evident in each interaction.

"Lucian," called an elderly woman, her voice frail but kind, "my roof has sprung a leak, and I fear the rain will only worsen it. Might you find some time to repair it today?"

"Of course, Mistress Alder," Lucian replied, his stern face softening as he beheld the aged woman. "I shall attend to it after our training session."

"Thank you, dear," she said, gratitude shining in her eyes. "I don't know what we'd do without you."

As the day progressed, Lucian found himself not only mending roofs but also aiding in the harvest, tending to sick animals, and offering counsel to those in need. With each act of service, he felt a sense of fulfillment that seemed to ease the burden upon his heart. Perhaps, he mused, it was possible to balance his duty as a warrior with the simple, yet meaningful life he had come to cherish in this village.

"Sometimes, Lucian," Mara's words echoed in his mind once more, "our destinies are not written in stone, but rather forged in the fires of our hearts."

As the sun began its descent, casting long shadows across the land, Lucian Valoria looked out upon the peaceful village he now called home, and with renewed determination, he vowed to protect it and the world beyond from the encroaching darkness. For here, amidst the tranquility of Elyria, he had discovered a purpose worth fighting for.

The sun dipped below the horizon, painting the sky in shades of crimson and gold. Lucian stood at the edge of the village square, his piercing blue eyes scanning the gathering crowd. It was the eve of the Festival of Light, an annual celebration held in Elyria to honor the gods and seek their protection against the encroaching darkness prophesied for centuries.

"Lucian!" Caelum called out, running towards him with a wide grin. "Are you ready for tonight? The pyres are almost prepared."

"Indeed, my young apprentice," Lucian replied, resting a hand on Caelum's shoulder. "Tonight, we must stand united and reaffirm our allegiance to the gods, lest the shadows consume us all."

As the villagers began lighting the massive pyres that would illuminate the night, Lucian couldn't help but ponder the fragile balance between light and darkness. Elyria was one of the last strongholds of the old faith, a bastion of hope in a world increasingly consumed by chaos and corruption. The political landscape beyond the village borders had become treacherous, with tyrants and false prophets vying for power and leading their followers astray.

"Your thoughts seem heavy, Lucian," Mara Willow observed, her wise eyes studying him as she approached. "Is it the festival or something more that weighs upon your heart?"

"Both, I suppose" Lucian admitted, his gaze fixed on the flickering flames. "I fear that our people have grown complacent, forgetting the ancient prophecies and the consequences of losing our connection with the divine."

"Yet here you stand," Mara countered gently, "a living reminder that not all is lost." Her words were a balm to his troubled soul, and Lucian drew strength from her unwavering faith.

"Thank you, Mara," he said softly. "I only wish I could do more to protect our people and the world beyond."

"Your dedication to this village and its people has not gone unnoticed," she assured him. "Your tireless efforts to train the next generation of fighters, your kindness in tending to the needs of the community- these are the actions of a true warrior, one who understands that the ultimate battle against darkness is fought not only on the battlefield but also within the hearts of men."

"Perhaps you are right," Lucian conceded, his resolve strengthening as he considered her words. "But I cannot shake the feeling that a greater challenge awaits us, one that will test the limits of our faith and the strength of our convictions."

"Then let us face it together," Mara declared, her voice filled with conviction. "For so long as we stand united, there is no force in this world or any other that can break us."

"May the gods grant us the wisdom and courage to prevail," Lucian intoned, his heart swelling with pride and determination as he watched the villagers gather around the blazing pyres, their faces alight with hope and reverence.

As the Festival of Light commenced, Lucian Valoria stood tall, a beacon of strength amidst the encroaching shadows. And though the darkness threatened to engulf them all, he knew that so long as they held fast to their faith and one another, the light would never truly be extinguished. For in the end, it was not the gods who would determine their fate, but the choices they made and the sacrifices they were willing to bear in the name of love and honor.

The sun dipped below the horizon, casting long shadows across the village square. Lucian Valoria stood alone, his mind preoccupied with the prophetic vision that had plagued him ever since he donned the ancient silver armor and took up the sword of pure light. The weight of destiny weighed heavily upon his shoulders, as if the world itself rested on the edge of his blade.

"Is this what I am meant for?" Lucian muttered to himself, staring into the dying embers of the Festival of Light's pyres. "To be a savior in these dark times, or simply another pawn in a cosmic game?"

"Troubled thoughts, my friend?" A familiar voice called out from the dimness. Gareth Ironside emerged from the shadows; his stocky frame silhouetted by the flickering flames. His graying hair was damp with sweat, evidence of a long day spent laboring over his forge.

"Ah, Gareth," Lucian sighed, resting the sword against his shoulder. "I find myself torn between duty and doubt, the path laid before me obscured by uncertainty."

"Tell me," Gareth said, drawing closer, his warm brown eyes reflecting genuine concern. "What troubles you so?"

Lucian hesitated, his blue eyes clouded beneath furrowed brows, then finally confided in his mentor. "I experienced a vision when I first wielded this sword, Gareth. A prophecy of darkness and destruction, a world bathed in blood and despair. And at its center... myself, clad in this very armor."

"Prophecies can be fickle things, Lucian," Gareth replied cautiously, rubbing his calloused hands together. "But I have always believed that we are masters of our own fate. If this vision has shown you a possible future, then it is within your power to change it."

"Perhaps," Lucian admitted, his grip tightening on the hilt of the sword. "But how can I be certain that my actions will not simply hasten the coming of this dark age?"

"Have faith in yourself, Lucian," Gareth urged, placing a hand on his shoulder. "You are a seasoned warrior and a man of honor. You have trained these young fighters and served this village with unwavering dedication. If anyone can face such darkness and prevail, it is you."

"Your words hearten me, old friend," Lucian said, offering a weak smile that did little to hide the turmoil within. "But still, I cannot help but fear that I am merely a pawn in some greater scheme, destined to fail and bring ruin upon us all."

"Destiny is what we make of it," Gareth insisted, his voice firm and resolute. "And if your vision is indeed a prophecy, then I say embrace it! Use it as a guide, a beacon to light your way through these troubled times. Let it serve as a reminder of the stakes at hand, and the responsibility you bear to protect Elyria."

"Perhaps you are right," Lucian conceded, his resolve strengthening as he considered the blacksmith's wisdom. "I shall face this threat head-on and do everything in my power to prevent the darkness from consuming our world."

"Then let us prepare for the journey ahead," Gareth declared, clapping Lucian on the back. "Together, we will forge a path towards a brighter future, and ensure that the light of hope never fades."

As they walked side by side back towards the heart of the village, Lucian's thoughts remained clouded by doubt and uncertainty. But amidst the shadows, a spark of determination burned ever brighter, fueled by the faith of a dear friend and the conviction that even the darkest of destinies could be challenged- and perhaps, ultimately, overcome.

The sun cast long shadows as it dipped below the horizon, painting the sky with an ominous palette of reds and purples. The village seemed to hold its breath in anticipation of the rapidly encroaching darkness. Lucian Valoria stood at the edge of town, his eyes fixed on the path that stretched out before him, leading into the great unknown.

"Are you certain about this, Lucian?" asked Mara Willow, her voice tinged with worry as she approached. Her emerald eyes searched his face for any hint of doubt but found only determination etched in every line and contour.

"More than ever," Lucian replied, barely suppressing a shudder as he recalled the haunting vision that had plagued him since he donned the ancient silver armor and grasped the sword of pure light. "I must face this threat head-on if we're to have any hope of stopping the impending darkness."

Mara nodded solemnly, understanding the gravity of the situation. She reached out to clasp his hand, her touch warm and reassuring. "Then I will help you prepare for your journey, Lucian. You won't face this alone."

"Thank you, Mara. Your support means more than you know." Lucian's voice trembled slightly, betraying the weight of responsibility he now bore.

Over the next few days, Lucian immersed himself in the preparations for his journey. He stocked up on provisions and supplies, making sure to pack enough food to sustain him on the long road ahead. He sharpened his sword, ensuring it would be ready to cut through the darkness when the time came. And he spent hours training with Caelum Stormrider, teaching the young fighter everything he knew about the ways of the blade, hoping to leave behind a capable protector for the village he would soon leave behind.

"Remember," Lucian told Caelum during one of their final sparring sessions, "the sword is an extension of your will. You must learn to wield it with both strength and precision."

"I'll make you proud, Lucian," Caelum promised, his eyes shining with determination as he parried a blow from his mentor. "I won't let the darkness take Elyria."

"Of that, I have no doubt." Lucian offered him a fierce smile, clapping him on the shoulder before turning away.

In the quiet moments when he found himself alone, Lucian wrestled with his thoughts. He questioned whether he was truly prepared for the challenges ahead, whether he had the strength to face the darkness and emerge victorious. And yet, despite his fears and doubts, an unyielding sense of purpose burned within him like a beacon of hope in the night.

"Lucian," Gareth Ironside called out as he approached, his weathered face etched with concern. "Are you ready?"

"Ready as I'll ever be," Lucian replied, his voice steady as he turned to face his old friend. "Thank you, Gareth, for everything."

"Come back to us, my friend," Mara whispered as she embraced Lucian tightly, her voice cracking with emotion. "Elyria needs you."

With one last look at the village that had been his home for so long, Lucian Valorian took the first step towards fulfilling his destiny. His journey had begun, and with each stride he took, the weight of the world seemed to grow heavier upon his shoulders.

But Lucian would not falter. He would fight against the encroaching darkness, against the forces of evil that sought to snuff out all hope and light from the world. He would stand tall, a guardian against the coming storm, and with every beat of his heart and every swing of his sword, he would send a message to the darkness:

"Bring forth your worst, for I am Lucian Valoria, and I shall not be broken."

Dark clouds gathered ominously overhead, casting the landscape in an eerie gloom as Lucian Valoria ventured forth from the village. His instincts sharpened by years of battle; he could feel that something was amiss. A frigid wind whipped across his face as he drew closer to a dense thicket, and as the air crackled with electricity, Lucian's heart pounded in anticipation.

"Show yourself!" he demanded, his voice echoing through the silent woods.

From the shadows emerged Elena Nightingale, her fiery red hair contrasting with her piercing green eyes. The bow held taut in her lithe hands spoke volumes about her skill as an archer, and it was clear she was not one to be trifled with.

"Who are you?" Lucian asked warily, gripping the hilt of his sword tightly.

"Someone who shares your goal," Elena replied tersely, her eyes narrowed in suspicion. "I've been tracking the darkness spreading across Elyria, and our paths were bound to cross."

Lucian studied her for a moment, weighing his options. Trust was not easily given in a world on the brink of chaos, and yet every fiber of his being told him that Elena could prove invaluable in his quest.

"Very well," he said slowly, extending his hand to her. "We shall join forces, but know this: I will not tolerate betrayal. If you wish to stand beside me, we must trust each other implicitly."

Elena hesitated, her gaze flitting between his outstretched hand and his steely blue eyes. She knew all too well the pain of treachery, and the wounds of her past still festered like a poisonous curse. But in Lucian's unwavering determination, she saw a flicker of hope—a chance to right the wrongs that haunted her.

"Agreed," she murmured, taking his hand and sealing their uneasy alliance.

As they journeyed together through the ravaged lands of Elyria, Lucian and Elena maintained a tense silence. Neither dared to speak of their fears or aspirations, for the walls they had built around themselves were fortified by mistrust and sorrow.

"Is this the path we must walk?" Lucian wondered silently, his thoughts racing like a tempest in his mind. "Must we bear the weight of the world alone, without solace or comfort?"

"Can I truly trust him?" Elena mused, her heart heavy with doubt. "Or is he just another false ally, waiting to strike when I am most vulnerable?"

The air grew colder as they ventured deeper into the darkness, their breaths visible in the chill night. Despite their initial distrust, Lucian and Elena began to appreciate the other's skills and resolve. In time, as the battles waged and victories were won, their alliance would strengthen, forged in the crucible of adversity.

"Perhaps," Lucian thought, "there is hope for us yet."

"Maybe," Elena allowed herself to believe, "we can find solace in one another."

For now, though, they pressed onward, two weary souls bound by a shared purpose, each haunted by the specter of an uncertain future. As the end of days loomed ever closer, their hearts beat in unison, resolute in their quest to save Elyria from the encroaching darkness.

The sun dipped below the horizon, casting the village in hues of gold and orange. Shadows stretched long across the cobblestone streets, as if reaching out to grasp at the fleeing light. Lucian stood tall, his muscular frame silhouetted against Elyria's final moments of tranquility.

Beside him, Elena shifted uneasily, her fiery red hair a stark contrast to the darkening sky.

"Are you ready?" Lucian asked, his voice low and tinged with determination.

hesitated, her green eyes searching his for any sign of deceit. "As ready as one can be when facing the end of days," she replied, her tone guarded.

"Then let us go forth," he said, turning toward the edge of the village where their journey would begin.

As they walked, the once-familiar sounds of laughter and camaraderie faded into a somber silence. The villagers had long since retreated to their homes, leaving Lucian and Elena to navigate the empty streets alone. It was as though the world itself held its breath, awaiting the first inklings of the apocalypse.

"Lucian," Elena whispered, breaking the stillness that enveloped them. "Do you ever doubt the prophecy?"

He did not answer immediately, his thoughts a whirlwind of uncertainty and fear. He pictured the ancient silver armor that now adorned his body and the sword of pure light, which hung at his side. How could he not doubt, when the weight of responsibility threatened to crush him beneath its heel? Yet, he knew he must remain steadfast, for the fate of Elyria rested on his shoulders.

"Every day," he finally admitted, his voice barely audible. "But I cannot allow those doubts to consume me. We are all that stands between our people and the darkness."

Elena nodded, her expression solemn. "I understand. I too carry the burden of responsibility, and I will fight by your side until our last breath."

"Then let us make a pact," Lucian said, extending his hand. "We shall face whatever trials come our way, together, as allies."

"Agreed," Elena responded, placing her hand in his. The warmth of their clasped hands seemed to chase away the chill that had settled over them.

As they stood on the outskirts of the village, the last vestiges of sunlight vanished from the sky, leaving only the cold glow of the moon to guide them. The world beyond was shrouded in darkness, a foreboding omen of the challenges that lay ahead.

"May the gods watch over us," Lucian murmured, his eyes fixed on the path before them.

"May they grant us the strength to prevail," Elena added quietly.

With a final glance back at the peaceful village they were leaving behind, Lucian and Elena set forth into the night, united in their mission to fend off the approaching apocalypse. The end of a thousand years of captivity loomed on the horizon, and they would face it head-on, defiant against the dying of the light.

The mystical world of Valyria was a place of enchanting beauty, where the very air seemed to shimmer with magic. Vast forests stretched as far as the eye could see, their ancient trees reaching towards the heavens like the fingers of giants. Rivers sparkled like silver ribbons, winding through lush meadows and valleys filled with flowers of every hue. The soft sigh of wind through the leaves and the bubbling laughter of brooks played a symphony that stirred the soul and filled the hearts of Valyria's inhabitants with wonder.

In this realm of splendor, a man of great stature stood watch over a village nestled at the edge of the boundless forest. Lucian Valeria was his name, and he was revered by many as a natural leader and skilled warrior. His tall, muscular physique exuded power, yet it was his piercing green eyes that captivated those who beheld him. Within their depths lay a calmness and wisdom that inspired trust and loyalty in all who knew him.

"Lucian!" called out a villager, "We need your guidance!"

As the cry reached his ears, Lucian turned and strode purposefully toward the gathering crowd. His shoulder-length dark hair billowed behind him like a raven's wing, adding an air of mystery to his already imposing presence. The villagers parted before him as if drawn by an invisible force, their eyes wide with respect and admiration.

"Tell me your concerns," Lucian commanded, his voice deep and resonant.

"Dark times are upon us, Lucian," a woman cried, wringing her hands anxiously. "Rumors of the apocalypse abound, and we know not what to do."

"Indeed, I have sensed the shadows lengthening," Lucian admitted, his brow furrowing in concern. "But fear not, for we shall face this darkness together. I will lead you through the storm and into the light."

His words washed over the villagers like a balm, soothing their troubled hearts. They knew that with Lucian Stargazer at their side, they stood a fighting chance against whatever darkness threatened their world.

As Lucian rallied his people to prepare for the approaching storm, he felt the weight of responsibility pressing down upon him. He knew that the fate of Valyria rested in his hands, and he was determined to do everything within his power to protect it. Though the shadows of doubt whispered in the recesses of his mind, Lucian refused to let them take root. He would be the beacon of hope that Valyria needed, and with unwavering resolve, he would guide his people through the trials ahead.

As Lucian turned his gaze away from the gathering crowd, his eyes fell upon a figure standing near the edge of the village. The sun's dying light illuminated her petite, graceful form, her long silver hair cascading down her back like a shimmering waterfall. Elena Nightshade, Valyria's most gifted healer, possessed a rare beauty that was only matched by her wisdom and kindness.

"Are you prepared for what is to come, Elena?" Lucian questioned, his voice tinged with concern as he approached her.

"None can ever truly be prepared, Lucian," she replied softly, her violet eyes meeting his green ones. "But I will do everything in my power to aid our people through this darkness."

Elena's delicate hands were calloused from years of tending to the sick and injured, and Lucian knew that her skills would be vital in the trials ahead. Her gentle spirit was a beacon of hope for the villagers, who looked up to her not only for her healing abilities but also for her unwavering dedication to their well-being.

The village itself was nestled on the edge of a vast, untamed forest, its quaint charm drawing the eye of any passing traveler.

Thatched-roof cottages lined cobblestone streets, while vibrant gardens burst with color against the backdrop of ancient trees. This close-knit community had weathered many storms throughout the centuries, and its inhabitants were bound together by love, loyalty, and shared values.

"Lucian," Elena spoke, her voice laced with urgency, "we must rally our people and prepare them for the struggle that lies ahead. Our world is changing, and we must stand together if we are to survive."

"Indeed," Lucian agreed, his jaw set in determination. "We shall lead them through this darkness, Elena, and with your wisdom and my strength, we will safeguard our beloved Valyria."

As they stood together, the glow of the setting sun fading behind the distant horizon, Lucian and Elena could feel the impending doom drawing nearer. The once vibrant colors of their world were now muted, replaced by an eerie stillness as shadows crept ever closer.

"May the gods be with us," Elena whispered, her eyes fixed on the encroaching darkness.

"May they grant us the strength to protect our people," Lucian added, his hand tightening around the hilt of his sword.

Their hearts heavy with both trepidation and determination, Lucian Stargazer and Elena Nightshade prepared to face the unknown, united in their unwavering commitment to save their people and their way of life from the looming apocalypse.

The air hung heavy with a palpable sense of dread as the villagers gathered in the village square, their faces etched with concern. Lucian stood before them, his piercing green eyes surveying the anxious crowd. He knew that the time had come to share the prophecy that he and Elena had uncovered– a revelation that foretold the impending apocalypse, and the end of the thousand years of captivity of Satan.

"Friends, neighbors," Lucian began, his voice firm yet compassionate, "we have discovered an ancient prophecy that speaks of a great darkness descending upon our world, a time when Satan will be released from his prison to wage war against us."

Murmurs of fear rippled through the crowd, but Lucian held up his hand for silence. "This is not a time for panic," he continued, "but for unity and resolve. We must prepare ourselves for the trials that lie ahead and stand together as one if we are to weather this storm."

Elena stepped forward, her petite frame exuding strength and wisdom beyond her years. "We must gather supplies, reinforce our defenses, and ensure that every man, woman, and child is ready for what lies ahead," she said, her violet eyes filled with determination.

As the villagers absorbed the gravity of their words, they sprang into action. Families banded together, exchanging worried glances as they hurried off to collect food, water, and other essential supplies. Others set to work fortifying their homes and the village's perimeter, determined to protect their loved ones from the encroaching darkness.

In the midst of the frenzy, Lucian found himself deep in thought, grappling with the weight of his responsibility. How can I lead these people through such a dark and uncertain time? he wondered, doubt gnawing at the edges of his confidence.

"Lucian," Elena whispered, sensing his inner turmoil. "You are the leader they need, now more than ever. Your strength and resolve will guide them through this darkness."

"Thank you, Elena," he replied, his voice barely audible above the din of the villagers' frantic preparations. "Your faith in me gives me hope."

As the sun dipped lower in the sky, casting long shadows across the village, Lucian and Elena watched their people work tirelessly to prepare for the coming apocalypse. Their hearts swelled with pride at the sight of their community's unity and resilience, but they knew that the true test still lay ahead.

"May the gods grant us the strength to prevail," Lucian murmured, clenching his fists in determination. And as darkness began to descend upon the village, the two warriors steeled themselves for the battle to save their world.

The final rays of sunlight stretched across the horizon, painting the sky in a masterpiece of gold and crimson. Lucian Stargazer stood tall at the edge of the village, his piercing green eyes focused on the dying light.

Beside him, Elena Nightshade's violet gaze mirrored his own, her silver hair dancing gently in the breeze. The two warriors, bound by shared purpose and unwavering resolve, faced the approaching darkness with steely determination.

"Once the sun sets, there will be no turning back," Lucian said quietly, his voice steady despite the turmoil surging within him. "We have prepared our people as best we can, but the battle ahead is like nothing we've ever faced before."

Elena nodded in agreement, her petite form radiating an inner strength that belied her delicate appearance. "But we must face it, Lucian. For our village, for our people, and for all of Valyria." Her words were laced with conviction, anchoring them both amidst the rising tide of fear.

As the last vestiges of sunlight clung to the heavens, the sky shifted from warm hues to cool shades of blue and gray. The vibrant colors retreated before the encroaching darkness, echoing the villagers' own retreat behind their hastily reinforced defenses. Lucian clenched his jaw, steeling himself for the trials to come.*I cannot falter now,* he thought,*for I am not only fighting for my life, but for the lives of everyone I hold dear.*

"Remember," Elena whispered, her voice barely audible, "we are not alone in this fight. Our ancestors fought against darkness in their time, and their spirits guide us now. Trust in your strength, Lucian- both the strength of your arm and the strength of your heart."

Lucian turned to look into Elena's eyes, finding solace in their violet depths. He nodded, his resolve firming. "Together, we will stand against the darkness. And we will prevail."

The final sliver of sunlight gave way to twilight, leaving Lucian and Elena bathed in the cool glow of the emerging stars. As the night enveloped them and the weight of their mission settled on their shoulders, they knew that the battle for Valyria- and for the fate of all mankind- had begun.

The encroaching darkness crept across the land like a malevolent serpent, consuming the once-bright world in its cold embrace. Shadows stretched and twisted into grotesque shapes as the final vestiges of daylight were swallowed by the night. Lucian could feel the unease that permeated the air, thick and suffocating, wrapping around his heart and threatening to choke the courage from him.

"Listen," Elena urged softly, her breath a ghostly whisper on the wind. "Can you hear it? The song of the stars, calling us to our destiny."

Lucian strained his ears, searching for the celestial melody amidst the eerie silence. Slowly, he began to discern the faintest strains of music, their haunting beauty a balm to his frayed nerves.

"By the gods," he murmured, awestruck. "I hadn't noticed it before, but now…it's like they're singing directly to us."

"Let their guidance fortify our hearts," Elena said, raising her arms skyward. "Great spirits of the heavens, lend us your strength and protection as we embark on this perilous journey to save our people and our world."

Lucian followed suit, lifting his gaze and his hands upward, feeling the tingling energy of the cosmos seep into his very being. "May we be worthy instruments of your divine will, and may we find the courage to face whatever darkness lies ahead."

As the quiet prayer left their lips, a sudden gust of wind swept through the village, stirring up a vortex of leaves and dust around them. Lucian felt an electric charge in the atmosphere, as if the gods themselves had heard their plea and granted them their blessings.

"Ready?" Elena asked, her violet eyes meeting his unwavering green gaze.

"Ready," Lucian affirmed, his voice steady with newfound determination.

Together, they stepped into the yawning abyss of darkness, guided by the whispered songs of the stars and the fire that burned within their souls. As they ventured forth on their mission to prevent the apocalypse, each step filled with trepidation and resolve, they knew that they were not only fighting for their village but for the very essence of humanity itself. And in that moment, they understood that the gods had chosen them for a reason, and they would not falter.

The bond between Lucian and Elena was like an unbreakable thread, woven through the fabric of their very beings. As they stood on the precipice of darkness, each heartbeat in sync with the other, their shared resolve to save their people and their way of life only served to strengthen that connection.

"Lucian," Elena said softly, her voice carrying the weight of their purpose. "Do you remember when we were children, playing in the meadows near the village? We promised to protect each other, no matter what."

He smiled at the memory, the innocence of their childhood promise now taking on a greater meaning. "I remember, Elena. And I intend to keep that promise." His piercing green eyes held hers, conveying his commitment not just to her, but to the entirety of Valyria.

A flicker of determination glinted in her violet eyes as she nodded, her hand reaching out to clasp his. "And so will I."

In that instant, as their hands intertwined, a surge of energy pulsed between them. It was as if every shared memory, every act of kindness, every moment of sacrifice had culminated into this one point in time. They knew, without a doubt, that they were destined to face this darkness together.

"Are you scared?" Lucian asked, his voice barely above a whisper.

Elena hesitated for only a moment before answering honestly. "Yes, but I know that we have the strength within us to overcome whatever awaits. And with you by my side, I fear nothing."

"Then let us face it together," Lucian replied, his chest swelling with pride at the woman he had come to love and respect more than anything in this world.

As they took their first steps into the unknown, the world around them seemed to hold its breath. The air grew still, and the shadows deepened, swallowing up the last vestiges of light. Yet, Lucian and Elena walked forward with unwavering determination, their eyes fixed on the horizon.

"Listen," Elena whispered, her voice trembling with trepidation and excitement. "The wind carries whispers of what's to come."

Lucian strained his ears, listening intently to the subtle rustling of leaves and the hushed murmurs of the encroaching darkness. Within those sounds, he could hear the distant echoes of prayers from their people, their faith in the gods and in them to save their world.

"May we be worthy," he thought, his heart aching with responsibility and hope.

"May we be strong," Elena added, her thoughts intertwining with his like silken threads.

With every step they took, the shadows seemed to gather closer, as though eager to test their resolve. But Lucian and Elena walked unwaveringly into the uncharted territory beyond their village, guided by their shared purpose and an unbreakable bond that would carry them through the trials ahead.

As they ventured deeper into the darkness, the last remnants of the sun's warmth vanished, replaced by a chill that seeped into their bones. But in the face of the unknown, Lucian and Elena pressed on, their hearts beating as one, their spirits alight with the fire of determination.

"Whatever awaits us," Lucian whispered into the darkness, his voice resolute, "we will face it together."

THE CITY OF GOD'S PEOPLE

The city of God's people trembled, as if the very earth beneath their feet sensed the impending doom. Whispers of fear and desperation rustled through the crowded streets like a sinister breeze. The armies of Gog and Magog were on the march, fueled by an ancient prophecy and set to fulfill their dark purpose– the destruction of the city.

"Have you heard?" an elderly woman whispered urgently to her neighbor as they huddled together in the marketplace. "They say Gog and Magog are coming. That we're all doomed, and there's nothing we can do to stop it!"

"Quiet!" hissed the other, her eyes darting nervously about. "You'll only spread panic among the people. We must stay strong and have faith that the Almighty will protect us."

Yet, despite her words of reassurance, she too felt her heart race with terror at the thought of the dread armies descending upon them. What hope could they have against such overwhelming odds?

Unbeknownst to the inhabitants of the city, a figure cloaked in darkness stood on a nearby rooftop, overlooking the chaos below. Azarael, his features hidden by the shadows that clung to him like a second skin, reveled in the turmoil he had so expertly orchestrated. He smiled, a cold, cruel smile, as he listened to the panicked whispers and cries of the people. Their fear was palpable, a living thing that thrummed in the air, and it fed his own twisted desires.

"Such sweet despair," he murmured to himself, his voice barely more than a whisper. "And yet, they cling so desperately to hope, like a dying ember in the cold night. How…pathetic."

Hidden from sight, Azarael reached out with his mind, probing into the thoughts and emotions of the unsuspecting citizens below. Like a puppet-master pulling invisible strings, he subtly manipulated the events unfolding within the city. A sudden altercation between two men escalated into a violent brawl, drawing the attention of the already frantic crowd. A mother, consumed by panic, lost sight of her child amidst the chaos, her cries for help adding to the cacophony of fear and despair.

"Such fragile creatures," Azarael mused, his unseen eyes narrowing as he continued to weave his dark web over the city. "So easily manipulated by their baser instincts. It's almost too easy."

He turned his gaze toward the horizon, where the first ominous signs of the approaching armies were visible– a billowing cloud of dust, accompanied by the distant rumble of marching feet and the jangle of armor. The final battle was at hand, and Azarael knew that he would play a crucial role in determining its outcome.

"Let the end begin," he whispered, his voice barely audible above the din of the terrified city below. And with that, he vanished into the shadows, leaving only a lingering sense of dread in his wake.

The streets of the city were a cacophony of despair, their once-vibrant colors now muted by the shroud of darkness that had descended upon the region. Shadows clung to every crevice and corner, whispering secrets to those who dared to listen. A palpable sense of unease hung in the air, as thick and suffocating as the ever-present gloom.

"Please, we need to leave this place!" cried a desperate mother, clutching her wailing child to her chest. "We cannot survive this!"

"What can we do?" shouted a young man, his voice cracking with barely contained fear. "Where can we run? There's no escape from this fate!"

As the people around them argued and despaired, Lilith stood amidst the chaos, her heart pounding in her chest. The dread she felt was nearly overwhelming, but she knew she couldn't succumb to panic. She had to remain strong for the sake of her people.

"Listen to me, everyone!" Lilith raised her voice, trying to cut through the din. "We have faced dark times before, and we have always emerged victorious! We must stand together now, united against this threat!"

"Easy for you to say," growled an old man, his eyes narrowing suspiciously. "You don't know what it's like to cower in fear, wondering if today will be your last."

"Indeed, I do not." Lilith's voice was firm, but gentle. "I have fought against the darkness my whole life, and I have seen its true face. That is why I am here– to help you find the strength within yourselves to survive this."

"Strength?" A woman laughed bitterly, the sound tinged with hysteria. "What strength do we have left? Look at us– we are all but broken already!"

"Enough!" Elias stepped forward, his scarred face a testament to his own battles against the darkness. "Lilith is right. We cannot give in to despair, for that is exactly what the enemy wants. We must find the courage to stand against them, even when it seems all hope is lost."

Silence fell over the crowd as they weighed Elias's words, the flicker of a fragile hope igniting within their hearts.

"Very well," said the old man reluctantly, casting a wary glance at the encroaching shadows. "We will fight, but we must be smart about it. The enemy is cunning and ruthless– we must be prepared."

"Agreed," Lilith nodded, her eyes scanning the city and its inhabitants, searching for any sign of weakness or vulnerability. "We will gather our allies, those who are strong and skilled in battle, and we will devise a plan to protect our people and our city. No matter how dark the future may seem, we will not go down without a fight!"

As the people began to rally around her, Lilith couldn't help but feel a chill run down her spine, as if unseen eyes were watching her every move. She knew that the true battle had yet to begin, and that the forces of darkness were waiting, biding their time before they struck.

But she also knew that she was not alone– her allies stood by her side, and together they would face whatever horrors awaited them. It would not be an easy fight, but it was one they could not afford to lose.

"Let us prepare for what is to come," she murmured, her voice barely audible above the whispers of the shadows. "For the end is upon us, and we must stand our ground, no matter the cost."

Far removed from the city's center, nestled within a desolate grove that seemed untouched by the sun's warmth, stood Azarael. Cloaked in shadows, his presence was almost imperceptible, an enigma that remained veiled from the world. An aura of darkness enveloped him, casting an eerie chill that permeated the air around him. Despite this, there was something undeniably alluring about him– a magnetic pull that drew even the most righteous of souls towards the abyss.

His face remained hidden beneath a hood, leaving only the faintest hint of his unnerving smile visible to any who dared look upon him. His eyes were pools of obsidian, impenetrable and void of any discernible emotion. Yet, those very same eyes held the power to pierce the soul, revealing one's deepest fears and desires with but a single glance.

Azarael's fingers danced gracefully over an ancient scroll, its parchment filled with cryptic symbols that seemed to writhe and twist before his very gaze. As he whispered incantations in a language long forgotten, his lips curved into a sinister grin, betraying his true intentions. For Azarael sought not just the release of Satan and the final battle, but dominion over a new world order– one where darkness reigned supreme and he, its undisputed ruler.

"Ah, sweet chaos," he murmured to himself, his voice smooth as silk yet laced with venom. "It has been far too long since your melody graced my ears."

As Azarael reveled in the impending destruction, the rustle of leaves caught his attention. A raven perched nearby, its beady eyes observing him intently. In that moment, Azarael shared a knowing look with the creature, as if they were both privy to a secret that the world would soon come to know.

"Watch carefully, my feathered friend," he whispered, the air around him crackling with malevolent energy. "For soon, this world shall tremble beneath our might."

The raven cawed in response, as if understanding the weight of his words, and took flight, vanishing into the darkening sky above.

Azarael's gaze followed the bird until it disappeared from sight, his thoughts drifting to the impending battle and the role he would play in its outcome. The city's people were already on edge, their fear and desperation palpable. He had but to nudge them ever so slightly, guiding them towards the abyss as they clung to hope's dying embers.

"Let them prepare," he mused, his voice barely audible even to himself. "For when the time comes, I shall cast aside the veil and reveal the true nature of their fate. And then, when all hope has been extinguished, we shall claim our rightful place upon this broken world."

With a flick of his wrist, the scroll vanished, leaving only a faint echo of darkness that lingered like a portent of doom. Azarael stood motionless, his thoughts already turning to the next phase of his plan— a plan that would bring about the end of an era and the birth of a new world order where shadows reigned supreme.

The city's once-bustling streets now lay shrouded in an eerie, oppressive silence, broken only by the occasional fearful whisper or muffled sob. The people of the city moved about with hunched shoulders and darting eyes, casting furtive glances at their fellow citizens as if expecting the enemy to appear amongst them at any moment. The air was thick with tension, a palpable sense of urgency gripping every man, woman, and child.

Lilith made her way through the city's winding alleys, her breath catching in her throat as she felt the weight of the people's fear press down upon her. Her gaze swept over the grim faces that surrounded her, each etched with the same desperate hope: that somehow, they would survive the impending onslaught.

"Have you heard the news?" a woman whispered to her companion, her voice quivering with barely suppressed panic. "They say the armies of Gog and Magog are on the march, led by that monster Valthor Malgath."

"God help us," the other replied, clutching at her shawl as if it could offer some measure of protection against the darkness that loomed on the horizon.

As Lilith continued her journey, the acrid scent of smoke stung her nostrils– the desperate attempts of the city's defenders to forge weapons for the coming battle. The clang of metal striking metal rang out through the air, the frantic rhythm echoing the frenzied beating of the people's hearts.

"Prepare yourselves!" Elias bellowed to the assembled warriors, his scarred face set in a grim expression. "We must stand strong and united if we have any hope of turning back this tide of darkness!"

As he spoke, Adaon stood off to the side, his long hair ruffling in the breeze as he stared into the distance, lost in thought. His keen eyes roved over the city's defenses, as if searching for any weakness that might be exploited by their foes.

"Can we truly withstand their assault?" Nara whispered to Lilith, her fiery hair a stark contrast to the fear that clouded her eyes. "If even half of what they say about Valthor Malgath is true, how can we hope to stand against such an implacable foe?"

"By standing together," Lilith replied, her voice steady despite the turmoil that roiled within her. "We will fight, and we will endure. It is all we can do."

"May the gods grant us the strength to see this through," Ariana murmured, her wise old eyes gazing skyward as if seeking divine guidance. "For if we fail, I fear there may be no tomorrow for any of us."

As the sun dipped below the horizon, casting its red glow upon the city like the blood of those who had already fallen, the air grew thick with the scent of fear and despair. The people of the city huddled together in the gathering darkness, seeking solace in one another's presence as they awaited the arrival of the enemy that would determine their fate.

"Let them come," Lilith whispered to herself, steeling her resolve. "We will face them, and we will not falter. For we are the children of light, and we shall not let the darkness claim our world without a fight."

But unbeknownst to her, a figure cloaked in shadow watched from a hidden vantage point, his intentions as dark as the night that encroached upon the city. And as the first stars began to twinkle in the sky above, he knew that soon, everything would change– and nothing would ever be the same again.

The streets of the city were eerily quiet, as if the very shadows themselves held their breath in anticipation. Lilith stood at a window, her gaze fixed on the horizon where the armies of Gog and Magog would soon appear. Her heart raced, pounding in her chest like a drumbeat foretelling doom.

"Are you certain it is tonight?" Nara asked, her voice barely above a whisper, as she joined Lilith by the window. Her fiery red hair seemed to blaze with the intensity of her emotions.

"Everything points to it," Lilith replied, her tone heavy with the weight of responsibility. "The prophecy, the omens… we must be prepared."

"Prepared for what?" Elias interjected, his scarred face a testament to the battles he had fought. "We cannot possibly stand against an army such as theirs."

"Hope, Elias," Ariana spoke up, her steady eyes meeting his. "We must have hope, even in the darkest of times. We will do whatever it takes to protect our people."

"Hope alone won't save us," Adaon murmured, running his fingers over his bow, as if seeking solace in its familiar touch. "We need a plan, a strategy."

"Then let's make one," Lilith said, determination burning within her. "Together, we can find a way to repel the darkness and protect our home."

As they gathered around a table, with candle light lightning the crowd, hastily strewn with maps and scrolls, their voices rose and fell in urgent discussion. Ideas were proposed, debated, discarded, and refined, each member of the group contributing their unique perspective and expertise.

"Perhaps we could use their own weapons against them," Nara suggested, her hands forming fists as she imagined grappling with the enemy. "If we can capture some of their arms, it might give us an advantage."

"An interesting idea," Ariana mused, her brow furrowed in thought. "But we must be cautious not to let the darkness taint us in the process."

"True," Lilith agreed, her eyes narrowing as she considered the risks. "We cannot allow ourselves to become corrupted by their evil."

"Then let us focus on strengthening our defenses," Elias proposed, his voice firm. "We can fortify our walls and prepare for a siege."

"Time is not on our side," Adaon pointed out, glancing anxiously toward the window. "Whatever we decide, we must act quickly."

"Indeed," Ariana nodded, her eyes filled with wisdom and resolve. "We must trust in one another and stand united against the coming storm."

The tension in the room grew palpable as they continued to strategize, each suggestion carrying the weight of countless lives hanging in the balance. The air seemed to grow heavier, like the very atmosphere was pressing down upon them, suffocating hope as the prophecy loomed ever closer.

"Enough!" Lilith finally exclaimed, slamming her fist onto the table. "We will spend no more time arguing about what might work. We have made our decisions, and now we must act. Everyone, gather your weapons and supplies. Tonight, we stand together as one, ready to face whatever comes our way."

As they dispersed to their various tasks, the city's people watched with a mix of fear and awe, sensing that the final confrontation between light and darkness was fast approaching. And as the sun dipped below the horizon, casting an ominous crimson glow over the world, the fragile barrier between hope and despair began to crumble.

For within the shadows, unseen by all but the most vigilant, Azarael lurked, his dark plans unfurling like the tendrils of a poisonous vine.

Soon, he knew, the battle would begin– and the fate of mankind would be forever altered.

As the crimson sun dipped below the horizon, Lilith stood at the edge of the city walls, her eyes scanning the distant, darkening landscape. The twilight sky seemed to reflect the turmoil in her soul, as if the heavens themselves were weeping for the fate of mankind. A cold wind whipped through her flowing hair, like a harbinger of the chaos that was about to descend upon them.

"Are you ready?" Elias asked, his scarred face set in grim determination, his muscular form silhouetted against the dying light.

"Can anyone ever truly be ready for the end of days?" Lilith responded quietly, her voice barely audible above the howling wind. "But I am prepared to fight with every fiber of my being."

"Good," Elias nodded, placing a reassuring hand on her shoulder. "We will stand together, united against the darkness." with soft tears trickling down her eyes.

The wind carried whispers of despair and dread through the streets of the city, stirring fallen leaves into swirling eddies that danced like lost souls. The tension in the air was palpable, a heavy weight pressing down on each and every heart.

"Look!" Nara cried out suddenly, pointing towards the east. "There, where the shadows grow deeper, do you see it?"

Lilith squinted, her eyes straining to pierce the veil of darkness that had begun to envelop the land like a shroud. And then, she saw it– a writhing mass of shadow that seemed to surge forward like a tidal wave, bringing destruction and terror in its wake.

"Valthor Malgath and the armies of Gog and Magog," Ariana intoned solemnly, her wise old eyes reflecting the flames of the torches that flickered around them. "The final battle is upon us."

"Then let us meet them head-on," Adaon declared, his tall, slender form poised like an arrow drawn in a bow, ready to be loosed upon the enemy. "We will not go gently into that dark night."

"Agreed," Lilith said, her voice resolute and strong. "Let us show them what it means to stand against the power of light."

As the warriors of the city armed themselves with sword, shield, and bow, they seemed to transform into living symbols of hope and defiance, their spirits shining like beacons in the gathering darkness. The approaching storm of evil was relentless, a black tide that threatened to consume all in its path– yet still they stood, steadfast and unyielding.

"Remember

Under the benevolent rule of Lord Eldryn, the city shone like a beacon in a world beset by darkness. Its high walls, constructed of white marble and adorned with golden accents, reflected the light of the sun, casting an ethereal glow across its bustling streets. The city's grandeur was matched only by the sense of community that pervaded every corner, from the cobbled paths of the marketplace to the flowering gardens that graced the palace grounds.

"More sandbags! We need to reinforce the eastern wall!" Lord Eldryn's voice boomed across the courtyard, his regal bearing evident even amidst the chaos of preparation. His eyes, as blue as the skies above, surveyed the scene with a calm determination, his long white beard fluttering in the cool breeze.

Citizens heeded his call, their hands roughened from days of labor, but their spirits unbroken. Mothers and fathers, siblings and friends, all united in their efforts to protect their beloved city. Wagons laden with supplies rumbled through the streets, their drivers calling out destinations as they navigated the throngs of people. Masons and carpenters worked tirelessly, fortifying the walls that had stood for centuries, preparing them for the battle that loomed on the horizon.

"Lord Eldryn, we've managed to gather enough provisions for three months," reported a weary, yet determined councilman, clutching a parchment scroll. "We're still working on securing more weapons and armor for our militia."

"Excellent work, Councilman," Lord Eldryn responded, his voice warm with gratitude. "See to it that our citizens are well-equipped and trained for the coming storm."

As the sun began to dip below the horizon, casting long shadows across the city, training sessions commenced under the watchful gaze of experienced soldiers. The rhythmic clang of sword against shield echoed through the air as men and women, young and old, honed their skills in defense of their home.

"Remember, keep your shield arm strong and your sword arm swift," instructed one seasoned warrior, sweat glistening on his brow as he demonstrated a parry. "We may be outnumbered, but we have righteousness on our side."

Elsewhere, archers drew their bows, arrows slicing through the air with deadly precision, while healers practiced their arts, mending wounds both physical and spiritual. And all throughout the city, prayers rose like incense, imploring the heavens for protection and deliverance.

Lord Eldryn stood atop the ramparts, his gaze sweeping across the city he had devoted his life to governing with wisdom and compassion. He knew that the days ahead would test the mettle of every citizen, but there was no doubt in his heart that they would face this trial with unwavering resolve.

"Let it be known," he murmured to himself, his voice barely audible above the din of preparation, "that even in the darkest hour, the light of our city shall never be extinguished."

As twilight descended upon the city, its citizens continued their tireless efforts to prepare for the impending attack. But amidst the chaos, there remained a steadfast belief in the power of unity and the indomitable spirit of humankind. In the face of certain doom, they would stand together, their hearts beating as one, ready to face whatever lay beyond the horizon.

As twilight's final embers faded into the night, three formidable warriors stood upon the city walls, their eyes scanning the horizon for the first signs of the prophesied onslaught. They were Valthor Malgath, Adaon, and Lilith– a trio forged in the fires of adversity, their unwavering resolve matched only by their deadly prowess in battle.

Valthor Malgath, a tall, muscular warrior with a fierce gaze and long, dark hair, clenched his fists at his sides, feeling the weight of his responsibility as the city's protector. His thoughts swirled like a tempest, but he was determined to stand firm, a bastion of hope amidst the gathering storm.

"Valthor," Adaon called out, his lean, agile form draped in shadows as he notched an arrow to his bow. The unusual sight of his blond hair caught the faint moonlight, and his sharp eyes remained ever vigilant. "I've got your back, friend. We'll hold this wall together, come what may." He flashed a wry grin, attempting to lighten the heavy atmosphere with his characteristic wit.

"Thank you, Adaon," Valthor replied, grateful for the camaraderie that had sustained them through countless trials. As his mind raced, he tried to focus on the task at hand, knowing that any lapse in concentration could prove disastrous.

Meanwhile, Lilith paced the battlements like a caged lioness, her fiery red hair a vivid contrast against the dark stone. Her sword gleamed in the moonlight, a testament to her skill and determination. She longed for the moment when she could unleash her fury upon the enemy, a storm of steel and wrath that would lay waste to all who dared threaten her home.

"Easy, Lilith," Valthor murmured, laying a reassuring hand on her shoulder. "We must remain patient. The time for action will come soon enough."

"Patience has never been my strong suit," she admitted, her voice like a smoldering ember as she glanced back at the city they were sworn to protect. "But I will stand by you both, to the bitter end."

The air was heavy with anticipation, each breath drawn in tandem with the beating of their hearts. As the trio stood upon the walls, they could feel the eyes of the citizens upon them— the unwavering faith of those who trusted them to defend their home against the coming darkness.

"May the heavens grant us strength," Valthor whispered, his words carried away on the night breeze. "For we shall need every ounce of it in the days to come."

"Strength, and maybe a bit of luck, too," Adaon added, his fingers drumming restlessly on his bowstring. "But together, there's nothing we can't face."

"Indeed," Lilith agreed, her eyes narrowing as she stared unflinchingly into the abyss beyond the city walls. "Let the enemy come. We are ready."

And with that solemn vow, the three warriors steeled themselves for the battle that would determine the fate of their world, the echoes of their defiance resounding through the darkened sky like the first peals of thunder before a cataclysmic storm.

From the shadows below, the citizens of the city gazed up at Valthor, Adaon, and Lilith as they stood sentinel upon the ramparts. Their eyes shone with a mixture of fear and awe, yet beneath it all was an unshakable faith in their champions. The trio represented the last bastion of hope, their very presence a beacon of defiance amidst the encroaching darkness.

"Look, there's Valthor," whispered a young boy, his small hand pointing skyward. "He's going to protect us from the evil that comes."

"Indeed," his mother replied, gently tousling his hair. "And with Adaon and Lilith by his side, they will stand strong against the forces of darkness."

"May the heavens bless them," murmured an old man, his voice frail but resolute. "For they are our shield and our salvation in these dire times."

As the words of encouragement and admiration drifted up to where the three warriors stood, Valthor couldn't help but feel both humbled and invigorated by the trust placed in them. He exchanged a glance with Adaon, who subtly nodded, acknowledging the weight of their responsibility.

Suddenly, trumpets blared, heralding the arrival of Lord Eldryn himself. The aged ruler strode forth with a regal bearing, his white beard flowing like a silken river. His eyes were alight with wisdom and determination as he addressed the gathered crowd, his voice carrying far beyond the city walls.

"Brave citizens of our beloved city!" he proclaimed, his words stirring the hearts of those who listened. "The hour of our greatest trial is upon us. It is true that the forces of darkness gather on the horizon, seeking to bring ruin to all we hold dear. But let us not cower in fear, for we have been blessed with mighty defenders!"

Lord Eldryn gestured toward Valthor, Adaon, and Lilith, his eyes filled with pride and admiration. The trio stood tall and resolute, their forms silhouetted against the twilight sky.

"Trust in them, for they are our hope and our salvation!" the noble ruler continued. "But do not rely on them alone— we must all stand together, united against the coming storm! Each of us has a part to play, a role in the defense of our home. Find courage in your hearts, and let it forge a shield that shall never break!"

As the crowd roared in response, Valthor felt a surge of determination course through him. He knew that the days ahead would test their resolve like never before, but with the support of their people and the guidance of Lord Eldryn, they would face the darkness head-on, no matter the cost.

"May the heavens watch over us all," he whispered to himself, certain that if they stood united, they would triumph over the apocalypse that threatened to consume their world.

Valthor's eyes scanned the sea of faces below, their expressions a mix of fear and determination. He looked to his companions, Adaon and Lilith, who stood resolute beside him. As they exchanged nods of understanding, a powerful sense of camaraderie washed over them.

"Remember," Valthor said, his voice low and steady, "we are the shield that guards this city. Together, we shall withstand the infernal tide."

"Indeed," Adaon replied, adjusting his quiver of arrows. "We've faced many trials, Valthor, but none so dire as this. Yet, I have no doubt that our bond will carry us through."

"Agreed," Lilith added, her hand resting on the hilt of her sword. "The darkness may be vast, but it has not met a force like us."

As they shared a moment of steadfast unity, several warriors and townsfolk approached the trio. Among them was Elara, a healer whose skill had saved countless lives, including Valthor's own during a past battle. Her silver hair framed a face marked by wisdom and experience.

"Valthor, Adaon, Lilith," she said with a warm smile, "we stand behind you in these final days. The people trust in your strength and valor, and I know that together, we shall overcome this darkness."

"Thank you, Elara," Valthor replied, nodding solemnly. "Your support means more than you know."

"Indeed," Adaon chimed in, "and should any of us falter, we know that your healing hands will be there to mend our wounds."

"Or to give us a stern lecture about taking better care of ourselves," Lilith added with a smirk.

Elara's eyes twinkled with amusement. "Well, someone must keep you three in check. Now, go and prepare for the battle ahead. We will be here, ready to aid you in any way we can."

As the trio turned to continue their preparations, a young boy with wide, awestruck eyes approached them. His hands clutched a small bundle of wildflowers— a symbol of hope amidst the chaos.

"Sir Valthor," he stammered, "I… I just wanted to say thank you. You're like heroes from the old stories, and I know you'll protect us all."

Valthor knelt down, taking the flowers with a gentle smile. "Thank you, young one. Your faith gives us strength. Remember, courage dwells within each of us. When the time comes, be brave and stand with your people."

The boy's chest puffed out with pride as he nodded, his gaze filled with admiration. In that moment, Valthor felt the weight of responsibility upon him, but also a renewed sense of determination. With the support and unity of their people, they would face the encroaching darkness and defend their city to the very end.

The sun dipped low in the sky, casting an eerie orange glow over the city's towering walls. Constructed of solid granite and reinforced with iron, they stood as a testament to the ingenuity and determination of its people. A sense of foreboding hung heavy in the air, but beneath it, the fires of defiance burned bright.

Valthor, Adaon, and Lilith walked along the ramparts, their eyes scanning the horizon for any sign of the encroaching enemy. They inspected each defensive measure meticulously, ensuring that every stone was secure and every trap primed for the impending battle.

"Adaon," Valthor said, his voice a rumble like distant thunder, "how fares our supply of arrows?"

"Plentiful, for now," Adaon replied, his fingers brushing against the fletching of an arrow. "But should this siege last long, we may need to ration them."

"Then let us hope our aim remains true," Lilith chimed in, her fiery red hair whipping about in the wind. Her grip tightened around the hilt of her sword, knuckles white with determination.

As they continued their inspection, a group of blacksmiths approached, bearing the trio's weapons and armor. The polished steel gleamed in the fading light, reflecting the steadfast resolve etched on their faces.

"Valthor Malgath," one of the blacksmiths began, presenting the warrior with a mighty war-axe. Its blade, cold and sharp as ice, promised a swift end to any who dared threaten their home. "May your strength never waver."

"Adaon," another blacksmith offered the archer a finely crafted bow of yew, its string taut and ready for battle. "May your aim be as swift and true as the wind."

"Thank you," Adaon replied, accepting the weapon with a nod.

Finally, Lilith received her gleaming longsword, its edge honed to a razor's sharpness. "May your courage never falter," the blacksmith said, and she nodded in agreement.

"Let us take a moment of silence to prepare ourselves," Valthor suggested, his deep voice sincere. The trio bowed their heads, each lost in their thoughts as they steeled themselves for what lay ahead.

The approaching storm of war threatened to engulf them all, but still, they stood resolute. For within each of them burned a fire fueled by love, loyalty, and an unyielding determination to protect their city and its people. And as long as that fire blazed, hope would never truly be extinguished.

"Come," Valthor said, lifting his gaze to meet those of his comrades, "let us stand firm against the darkness and fight for our home!"

An eerie silence fell over the training grounds, pierced only by the quiet rustle of leaves dancing in the wind. Under a blood-red sky, Valthor, Adaon, and Lilith stood side by side, their weapons gleaming in the fading light. Their breaths came out in tense, measured puffs, as if each exhale contained the weight of their determination.

"Remember," Valthor began, his voice low but steady, "when the battle comes, we fight not just for ourselves, but for our families, our loved ones, and every soul within these walls." He raised his war-axe, its blade reflecting the darkening sky like a mirror, and swung it with practiced precision, slicing the air before him.

"Right," Adaon agreed, nocking an arrow onto his bowstring and drawing back with ease. His eyes narrowed, focused on an invisible target in the distance. "We are the last line of defense, the final hope for our people. We cannot fail them." He released the arrow, and it whistled through the air, striking an unseen mark with deadly accuracy.

Lilith's gaze flitted over the pair as she tightened her grip on the hilt of her longsword. Her heart thundered in her chest, but her resolve remained steadfast. "No matter what horrors come our way," she declared, her voice resolute and unwavering, "we will stand strong against them."

"Let us sharpen our skills and steel our minds," Valthor said, nodding in agreement. "Together, we shall become an unbreakable fortress against the darkness that threatens our home."

The trio launched into a flurry of action, their weapons singing through the air as they honed their individual skills. Valthor's axe cut through the air in powerful arcs, each swing precise and lethal. Adaon's arrows flew with unerring accuracy, piercing the heart of each target he set his sights on. Lilith's sword danced with a deadly grace, her movements fluid and agile as she carved through imaginary foes.

As they trained, thoughts of those they held dear filled their minds, fueling their determination to protect them at all costs. Valthor thought of his aging parents, still brimming with pride for their son who had become a symbol of hope for the city. Adaon recalled the laughter of his young siblings, innocent and carefree despite the looming threat. And Lilith, though hesitant to trust others easily, found solace in the bonds forged between her and her fellow warriors, knowing that together they formed an unbreakable alliance against the darkness.

"Promise me," Lilith said suddenly, her voice barely above a whisper, "that no matter what happens, we will not let our people down."

Valthor and Adaon exchanged glances before nodding determinedly. "We promise," Valthor replied, his voice firm and unwavering. "Together, we will stand strong against whatever challenges come our way. We will fight to the death, if necessary, to protect our home."

"May the heavens grant us strength," Adaon murmured, gazing up at the blood-red sky, where storm clouds gathered ominously on the horizon. "For the fate of our city rests upon our shoulders, and we must be prepared to bear that burden with honor and courage."

As the trio continued their training, the weight of their responsibility settling heavily upon them, they felt an unwavering resolve solidify within their hearts. Their skills were honed, their minds focused, and their spirits aflame with the burning desire to defend their home and loved ones against the impending onslaught.

And so, under the watchful eye of a blood-red sky, the last defenders of the besieged city prepared themselves for the battle that would determine the fate of their world.

The narrow, cobblestone streets of the city teemed with life as the citizens went about their daily routines. Market stalls overflowed with fresh produce and fragrant spices, while blacksmiths hammered away at glowing metal, forging weapons for the upcoming battle. Children chased each other through the alleys, their laughter a stark contrast to the somber expressions on their parents' faces. Despite the semblance of normalcy, an undercurrent of tension and anticipation thrummed through the air.

Valthor surveyed the scene from atop the city walls, his dark eyes darting between the bustling streets below and the ominous storm clouds above. The people needed hope now more than ever, and he knew it was up to him, Adaon, and Lilith to provide that glimmer of light in the darkness.

"Are you ready?" Adaon asked, his voice steady and calm as he approached Valthor, bow slung over his shoulder. "The people are gathered."

"Let us remind them what we stand for," Lilith chimed in, her red hair whipping around her face as she joined them on the battlements. "Together, we can face any threat."

Valthor took a deep breath and nodded, steeling himself for the task ahead. He led Adaon and Lilith down the steps to the central square, where a sea of anxious faces awaited them. As they approached, the crowd parted, and a hush fell over the assembly.

"Listen well, my friends," Valthor began, his voice booming across the square. "We know the enemy draws near, but fear not! We have prepared, we have trained, and we are ready to defend our home!"

"Look around you," Adaon added, gesturing to those gathered. "Your brothers, your sisters, your neighbors– we all share the same purpose, the same determination. Together, we are strong, and together, we will stand against the tide of darkness!"

"Remember," Lilith continued, her voice fierce and unwavering, "you are not fighting alone. We stand beside you, ready to face whatever may come. Our resolve is unbreakable, our loyalty boundless, and our courage unyielding."

"Let us stand united as one, shoulder to shoulder in this darkest hour," Valthor declared, his eyes blazing with conviction. "We have faced challenges before, and we have always emerged victorious. This time shall be no different!"

"May the heavens grant us strength," Adaon whispered, echoing his earlier sentiment. "And may our unity be a beacon of hope that shines through the storm."

As the trio's words washed over the gathered crowd, a ripple of determination spread through the people. Heads lifted, shoulders squared, and eyes gleamed with newfound resolve. In that moment, the beleaguered citizens took heart, the seeds of hope sown within their souls.

With the threat of annihilation looming ever closer, the people of the city drew strength from their unity and the unwavering commitment of their protectors. As the last rays of sunlight vanished beneath the horizon, plunging the world into darkness, the citizens stood resolute, prepared to face whatever fate awaited them at the dawn of this final battle.

As Valthor surveyed the city below, he could not help but marvel at the determination etched upon the faces of its inhabitants. They went about their daily routines, yet their eyes remained ever watchful, a constant reminder of the impending threat. The air hummed with an undercurrent of resolute energy that pulsed like a heartbeat, uniting them all.

"Adaon," Valthor called, his voice steady and strong. "Lilith, gather around. There's something we must do."

The trio convened atop the city walls, their gazes fixed on the horizon. A crimson sunset bathed the sky in a fiery glow, casting ominous shadows across the land. Valthor drew a deep breath, feeling the weight of responsibility settle heavily upon his shoulders.

"Friends," he began, his tone solemn and commanding, "we have spoken to our people and given them hope, but now it is time for us to prepare for what lies ahead. We must be ready to face the enemy together, as one."

"Indeed," Adaon replied, his eyes narrowing as he scanned the darkening landscape. "We cannot let the fear of the unknown grip our hearts. Our people depend on us."

Lilith nodded, her jaw set firmly. "Whatever may come, we shall stand against it." Her hand instinctively tightened around the hilt of her sword.

Valthor looked at his fellow warriors, pride swelling within him. "Let this moment serve as a vow, a sacred bond between us. No matter how great the darkness, we will fight until our last breath, until our final heartbeat."

"Agreed," Adaon said, clasping Valthor's shoulder.

"May death itself tremble before our might," Lilith whispered, her eyes blazing with ferocity.

As the last remnants of daylight faded beneath the horizon, a sudden chill swept through the air. The scent of impending doom lingered like a shroud, suffocating and ominous. Valthor's heart raced, an instinctive warning echoing within the depths of his soul.

"Something approaches," he murmured, his gaze locked on the now pitch-black expanse beyond the city walls.

Adaon and Lilith tensed, their eyes scanning the darkness for any sign of movement. A heavy silence enveloped them, broken only by the distant howl of a lone wolf.

"Ready yourselves," Valthor whispered, his hand gripping the hilt of his sword so tightly that his knuckles turned white. "The enemy is upon us."

As the words left his lips, a cacophony of malevolent laughter erupted from the shadows, heralding the arrival of the army they had feared for so long. With mounting dread, Valthor realized that the final battle had begun– a battle that would decide the fate of not just their city, but of humankind itself.

"May the heavens have mercy on us all," he breathed, steeling himself for the cataclysmic confrontation that lay before them.

V

THE WORLD IN CHAOS

The world had become a forsaken wasteland, its surface scarred by the merciless wrath of Satan, Gog, and Magog. The once-thriving cities lay in ruins; their towering skyscrapers now reduced to lifeless skeletons, mere shadows of their former grandeur. The air reeked of smoke and ash, suffocating the few remaining survivors as they choked on the remnants of their shattered existence. Rivers flowed crimson with the blood of the fallen, while the sun, obscured by an eternal veil of darkness, cast no light upon the chaos that had befallen humanity.

In the midst of this devastation, a lone figure stood tall and defiant against the backdrop of ruin. Lucian Donovan, a young man in his mid-40s, surveyed the carnage with a fierce determination burning in his chest. His height was not lost among the rubble, his tall stature commanding attention even in the face of Armageddon. Dark hair crowned his head, wild and untamed, much like the spirit that drove him forward through the desolation.

Lucian's steely gray eyes scanned the horizon, taking in the destruction wrought by the release of the unholy trinity. His strong-willed nature, once suppressed beneath layers of doubt and fear, had risen to the surface, forged anew by the fires that consumed the world around him. He knew that he could no longer stand idly by while evil ravaged all that he held dear. He bore the weight of humanity on his broad shoulders, aware that it rested upon him to restore order from the chaos that threatened to swallow them whole.

"Enough," Lucian muttered under his breath, clenching his fists at his sides. "This ends now."

His voice carried over the wind, a beacon of hope amid the desolation. It was a declaration of war against the force of darkness, a promise to fight until his last breath to protect the world and all who remained in it from the relentless onslaught of Satan, Gog, and Magog.

A cacophony of screams and wails echoed through the air as chaos reigned supreme. Buildings crumbled, fires raged, and the earth itself seemed to shudder in protest against the malevolent forces unleashed upon it. Amid this maelstrom of destruction stood Lucian Donovan, his heart pounding in his chest like a war drum, his breath catching in his throat.

"Dear God," he whispered, his voice barely audible over the din that surrounded him. "What have they done?"

His strong-willed nature initially paralyzed by shock and disbelief, Lucian could only stare as he watched the world unravel before him. A young mother clutched her infant tightly to her chest, tears streaming down her face as she fled from an oncoming wall of flame. An elderly man stumbled and fell, unable to rise as the ground beneath him cracked and split open.

"Please... someone help them!" Lucian cried out, his voice choked with emotion.

Though he was but one man against a seemingly insurmountable tide of darkness, Lucian's spirit refused to be crushed. Through his eyes, the reader bore witness to the full extent of the devastation wrought by Satan, Gog, and Magog. Cities lay in ruin, their once-majestic skylines now little more than smoldering husks. The very land itself appeared poisoned, the once-verdant fields now barren and lifeless.

"Is there no one left to stand against them?" Lucian wondered aloud, his voice tinged with desperation. "Are we truly so powerless?"

"Lucian," a voice called out weakly from behind him. He turned to see a ragged figure huddled amid the ruins, his clothes torn and bloodied.

"Who are you? How do you know my name?" Lucian asked, his heart racing with equal parts dread and hope.

"Does it matter?" the stranger replied, grimacing in pain. "What matters is this: you are not alone in your fight. But we must act quickly, or all will be lost."

"Then tell me what to do," Lucian demanded, fire igniting within him once more. "Tell me how to stop them."

"Take this," the stranger said, pressing a small object into Lucian's hand. "It is the key to their undoing."

As Lucian stared at the item, his mind raced with questions and fears. The weight of the entire world bore down upon him as he faced the daunting task ahead. He knew that he could not afford to fail– humanity's very survival depended on it.

"May God have mercy on us all," Lucian murmured, steeling himself for the battle that lay ahead. With a final glance at the destruction that surrounded him, he turned and walked towards his horse and began his journey into the heart of darkness itself.

As Lucian stared at the small object in his hand, the key to their undoing, he felt the weight of responsibility settle upon his shoulders like a leaden cloak. He knew that this was his moment, his chance to rise above the ashes of a broken world and stand as its protector and defender. The destructive forces of Satan, Gog, and Magog had been unleashed, and now it was up to him to face them head-on.

"Are you certain this will work?" Lucian asked the stranger, his voice wavering slightly.

"Nothing is certain," the stranger replied, "the only thing that is certain,..... is the love.... of my God". His eyes filled with sorrow. "But it is our best hope."

Lucian clenched his fist around the object, his knuckles turning white. He took a deep breath, exhaling slowly as he steeled himself for the trials ahead. Though doubt gnawed at the edges of his resolve, he refused to let it consume him.

"Then I will use it," he declared boldly, his gaze fixed on the horizon. "I will confront these enemies of mankind and put an end to their reign of terror."

"Be brave, Lucian," the stranger urged, resting on a pool of blood, several dead people lying all around him, a hand on his shoulder. "The fate of the world rests on your shoulders."

"Bravery alone won't be enough," Lucian admitted, his inner turmoil churning like a stormy sea. "I'll need every ounce of strength I possess, both physical and mental, to overcome what lies ahead."

"Remember that you are not alone," the stranger reminded him, his voice laced with compassion. "There are others who will stand by your side when the time comes."

"Will they be enough?" Lucian asked, his eyes searching the stranger's face for reassurance.

"Only time will tell," came the somber response.

With that, the stranger melted back into the shadows, leaving Lucian to face his destiny. As he stood amidst the desolation, his heart heavy with the burden of his task, Lucian resolved to confront his doubts and fears head-on, transforming them into a source of strength rather than weakness.

"God! grant me the courage to face this darkness," he whispered, his voice barely audible above the howling winds that whipped around him. "For though I am but one man, I know that I must stand against these monstrous forces for the sake of all humanity."

And so, with a steely determination that belied the fear in his heart, Lucian Donovan set forth on his perilous journey, driven by a newfound purpose that burned within him like an unquenchable flame. Only time would tell if his resolve would be enough to stem the tide of destruction, but he knew one thing for certain: he would not go down without a fight.

As Lucian surveyed the wreckage of what was once a thriving world, his heart swelled with a mix of fear and determination. He knew that he could not stand idly by while the forces of evil wreaked havoc upon the world, leaving only death and despair in their wake. Despite the odds being stacked against him, Lucian made a conscious decision to protect humanity and all that was good in this world.

"Though I face great challenges and dangers," he murmured to himself, "I will stand as a beacon of hope amidst this darkness."

His first plan of action was to gather information about the enemy he was to face. Satan, Gog, and Magog were a formidable trio– each with their own unique strengths and weaknesses. Lucian knew that knowledge would be key in finding a way to confront and ultimately defeat them.

"Those who fight blindly are doomed from the start," he thought, steeling his resolve. "I must learn all I can about these fearsome adversaries if I am to have any hope of victory."

Lucian's initial investigation led him to seek out ancient texts and wise scholars, delving deep into the lore surrounding each of the three antagonists. He spent countless hours poring over dusty scrolls and manuscripts, searching for any hint of a weakness that he could exploit.

"Every foe has a flaw," he told himself as he studied, the flickering candlelight casting eerie shadows across the parchment before him. "I just need to find theirs."

In his quest for knowledge, Lucian also sought out allies who might aid him in his battle against evil. He traveled far and wide, speaking with warriors, mages, and priests, hoping to form a coalition strong enough to challenge the relentless onslaught of darkness.

"United, we may stand a chance against these monstrous foes," he declared, rallying those who shared his cause. "For when the light of hope is joined together, it can pierce even the blackest night."

Throughout his journey, Lucian's thoughts often returned to his own doubts and fears. He knew that he was but one man– a single warrior against an enemy of immense power and wickedness. Yet each time those nagging thoughts threatened to overwhelm him, he pushed them aside, drawing strength from the conviction that lay deep within his soul.

"Though I tread a path of uncertainty," he pondered as he stared into the endless night sky, "I will not let fear rule me, for I am driven by a purpose greater than myself."

With every new piece of information and each ally gained, Lucian felt his resolve growing stronger. He knew that the battle ahead would be long and arduous, filled with pain and sacrifice. But he also knew that he could not turn back now— the fate of the world hung in the balance, and he would not rest until the forces of evil had been vanquished once and for all.

"By my blood, I swear to protect this world," he vowed, steel flashing in his hand as he gazed out over the desolate landscape. "And may the heavens above grant me the strength to see this task through to its bitter end."

Lucian stood at the edge of a crumbling precipice, his dark eyes surveying the charred and desolate wasteland before him. The acrid scent of smoke hung heavy in the air, stinging his nostrils and throat as he drew in a sharp breath. This was no world for the weak or hesitant— it was a land torn apart by chaos and destruction, where only the strong could hope to survive.

"Time is short," he whispered, his voice barely audible above the howling winds that whipped around him. "I must act."

With one last glance at the hellish landscape, Lucian turned on his heel and strode purposefully toward the heart of the chaos. Each step felt like a declaration, a promise to uphold his vow to protect the world from the malevolent forces that threatened to consume it.

As he ventured deeper into the maelstrom, the cries of suffering souls echoed in his ears, a haunting reminder of the urgency of his mission. He knew that each moment he spent preparing was another that the world teetered on the brink of annihilation.

"Every second counts," he muttered, quickening his pace.

"Where do you think you're going?" A gruff voice called out from the shadows, causing Lucian to halt abruptly.

"Who's there?" He demanded, his hand instinctively reaching for his weapon.

"Easy, lad," the voice replied, its owner emerging from the darkness. The man was old and wizened, with a long gray beard and piercing blue eyes that seemed to bore into Lucian's very soul. "I've been waiting for you."

"Waiting for me?" Lucian questioned, his brow furrowing in confusion. "Why?"

"Because you are the one who can stand against Satan, Gog, and Magog," the old man replied solemnly, his gaze never wavering. "You are the one destined to save us all."

"Then I must act quickly," Lucian insisted, his mind racing with thoughts of what he needed to do. "There is no time to waste."

"Indeed," the old man agreed, nodding sagely. as the darkness covered his face "But first, you must learn. You cannot face them unprepared, for they are cunning and ruthless in their quest for power."

"Teach me, then," Lucian implored, urgency clawing at his chest. "Tell me what I must do to defeat them and restore order to this world."

"Very well," the old man said, with the hood covering his face, a flicker of a smile gracing his weathered features. "But know that the path you walk will be fraught with danger and hardship. Are you prepared for that?"

"Whatever it takes," Lucian vowed, his voice fierce and unwavering. "I will not rest until they are vanquished and peace once again reigns."

"Then let us begin," the old man declared, his eyes shining with determination as he led Lucian away from the ravaged landscape.

As they walked together, the weight of the world rested heavily upon Lucian's broad shoulders. Yet despite the gravity of his task, he felt a spark of hope ignite within him— the first glimmer of light in a world consumed by darkness. He knew that the journey would be long and treacherous, but with each step he took, he felt his resolve grow stronger.

"I will not fail," he whispered into the howling winds, his words carried forth like a promise to the heavens above. "I will fight, and I will prevail."

The sky above them churned with the tumult of a thousand storms, casting an eerie pallor over the desolate landscape. Lucian and his mentor stood on a precipice overlooking a vast expanse of scorched earth, punctuated by the twisted remains of what once were cities and towns. The air was thick with the stench of smoldering ash and charred flesh.

"Look closely, Lucian," the old man instructed, his voice barely audible above the cacophony of thunder and wind. "This is the result of their malevolence– the fate that awaits us all if we do not act."

Lucian's dark eyes roved over the destruction, and a bitter taste filled his mouth as he swallowed down the bile that rose in his throat. He raised a trembling hand to his face, wiping away the tears that threatened to spill over.

"I understand," he said, his voice cracking with emotion. "We must stop them before it's too late."

"Indeed," the old man replied, his expression grim. "But first, you must learn how to wield your newfound power. It will not be easy, but I have faith in your strength and determination."

They began their training in haste, with the old man teaching Lucian the ancient arts of combat and strategy. Each day, they pushed themselves harder, honing their skills in preparation for the battle that lay ahead. And though his body ached with fatigue, Lucian never wavered in his commitment to their cause.

As days turned to weeks, and weeks gave way to months, Lucian became stronger, faster, and more adept at wielding his powers. Yet even as he grew in confidence, he knew that time was running out, and the forces of darkness continued to gather strength.

One fateful night, beneath the blood-red glow of a lunar eclipse, Lucian stood alone on the edge of a cliff, gazing out at the chaos that lay before him. Despite his progress and newfound abilities, doubt still gnawed at the edges of his resolve.

"Am I truly ready?" he whispered into the darkness, his voice barely audible above the roar of the wind. "Can I really save this world?"

"Your heart is strong, Lucian," the old man's voice echoed from behind him, steady as stone. "You have made tremendous progress, but now you must trust in yourself and believe in your destiny."

Lucian closed his eyes, taking a deep, steadying breath as he reached inside himself for the strength he knew he possessed. He felt the power coursing through his veins, surging like lightning beneath his skin.

"Then let it begin," he said, his words resolute and clear as he turned to face his mentor. "I am ready to confront them— to fight for all that is good and just in this world."

"Very well," the old man replied, his expression solemn. "But know that once you embark on this path, there can be no turning back. You are our last hope, Lucian Donovan. The fate of humanity rests in your hands."

As the moon cast its eerie glow upon their faces, the two figures stood side by side, their gazes locked on the horizon where darkness loomed like a shroud. And as they prepared to enter the fray, an unspoken vow passed between them— a promise to fight until their dying breaths, or until the world was free from the shadows that sought to consume it.

"Let us go forth," Lucian declared, his voice ringing with determination. "Together, we shall face the storm, and emerge victorious."

The sky overhead was a tumultuous canvas of swirling black clouds, pierced by the fiery tendrils of lightning. The ground trembled beneath Lucian's feet, as if the very earth itself groaned under the weight of its impending doom. Despite the chaos surrounding him, Lucian stood tall, his dark hair whipped about by the gale-force winds that threatened to uproot the last vestiges of humanity's hope.

"Are you sure this is where they'll be?" Lucian asked, his voice barely audible above the howling storm.

"Indeed," the old man replied, his own voice strained but resolute. "Satan, Gog, and Magog will converge at this place, seeking to complete their unholy trinity and unleash destruction upon us all."

Lucian scanned the desolate landscape before them, his heart heavy with the weight of responsibility. He knew the price that would be paid if he faltered, if he allowed fear or doubt to consume him. But as he stared into the abyss, he felt an ember of defiance flicker within him— a spark of determination that burned brighter with each passing moment.

"Then we must not waste any more time," Lucian stated, his resolve hardening like steel around his heart. "We will stand our ground here, and face them head-on. Together, we shall drive back the darkness and restore the light."

Before Lucian could take another step, a sudden flash of crimson illuminated the sky, casting an eerie, blood-red hue over the battlefield. A deafening roar shook the heavens, and from the maelstrom of shadows emerged the twisted forms of Satan, Gog, and Magog.

"Come, then!" Lucian bellowed, his voice filled with the fire of unyielding conviction. "Face me, and know that I am the end of your reign of terror!"

"Lucian," the old man whispered, his eyes filled with sorrow yet shining with pride. "It has been an honor to stand by your side."

"Likewise," Lucian replied, sparing a glance at his mentor before turning his attention back to the approaching abominations. As the unholy trinity closed in, Lucian could feel the terror clawing at the edges of his consciousness, but he refused to give in.

"Remember," he thought to himself, "I am the defender of this world, and I will not falter."

With a roar that echoed through the storm-stricken skies, Lucian charged headlong into the fray, each step a testament to his unwavering determination to save humanity.

"Come forth, you monsters!" he cried, his voice a clarion call of defiance against the darkness. "I am Lucian Donovan, and I shall be your end!"

As the battle raged on, the very fabric of reality seemed to shudder under the onslaught of demonic forces. But as long as Lucian's heart continued to beat with fierce resolve, there remained a glimmer of hope– a beacon of light amidst the encroaching shadows of despair.

The air was thick with the acrid stench of burning flesh, sulfur and brimstone, an unholy miasma that clung to the lungs like a drowning man's last breath. The once verdant landscape had been reduced to a desolate wasteland, its fragile beauty ravaged by the unrelenting forces of darkness.

Lucifer's twisted laughter echoed through the charred remains of cities, his triumphant howl a harrowing reminder of humanity's approaching doom.

"Lucian! We need to move!" a voice cried out, cutting through the cacophony of chaos.

"Right!" Lucian grunted, his dark hair matted with sweat as he pushed himself to his feet. His tall frame towered over the smoldering ruins, his piercing eyes scanning the horizon for any sign of hope amidst the devastation.

"Look!" shouted one of his companions, pointing toward a small group of survivors huddled together in fear. "We can't just leave them here!"

"Agreed," Lucian replied, his strong-willed nature refusing to abandon those who still drew breath. With swift determination, he strode toward the terrified civilians, extending a hand of reassurance as he spoke. "I am Lucian Donovan. I will protect you."

"Please please save us," a woman sobbed, her tear-streaked face reflecting the depths of her despair.

"Stay close and keep moving," Lucian instructed, his heart aching for the innocent lives caught in the crossfire of celestial war.

As they pressed on, the ground trembled beneath their feet, each quake heralding the approach of Satan's most fearsome generals: Gog and Magog. Their monstrous roars were like the crack of thunder, reverberating through the air and igniting a primal fear within the very marrow of Lucian's bones.

"Go! Keep moving!" Lucian shouted to the survivors, his voice a blend of urgency and steely resolve. "I'll hold them off!"

"Lucian!" one of his companions protested. "You can't face them alone!"

"Watch me," he growled, his eyes narrowing with determination.

"Think quickly, Lucian! There's no time to lose!" whispered the old man who had been by his side since the beginning of this nightmare, his mentor and guide in this apocalyptic world.

"Remember your training, and remember who you are," Lucian replied, his own voice barely audible amidst the deafening roar of the approaching doom. The weight of responsibility settled heavily upon his shoulders, but Lucian refused to buckle under its pressure.

"Let them come," he muttered to himself, clenching his fists as he prepared to face the oncoming storm. "I am ready."

The maelstrom of destruction swirled around him, but within Lucian's heart burned a fierce defiance that refused to be extinguished. As the hordes of hell bore down upon him, he knew that the fate of humankind rested upon his broad shoulders.

The sun hung low in the sky, casting an eerie red glow over the remnants of a world ravaged by chaos and destruction. Smoldering ruins stretched as far as the eye could see, while the air was thick with the acrid stench of smoke and decay. The once lush landscape had been reduced to a desolate wasteland, marred by deep craters and jagged fissures that snaked their way across the charred earth.

Lucian Valeria surveyed the apocalyptic scene before him, his heart heavy with the burden of survival. He stood amidst a small group of survivors who had banded together in the face of this devastation, their faces etched with despair and fatigue. Their eyes, hollow and haunted, held flickers of hope that seemed to wane with each passing day.

"Is there any chance we'll ever see the end of this nightmare?" one survivor asked, her voice barely a whisper.

Lucian's gaze hardened, and he spoke with quiet conviction. "There is a prophecy—ancient and almost forgotten—that speaks of a time when the forces of evil will be vanquished and peace restored to the Earth."

"Tell us more," urged another survivor, desperation seeping into his tone.

"Legend has it that there will come a day when Satan's generals, Gog and Magog, shall rise and unleash a storm of destruction upon the world. As they lay waste to all that stands in their path, a warrior of unwavering resolve will emerge from the ashes—a beacon of hope for humanity."

"Is that… Are you that warrior, Lucian?" Amara Sinclair asked, her eyes wide with awe and terror.

"Only time will tell," he replied solemnly, "but I swear to you all, I will do everything in my power to protect you and stand against the darkness that threatens to consume us."

As Lucian spoke these words, the survivors exchanged furtive glances, daring to believe that perhaps there was a chance for redemption amidst the ruin. The prophecy, though vague and steeped in myth, brought a glimmer of hope—a lifeline for those who had lost everything.

"Then we stand with you, Lucian," declared Gideon Blackwood, his voice firm with resolve. "Together, we will face whatever trials lie ahead."

And as they stood together, a ragtag group of survivors united by a shared fate, the first faint stirrings of hope began to take root.

The wind tore at Lucian's tattered clothing as he stood amidst the ruins, his gaze sweeping over the devastated landscape that stretched out before him. His chiseled face bore the marks of countless battles— jagged scars tracing a brutal roadmap of survival across his skin. Piercing eyes, a steely gray reflecting the turmoil of the world around him, were narrowed in determination.

"Lucian," Amara called out to him, her voice barely audible over the howling wind. "We can't stay here much longer."

"I know." His deep voice carried the weight of unyielding resolve. "But we cannot run forever. We must find a way to stand against this darkness."

"Is it even possible?" Gideon asked, his voice laced with both doubt and hope. "Can we truly fight against Satan's generals?"

"Only if we are united," Lucian replied, his words like solid steel. He stood tall and resolute, an unwavering figure amidst the chaos that enveloped them. The survivors couldn't help but be drawn to him, his presence radiating a sense of strength and purpose that was almost palpable.

"United, then," Amara agreed, her eyes shining with newfound determination. "What do we do next?"

"First, we must gather our strength. Find food and shelter. Prepare ourselves for what lies ahead," Lucian said, his tone brooking no argument. "Then we train. Learn to fight as one. To protect each other."

"Sounds like a plan," Gideon muttered, looking around at the others who nodded in agreement.

"Good," Lucian said, clapping a hand on Gideon's shoulder. "It won't be easy, but we have no other choice. The prophecy speaks of a warrior who will rise to defy the darkness. I will do everything in my power to fulfill that role, but I cannot do it alone."

"None of us can," Amara murmured, her eyes meeting Lucian's in a moment of shared understanding. "We're with you, Lucian, no matter what."

"Then let's move," Lucian commanded, his voice resonating with authority. "We have much to do and little time to waste."

As the group of survivors began their journey through the desolate wasteland that was once their world, they took solace in the knowledge that they were not alone. They had each other, and they had Lucian—their unwavering beacon of hope.

And in his heart, Lucian knew that as long as he could draw breath, he would fight. He would stand against the darkness, refusing to submit, refusing to surrender. For himself, for the ones he had sworn to protect, and for all of humanity.

The sun hung low in the sky, casting a blood-red hue over the decimated landscape. It was as if the very heavens themselves mourned for the world that had been lost. The survivors moved forward in silence, each haunted by their own private terrors. Among them were Amara Sinclair, with her fierce green eyes and dark hair that whipped around her face like a battle standard, and Gideon Blackwood, his beard unkempt and ragged from countless days on the run.

Lucian led the group with unyielding determination, his chiseled face set into an unwavering expression. His eyes scanned their surroundings, alert to any signs of danger, while his mind raced with plans and strategies. He knew they faced an enemy unlike any other: Gog and Magog, Satan's generals, who had been unleashed upon the earth to wreak havoc and despair.

"Stay close," he whispered to Amara, who nodded silently, her hand gripping the hilt of her sword.

Gideon's eyes flicked warily between Lucian and the horizon, his fingers drumming nervously against the shaft of his makeshift spear. "We're not ready for this," he muttered, mostly to himself. "How can we possibly stand against such evil?"

"By remembering what we're fighting for," Lucian replied, his voice steady and resolute. "And by trusting in the prophecy."

As if summoned by their fears, a deafening roar shattered the eerie silence, and the ground trembled beneath their feet. In the distance, two monstrous figures approached, their forms barely discernible through the gathering darkness. Gog and Magog had come.

The survivors' hearts pounded within their chests, each beat a testament to the terror that coursed through their veins. Desperation clawed at their throats as they stared down the approaching doom, but in that moment of darkness, Lucian's resolve shone like a beacon, drawing them closer to him.

"Stand your ground," he ordered, his voice barely audible over the howling wind. "We've come too far to let fear win now."

Amara's grip on her sword tightened, and her eyes flashed with determination as she stood beside Lucian. Gideon swallowed hard, steadying himself as he raised his spear. The other survivors followed suit, their faces etched with grim resolve.

As Gog and Magog drew nearer, an oppressive aura of evil radiated from them, threatening to smother all hope that remained. Yet in the face of such darkness, Lucian's heart burned with fierce defiance. He would not allow these monstrous beings to claim any more lives—not while he could still fight.

"Are you with me?" he asked, his eyes meeting each of theirs in turn.

"We stand with you, Lucian," Amara vowed, her voice unwavering. "To the bitter end."

"Then let us show these demons what we're made of," Lucian declared, steeling himself for the battle to come. And as Gog and Magog closed in, the survivors prepared to fight for their very existence, united by the unbreakable bond forged in the fires of this apocalyptic world.

The ground trembled beneath their feet, a violent quaking that threatened to tear the very earth asunder. Cracks snaked across the desolate landscape, swallowing what little remained of the world they had once known. Lucian's heart raced in his chest as he felt the raw power of Gog and Magog's approach– the prophecy was beginning to unfold.

"Everyone, listen!" Lucian shouted, his voice carrying above the cacophony of destruction. "You must flee! I will hold them off as long as I can!"

Yet even as he spoke, he saw Amara, Gideon, and the others exchange glances filled with resolve. They had faced so much together, had sacrificed so much in the name of this desperate mission. To abandon it now would be to forsake all they had endured.

"No, Lucian," Amara replied, her voice steady despite the chaos erupting around them. "We won't leave you."

"Amara's right," Gideon added, gripping his spear tightly. "We've come this far together. We'll see it through to the end, no matter what."

Lucian searched their faces, seeing the unwavering determination etched there. He knew then that there would be no persuading them, and a fierce pride swelled within him at their collective courage.

"Very well," he conceded, his eyes never leaving the horizon where Gog and Magog continued their relentless advance. "But know this: we are not simply fighting for our lives. We are fighting for the souls of all mankind. Our victory here will mark the end of Satan's thousand-year captivity."

As he spoke, the survivors nodded, their gazes hardening with renewed purpose. They understood the gravity of their task, and the weight of the world rested upon their shoulders.

"Let's make our stand," Amara whispered, her grip on her sword tightened, knuckles turning white.

"Here and now," Gideon agreed, his eyes locked on the approaching menace.

The ground shuddered once more, the tremors growing stronger as the monstrous forms of Gog and Magog loomed ever closer. Lucian could see the fear in his companions' eyes, but also their unwavering resolve— they would stand with him until the very end.

"Then let us give these demons a battle they will never forget," Lucian declared, his voice filled with a fierce certainty that seemed to galvanize those around him. "For the sake of all humanity, we will not fail!"

And with that, they braced themselves for the coming onslaught, each one ready to face whatever horrors awaited them in this final confrontation. For the world was crumbling around them, and only through their courage and unity could any hope remain.

The air hung heavy with foreboding as the tremors grew ever stronger, the apocalyptic landscape a stark reminder of the world's shattered state. Lucian Valeria stood at the precipice, his piercing eyes scanning the horizon for any hint of the approaching hellish generals. His muscular frame was tense, poised like a coiled spring, ready to leap into action at a moment's notice. The scars that adorned his chiseled face and body were a testament to his battles fought and won, each one a story of survival in this desolate world.

"Lucian," Amara Sinclair's voice was soft but firm, her expression a mix of concern and admiration. "You don't have to do this alone. We can still run, find somewhere safe."

"Safe?" Lucian scoffed, his gaze never leaving the darkening sky as Gog and Magog continued their relentless advance. "There is no safe anymore, Amara. This is our last stand."

"Then let us help you," Gideon Blackwood interjected, his brow furrowed with determination. "Together, we can make a difference."

Lucian looked at his companions, seeing the fire in their eyes, the same fire that had burned within him all these years. He knew they were right— he couldn't do this alone. But he also knew the price of their loyalty, the lives that could be lost in the coming battle.

"Listen," Lucian began, his voice low and steady. "I appreciate your courage, but this is my fight. I've trained for this moment, for the fulfillment of this prophecy. I will not allow you to risk your lives in vain."

"Lucian," Amara said, her voice quivering with emotion. "We've come this far together. We will not stand by and watch you face this alone. If we die, we die fighting for something greater than ourselves."

"Besides," Gideon chimed in, a wry smile playing on his lips. "Who else is going to watch your back?"

Lucian couldn't help but chuckle at Gideon's words, despite the gravity of the situation. He knew that their bond, forged through shared adversity, was unbreakable. And perhaps, with their combined strength, they stood a chance against the approaching doom.

"Alright," Lucian conceded, his heart swelling with gratitude and pride. "Together, we'll hold them off for as long as we can. But remember: we're fighting not just for our lives, but for the souls of all mankind."

"Then let us make our stand," Amara whispered, her grip on her sword tightening.

"Here and now," Gideon agreed, his eyes locked on the encroaching darkness.

As the ground shook violently beneath them, Lucian steeled himself for the coming battle. He would not falter, not under pressure nor threat of death. With his companions by his side and the fate of humanity in the balance, he would face Gog and Magog with unwavering resolve. The end of Satan's thousand-year captivity was at hand, and he would do everything in his power to ensure that it remained so.

The ground trembled beneath them, as if the very earth itself were crying out in terror. A chilling wind swept through the battlefield, carrying with it the scent of sulfur and the distant echoes of agonized screams. The sky above was a swirling vortex of darkness, casting eerie shadows across the desolate landscape.

"Here they come," Gideon whispered, his voice barely audible over the howling wind.

Emerging from the blackness like a nightmare brought to life, the monstrous forms of Gog and Magog loomed ever closer. Their twisted visages bore expressions of pure malevolence, their eyes shining like red-hot embers amid the encroaching gloom. They moved with unnatural speed and agility, each step shaking the ground beneath them.

"Stay close," Lucian shouted to his companions, drawing upon every ounce of courage he possessed as the generals of Satan closed in. "We must hold our ground!"

With a deafening roar, Gog lunged at Lucian, its razor-sharp claws slashing through the air. He barely managed to dodge the lethal attack, feeling the wind from the near miss brush against his face. As he rolled to his feet, Magog joined the fray, unleashing a barrage of dark energy that tore through the earth like wildfire.

"Is this all you've got?!" Lucian bellowed defiantly, parrying another blow from Gog and swiftly countering with a powerful strike of his own. His sword hummed with divine energy, leaving searing trails of light in its wake as it struck true against the hideous creature.

"Lucian!" Amara cried out, her voice laced with both concern and admiration. She fought valiantly alongside him, her own blade clashing against Magog's fearsome form with unyielding determination. "We stand with you!"

"Then let's make these monsters regret ever crossing our path!" Gideon shouted, weaving in and out of the chaos with deadly precision. His daggers danced through the air like twin vipers, striking at the vulnerable joints of the hellish beasts.

As the battle raged on, Lucian found himself pushed to his limits. The relentless assault from Gog and Magog threatened to overwhelm him, and he could feel the strain of their onslaught beginning to wear him down. But he refused to succumb to fear or despair, for he knew that the fate of all humanity rested upon his shoulders.

"Stay strong," he whispered to himself, driving away the creeping tendrils of doubt with a fierce surge of determination. "For them."

With renewed vigor, Lucian fought back against the monstrous tide, his every movement a symphony of violence and grace. Each blow struck with unwavering resolve, each parry executed with a master's skill. And as he held off the terrifying forces of darkness, he became a beacon of hope amid the desolation, a symbol of mankind's indomitable spirit in the face of ultimate evil.

The deafening clash of Lucian's sword against the monstrous beast's hideous scales reverberated through the shattered landscape, a symphony of steel and fury. The once vibrant earth now lay in ruins, its cracked surface spewing forth plumes of smoke and ash– a testament to the apocalyptic events that had transpired.

"Lucian, you can't keep this up forever!" Amara cried out, her voice barely audible above the cacophony of battle. Her eyes were wide with fear as she watched him struggle against the relentless onslaught of Gog and Magog.

"I will not let them win," Lucian growled, his heart burning with fierce defiance. Each blow he struck carried the weight of his determination, the resounding echoes of his roars mingling with the cries of the beasts he fought.

"Fall back! We need a plan!" Gideon shouted, his daggers slicing through the air like lethal shadows. But Lucian refused to yield, digging his heels into the scorched earth as he held the line against the terrifying enemies before him.

"Stand your ground!" Lucian commanded, his eyes locked on Gog's nightmarish visage. "We will not let these abominations claim our world!"

His words echoed through the hearts and minds of the survivors, igniting a spark of courage within their souls. They charged forward, their weapons raised high, determined to fight alongside Lucian until their last breaths.

"Amara, Gideon, flank them!" Lucian ordered, his blade flashing in the hellish light as he continued to battle the demonic generals. His companions moved with deadly precision, weaving through the battlefield to encircle their foes.

"Your bravery is commendable, but ultimately futile," Gog snarled, his voice dripping with malice. He lunged at Lucian, who parried the attack with expert skill.

"Your kind will never triumph," Lucian replied, his voice unwavering. "For every one of you that rises, there are a thousand humans who would gladly give their lives to see you cast back into the abyss."

"Then let them come," Magog roared, its grotesque form twisting and writhing as it surged towards Lucian.

"Let them come indeed," Lucian whispered, his heart ablaze with resolve. As he fought, each swing of his sword carried the desperate hopes of those he sought to protect– a resounding promise that he would not falter in the face of evil.

The survivors watched in awe as Lucian continued to hold his ground against the monstrous tide. His bravery became a rallying cry, inspiring them to fight with renewed determination.

"Lucian, we stand with you!" Amara called out, her sword flashing in tandem with his as they fought back to back.

"Then stand strong," Lucian urged, his heart pounding like the drums of war. "Together, we will turn the tides of this battle and send these monsters to their doom!"

The grueling battle raged on, the scorched earth trembling beneath their feet as they fought. Lucian's muscles burned with fatigue, sweat and blood mingling to stain his skin. Yet, despite the odds against him, he persevered, driven by an unwavering resolve to protect those who had placed their faith in him.

"Face it, mortal!" Gog taunted, his voice echoing across the battlefield like thunder. "You cannot hope to stand against us!"

"Perhaps not alone," Lucian retorted, his eyes blazing with defiance. He struck at Gog with a roar of determination, his sword shimmering like a silver lightning bolt in the apocalyptic gloom. "But together, we are more than you can ever hope to overcome!"

"Your hope is misplaced," Magog sneered, lunging at Lucian with terrifying speed. But as if anticipating the attack, Lucian dodged just in time, his nimble movements belying the exhaustion that threatened to consume him.

"Is it?" Lucian questioned, the pain in his body momentarily forgotten as he focused on the task at hand. "For all your power, you have failed to break our spirit. In the end, that is what will lead to your undoing."

The warriors around him, heartened by Lucian's unyielding spirit, redoubled their efforts. They moved like a well-oiled machine, each blow struck with precision and strength borne from the knowledge that this was a battle for the very soul of humanity.

"Enough of this!" Gog roared, his monstrous form seething with rage. With a swift motion, he attempted to swipe Lucian off his feet, but the seasoned warrior anticipated the move, leaping high into the air to avoid the deadly claws.

"Your time is at an end, foul creatures!" Lucian shouted, using the momentum of his leap to deliver a powerful, downward strike at Gog's exposed neck. The force of the blow reverberated through the air, and Gog crumpled to the ground, defeated.

"NO!" Magog screamed, his face twisted into an expression of pure hatred. He charged at Lucian, but before he could reach him, Amara and Gideon intercepted the monstrous general, their combined strength enough to bring him down as well.

As Magog fell, the ground finally ceased its violent shaking. Lucian stood tall amidst the carnage, his chest heaving as he tried to catch his breath. The survivors around him began to cheer, their voices rising in unison like a triumphant anthem.

"Today, we have shown them that we will not go quietly into the night," Lucian declared, his eyes scanning the faces of those who had fought beside him. "This victory is ours, but let it also serve as a reminder that we must always be prepared for the battles ahead."

The survivors erupted into elated shouts and embraces, their eyes alight with hope as they basked in the improbable victory. In the center of it all stood Lucian, sweat glistening on his chiseled face, his piercing eyes observing the joy that surrounded him. He allowed himself a small smile, acknowledging the significance of their triumph.

"Lucian, you did it!" cried Amara Sinclair, rushing to his side, her eyes shimmering with unshed tears. "This is a new beginning for us all!"

"Indeed," Lucian agreed, his voice steady despite the fatigue that weighed heavily upon him. "But we must remain vigilant, for our enemies are relentless."

He turned to Gideon Blackwood, whose muscular frame still bore the scars of recent battle. "Gideon, what's our next move?"

"Brother," Gideon replied solemnly, clasping Lucian's forearm in a warrior's grip, "we regroup and rebuild. This victory has bought us time, but we must use it wisely."

"Very well," Lucian nodded, his gaze drifting to the distant horizon where dark clouds still gathered, threatening to cast shadows over their newfound hope. He knew in his heart that this was not the end; it was merely the beginning of a long and arduous journey.

As the celebration continued around him, Lucian could not help but feel the weight of responsibility bearing down upon him. The prophecy had been fulfilled, but he understood that more trials awaited them in the days to come. He clenched his fists, resolving to stand firm against whatever horrors might emerge from the darkness.

"Amara, Gideon," he said, his voice low and urgent, "gather the people. It's time to move forward, to forge a new path for humanity."

"Where will we go?" Amara asked, her brow furrowed with concern.

"Wherever we must," Lucian replied, his eyes burning with determination. "We will traverse this desolate land, seeking out those who have survived the destruction. We will stand against the forces of evil, united in our purpose."

"Lucian, are you certain?" Gideon queried, uncertainty flickering across his battle-hardened visage. "The dangers that lie ahead are immense."

"Of course I am," Lucian stated firmly, his unwavering resolve inspiring confidence in his companions. "I have been chosen for this mission, and I will not falter. The future of humanity depends on it."

With renewed vigor, the survivors rallied around their leader, prepared to face the unknown and defend their fragile existence against all odds. And so, they marched on, guided by the indomitable spirit of Lucian Valeria, their beacon of hope amidst the ashes of a fallen world.

THE PROPHECY
AND THE KINGDOM OF ELDORIA

Once a realm of prosperity and tranquility, the kingdom of Eldoria flourished under the wise rule of King Arcturus. The streets were lined with lush gardens, vibrant marketplaces, and stately homes. Laughter echoed through the air as children played, their innocent hearts unburdened by fear or strife. Farmers tilled the fertile soil, and artisans lovingly crafted wares that brought joy to their fellow citizens. In this haven, people lived in harmony, their lives interwoven like the threads of a rich tapestry.

"Peace be upon you, good sir," a merchant called out to Lucian Valerius as he strode through Eldoria's bustling marketplace. With a nod of acknowledgment, Lucian continued on his way, his thoughts consumed by the shadow that had begun to darken their once-bright world.

It was whispered in hushed tones, fear trembling on each syllable: an ancient prophecy, long-forgotten, now resurfaced like a serpent from the depths. It foretold of a great battle, one that would ravage the land and threaten to engulf the kingdom in chaos and destruction. Panic gripped the hearts of Eldoria's citizens as they grappled with the terrifying prospect of their peaceful existence being shattered.

"Can you believe it, Lucian?" Cora Leventis asked, her voice taut with worry, as she joined him on his walk. "The end of our peace, just like that?"

"Prophecies have a way of stirring unrest," Lucian replied, his piercing blue eyes scanning the faces around them. He could see the distress etched on each brow, the uncertainty gnawing at their souls.

"Damn that prophecy," muttered Eamon Fitzroy, who had slipped into step beside them. "It's got everyone on edge."

"Perhaps it is not the prophecy we should curse, but our complacency," Aurelia Callas chimed in, her warm brown eyes filled with wisdom. "We have grown comfortable in our peace, forgetting the lessons of the past."

"Whether we curse it or not, we must face it," Lucian said, his voice resolute. "King Arcturus has entrusted us with the task of preparing for this battle, and we will do everything in our power to protect our home."

As they walked, the weight of their responsibility hung heavy on their shoulders, each knowing that the fate of Eldoria rested upon them. But they were not alone; others joined their ranks, united by a common purpose: to defend their kingdom against the coming storm.

"Remember, my friends," Lucian whispered as they turned to face the uncertain future, "we are Eldoria's last hope. Together, we shall stand against whatever darkness lies ahead."

King Arcturus stood at the edge of his balcony, gazing out over the peaceful kingdom of Eldoria. The golden fields swayed in the gentle breeze, and the laughter of children filled the air as they played by the riverbanks. But beneath the tranquility, a sense of foreboding gripped the hearts of the people.

"Your Majesty," whispered the king's advisor, entering the chamber. "The prophecy has spread like wildfire through the kingdom. The people are frightened."

"Of course they are," King Arcturus murmured, clenching his fists. "They have every right to be. It is my duty to protect them, but how can I prepare for a battle I know nothing about?"

"Perhaps we should consider seeking allies," suggested the advisor. "Surely there are those who would stand with us against this uncertain enemy."

"Indeed," the king replied, his eyes narrowing. "We must gather our forces and face this darkness together. But who can I trust with such an important task?"

"Your Majesty," interjected the captain of the guard, stepping forward. "There is only one man skilled enough to undertake this mission: Lucian Valerius."

"Ah, yes," King Arcturus mused, stroking his beard. "Lucian, our finest warrior. His loyalty is beyond question, and his skills in battle unmatched." He turned to the captain. "Summon him to me."

As the sun dipped below the horizon, casting shadows across the royal courtyard, Lucian Valerius approached the throne. His muscular build and strong jawline spoke of years spent honing his craft, while his neatly arranged dark hair and piercing blue eyes betrayed a sharp mind and unwavering resolve.

"Lucian Valerius," King Arcturus boomed, his voice echoing throughout the chamber. "I have summoned you here because our kingdom faces an unprecedented threat. An ancient prophecy foretells of a great battle, one that could bring destruction to all we hold dear."

"Your Majesty," Lucian replied, his voice steady. "I am at your command. What would you have me do?"

"Your mission is to gather allies from our neighboring kingdoms and tribes," the king explained. "We must stand united against this encroaching darkness, and I can think of no one better suited for this task than you."

"Thank you, Your Majesty," Lucian said, bowing deeply. "I will not fail you or our people."

As Lucian took his leave, King Arcturus watched him stride confidently across the courtyard, his heart heavy with the weight of responsibility. The fate of Eldoria now rested on the shoulders of one man, and as the king retreated into his chambers, he offered a silent prayer for their deliverance.

The sun hung low in the sky, casting a blood-red hue over the royal courtyard. Lucian Valerius stood silently before King Arcturus, his piercing blue eyes locked onto the king's own, reflecting unwavering loyalty and determination.

"Lucian," King Arcturus spoke with urgency. "Our kingdom stands on the precipice of destruction, foretold by the ancient prophecy. I entrust you with the monumental task of gathering allies to face this impending battle. Your bravery and skill have been proven time and again– Eldoria needs you now more than ever."

"Your Majesty, I am honored by your confidence in me," Lucian replied, his voice steady, yet tinged with the gravity of the situation. "I will do everything in my power to protect our people and secure the future of our kingdom."

With a solemn nod from the king, Lucian turned and strode out of the courtyard, his heart heavy but his resolve unshaken. As he passed through the city streets, the atmosphere of fear and uncertainty clung to every corner like a suffocating fog. It was clear that the weight of the prophecy had settled upon the citizens of Eldoria.

In his travels, Lucian encountered various challenges as he sought to forge alliances with neighboring lands. At every turn, he faced skepticism and reluctance from those who doubted the prophecy or feared the consequences of aligning with Eldoria.

"Join us in our fight against this darkness," Lucian implored one ruler after another. "Together, we can overcome the threat that looms over us all."

But even as he persisted, Lucian grappled with his own doubts. He knew that in war, there were no guarantees, and the path ahead was fraught with danger. Yet he pushed onward, driven by his unwavering dedication to his kingdom and its people.

As he journeyed far and wide, Lucian discovered that the challenges he faced were not merely physical, but also a test of his inner strength and conviction. He could sense the shadows of doubt creeping into his mind, threatening to break his spirit.

"Can I truly succeed in this mission?" he wondered, as he sat by a dying campfire one night. "What if my efforts are not enough?"

But even in the face of these doubts, Lucian's steadfast determination refused to falter. As the sun rose each day, so too did his resolve, renewed with the knowledge that the survival of Eldoria depended upon him.

"Failure is not an option," he whispered to himself, steeling his nerves for the battles yet to come. "I will protect my kingdom at all costs."

And so, with each passing day, Lucian Valerius pressed forward on his quest. The trials he faced only served to strengthen his determination, as he sought to gather the allies Eldoria so desperately needed to confront the darkness that threatened to consume them all.

As Lucian's footsteps echoed through the grand halls of neighboring kingdoms, the weight of his mission bore down upon him. He stood tall and proud before the rulers of these lands, his piercing blue eyes filled with unwavering determination.

"Your Highnesses," Lucian began, his voice strong and resolute, "I stand before you today as a humble servant to King Arcturus and the people of Eldoria. I implore you to hear my plea and join our cause in the battle that will decide the fate of our world."

The leaders exchanged glances, their expressions a mixture of concern and curiosity. Lucian could sense their apprehension, but he pressed on, for he knew that the future was at stake. With each word, he painted a vivid picture of the darkness that threatened to consume them all, drawing upon the ancient prophecy and its foreboding message

"An age of suffering and despair will befall us if we do not act now," Lucian warned, his voice barely concealing the urgency that coursed through him. "But together, united in purpose, we can stand against this tide and protect our people from the horrors that await."

His impassioned plea struck a chord within the hearts of those who listened, and one by one, they pledged their allegiance to Eldoria. Negotiations were held, alliances forged, and agreements signed as Lucian's charisma and dedication inspired the leaders to join forces with his kingdom.

With the support of these newfound allies, Lucian returned to Eldoria to prepare the warriors for the approaching storm. They gathered in the training grounds, faces etched with both fear and anticipation, awaiting his guidance.

"Brothers and sisters in arms," Lucian shouted, addressing the assembled warriors, "we have been chosen to defend our people against an enemy that seeks to destroy us. We must be ready to face this threat, to stand firm in the face of darkness and persevere."

He began to train them, demonstrating his mastery of the sword and sharing the wisdom he had gained through years of combat. Lucian pushed them to their limits, knowing that only rigorous training would prepare them for the horrors that lay ahead.

"Remember," he told them as they practiced their forms, sweat dripping from their brows, "the strength of a warrior is not measured by the sharpness of his blade, but by the resilience of his spirit."

The warriors listened intently, their eyes filled with determination as they absorbed Lucian's teachings. They drilled tirelessly, honing their skills and developing strategies that would give them the advantage when the time came.

As the sun set each day, casting long shadows across the battlefield, Lucian could feel the weight of responsibility resting upon his shoulders. Yet within him burned a fire that refused to be extinguished—a fire fueled by his unwavering dedication to his people and his kingdom.

"Failure is not an option," he whispered to himself as he surveyed the preparations, his heart heavy but steadfast. "We will stand united, and we will prevail."

The sun dipped below the horizon, casting an eerie glow over the kingdom of Eldoria. The air was thick with anticipation, as soldiers and civilians alike prepared for the battle foretold by ancient prophecy. Lucian Valerius stood on a hill overlooking the bustling camp, his eyes reflecting the resolve that burned within him.

"Tmorrow," he whispered to himself, "we prove our worth."

Below, the people of Eldoria moved with purpose, their fear replaced by a steely determination. They had come together in the face of adversity, forging bonds stronger than iron. Women and men worked side by side, fortifying the city and assembling weapons, while children gathered supplies, their faces set and serious.

"Sir," called out Eamon Fitzroy, approaching Lucian with a confident stride. "The battlements are nearly finished, and the archers have taken their positions."

"Excellent," replied Lucian, his voice steady despite the turmoil within. "Cora, how fare the scouts?"

Cora Leventis, her fiery red hair tied back, stepped forward. "Our scouts have returned, Sir. Enemy forces approach and will be upon us within hours."

"Very well," Lucian murmured, feeling the weight of responsibility settle further on his shoulders. "We must ensure everyone is prepared."

As he descended the hill, Lucian's mind raced with the plans they had made, the strategies they would employ. It was an uncertain future that awaited them, but they would face it united.

"Lucian," Aurelia Callas said, touching his arm gently, her wise brown eyes filled with empathy. "Remember to breathe. We believe in you."

"Thank you, Aurelia," Lucian managed a small smile, bolstered by her unwavering support.

"Captain Thorne," Lucian addressed Elara, who stood tall and proud, her scars testament to her previous battles. "Have your soldiers report to their stations."

"Understood, Sir," she replied, her voice strong and clear.

The night wore on, the tension among Eldoria's people palpable. Kairos, the enigmatic figure, watched from a distance, his violet eyes unnervingly calm. As the first light of dawn appeared, Lucian called his warriors together.

"Friends, allies," he began, his voice resonating with conviction, "today we face our destiny. We stand united, not just for ourselves but for the generations to come. Our enemy may be fearsome, but together, we are stronger."

As he spoke, the faces around him transformed—fear and doubt giving way to courage and determination. They would fight, and they would survive.

"Ready yourselves," Lucian commanded, feeling the fire within him blaze anew. "Together, we will defend our homeland. Together, we shall write our own prophecy."

"FOR ELDORIA!" The cry went up from the soldiers, echoing across the land as they took their positions.

As battle drew near, the air buzzed with anticipation and fear. Hearts pounded in chests, hands shook with adrenaline. But through it all, their unity held strong, for they were Eldoria, and they would not be broken.

The land of Eldoria stretched out before them, a vast expanse of lush greenery and tranquil waters. The once-pristine beauty of the landscape was now marred by hastily erected barricades and the constant movement of soldiers preparing for the battle that would determine the fate of their world. Flashes of sunlight glanced off the tips of spears and arrows as they pierced through the canopy of trees, casting an otherworldly glow on the faces of those who stood ready to defend their homeland.

A palpable tension hung heavy in the air, like the weighty stillness before a storm. Men and women whispered fervent prayers under their breath, their voices barely audible above the rustle of leaves and the sounds of steel meeting stone. They could not shake the creeping sense of dread that gnawed at the edges of their minds, threatening to swallow them whole as they braced themselves for the impending apocalypse.

Against this backdrop of chaos and uncertainty, Lucian, the charismatic leader of Eldoria, stood tall and proud before his people. His every movement seemed deliberate and measured, exuding an air of authority that demanded attention and respect. As he surveyed the scene before him, his eyes lingered for a moment on each face, searching for any signs of fear or doubt. He knew all too well the burden of responsibility that rested upon his shoulders, and he understood the importance of projecting strength and resilience in these final moments before the battle began.

"Today," Lucian called out, his voice resonating with conviction and echoing across the valley, "we stand together as one. United by our shared love for this land and our unwavering determination to protect it from the forces that seek to destroy us."

As Lucian spoke, his words seemed to weave a spell over those who listened, instilling within them a newfound sense of hope and purpose. Their eyes shone with renewed vigor, their hands steadying as they gripped their weapons with a fierce determination. For the first time in days, the people of Eldoria began to believe that they might have a chance against the terrifying enemy that loomed on the horizon.

"Remember," Lucian continued, his voice steady and strong despite the storm of emotions that raged within him, "we are not mere pawns in some cosmic game, powerless to change our fate. We are the children of Eldoria, born from the very earth upon which we stand. And today, we will fight with every ounce of strength and courage that courses through our veins."

With each word that passed his lips, Lucian felt the weight of his people's hopes and fears settling upon him like an invisible cloak. He knew that the path ahead was fraught with danger and despair, but he also knew that it was his duty to guide them through the darkness and into the light of a new day.

"Stand together, my friends," he said, his eyes sweeping across the sea of faces before him, "and let us write our own prophecy."

Lucian towered above the assembled crowd, his imposing figure casting a long shadow as the sun dipped lower in the sky. His broad shoulders were draped in a majestic crimson cape that flowed like a river of blood down his back, signaling his authority as leader of Eldoria. The fading sunlight glinted off his raven hair, and his piercing blue eyes seemed to hold within them the very essence of the vast ocean– a tempestuous blend of strength, determination, and an undercurrent of vulnerability known only to those who dared to look deep enough.

"Children of Eldoria," he began, his voice resonating with the kind of conviction that could sway even the most jaded of hearts. "The time has come for us to stand united against the darkness that threatens our world."

As Lucian spoke, a hush fell over the gathered masses, each person hanging on his every word. The air was thick with anticipation, the electricity of their collective nerves almost tangible. They knew that the fate of not only their beloved homeland but also mankind itself hung in the balance, and it was up to them to tip the scales towards salvation.

"Long have we lived under the crushing weight of fear," Lucian continued, his gaze sweeping across the sea of faces before him. "But no longer shall we cower in the shadows. Tonight, we march forth into battle, not as mere mortals, but as warriors of destiny, chosen by the heavens themselves to turn the tide of this apocalyptic war."

As his words echoed through the evening air, a fire ignited within the hearts of his people, burning away the lingering tendrils of doubt and despair. In their place grew a newfound sense of purpose and unity, forged from the flames of hope and determination.

"Let the enemy tremble at our approach, for they shall soon learn that they have underestimated us," Lucian declared, his steely resolve sending a shiver down the spines of all who heard him. "We are Eldoria, and we shall not falter."

"Lead us, Lucian!" came a battle cry from within the crowd, quickly taken up by others until it swelled into a deafening roar. The earth seemed to tremble beneath their feet, as if even the land itself recognized the gravity of the moment.

"Then let us march forth," Lucian proclaimed, his voice rising above the clamor, "and may our victory usher in a new era of freedom and prosperity for all mankind!"

With that, he raised his sword high, the gleaming steel reflecting the dying light of the setting sun. The assembled warriors followed suit, their weapons held aloft like a forest of defiant steel, ready to face whatever challenges lay ahead in this final chapter of humanity's struggle against darkness.

Through it all, Lucian's inner turmoil churned beneath the surface, hidden behind the mask of authority he wore so well. Yet despite his fears and doubts, he knew that he must stand strong– not just for himself, but for the countless lives that depended on him. As the sun dipped below the horizon, plunging the world into twilight, he squared his shoulders and took the first steps towards destiny, his loyal followers close at his heels.

As the sun's final rays dipped below the horizon, Lucian stood tall amidst the sea of warriors, his piercing blue eyes scanning the crowd. His heart raced with anticipation, but he refused to let it show. They needed him now more than ever.

"Captain Mallory!" He bellowed, his voice reverberating through the cool evening air.

A figure emerged from the throng, her muscular frame casting an imposing shadow on the ground. Thorne Mallory was a force to be reckoned with– her short-cropped auburn hair framing steely gray eyes that had seen countless battles and stared down death itself. As she strode confidently towards Lucian, her numerous scars told the tale of her unwavering dedication to their cause.

"Lucian," she replied simply, nodding her head in respect as she took her place by his side. Her presence emanated strength and loyalty, offering a silent reassurance to those gathered around them.

"Tonight," Lucian began, his voice laced with determination, "we witness the culmination of our destiny. Look upon your brothers and sisters in arms, each one unique, yet bound together by a single purpose– to defend Eldoria against the darkness."

And so they did. The skilled warriors before them were a tapestry of strength and valor, each individual thread woven together to create a formidable force. A giant of a man with arms like tree trunks swung a massive hammer with ease, while a lithe woman with a wickedly sharp spear danced gracefully around him. Nearby, an archer with keen eyes and a steady hand drew back an arrow, his aim unerring as he released it into the night sky.

"Remember," Lucian continued, his eyes locked onto Mallory's as if sharing a secret only they understood, "while we may come from different walks of life and possess diverse abilities, it is our unity that makes us unstoppable."

"Indeed," Mallory agreed, her voice firm and reassuring. "We are Eldoria's shield and sword, forged in the fires of adversity. Together, we shall cast down our enemies and reclaim our land."

"Let this night bear witness to our resolve," Lucian declared, his words igniting a flame within the hearts of those who listened. "For today, we stand on the precipice of history, ready to carve our names into the annals of time."

As Mallory raised her own weapon in solidarity, Lucian could feel the unyielding determination that coursed through her veins. He knew that, with warriors like her by his side, they stood a chance against the encroaching darkness.

"Then let us march forth as one," he roared, brandishing his sword once more, "and may the heavens tremble at our might!"

The warriors erupted in cheers, their spirits lifted by Lucian's unwavering conviction. As they prepared to depart, their hearts pounded in their chests, adrenaline coursing through their veins. The end of the thousand years of captivity of Satan was upon them, and they were ready to face it head-on.

In the face of such cataclysmic events, Lucian offered a silent prayer for strength, knowing that though the road ahead would be fraught with peril, he would lead his people through the darkness and into the light.

The sun dipped beneath the horizon, casting long shadows on the gathered warriors who stood in a circle around Lucian. Each one of them held their weapons at the ready, their eyes locked on their leader as they prepared to make their pledge. The wind whispered through the tall grasses of Eldoria, carrying with it the scent of impending battle.

"Brothers and sisters," Lucian began, his voice steady and strong, "before we march into the abyss, I ask that you pledge your loyalty not just to me, but to the land we fight for and the people we protect."

One by one, the warriors stepped forward. First came Mallory, her gray eyes locking onto Lucian's as she knelt before him, her sword held out in offering. "I pledge my loyalty to you, Lucian, and to Eldoria. With every breath in my body, I will fight to defend our homeland and vanquish the darkness that threatens us."

As Mallory rose, a tall man with olive skin and a thick beard approached. His name was Aiden, a skilled archer with an unwavering focus. Despite his impressive skills, he bore the weight of his past mistakes, forever striving to prove himself worthy. "My bow is yours, Lucian," he said, his voice tinged with determination. "I pledge my loyalty to Eldoria and vow to protect our people until my final breath."

Next came Elara, a lithe warrior with dark hair and eyes that seemed to pierce the very soul. Her agility and speed were unmatched among the ranks, but her overconfidence could sometimes be her undoing. She bowed her head to Lucian, her twin daggers glinting in the fading light. "I pledge my loyalty to you and to Eldoria, and promise to use my blades to carve a path to victory."

And so it went, each warrior stepping forward to offer their unique gifts and unwavering loyalty. There was Kael, the steadfast shield-bearer whose courage was tempered by a deep-rooted fear for his family's safety; Lila, the gifted healer whose kind heart sometimes struggled with the harsh realities of war; and countless others who brought their own strengths and weaknesses to the battlefield.

As Lucian listened to their pledges, he could not help but be moved by their dedication and resolve. These were not mere soldiers, bound together by duty alone– they were a family, forged in the fires of adversity and united by a shared purpose. He looked into the eyes of each warrior as they pledged themselves to him and felt the weight of their trust press heavily upon his chest.

"Thank you," he said, his voice thick with emotion. "Your loyalty and commitment honor me more than you can know. Together, we will face the darkness and emerge triumphant."

With the ceremony complete, the warriors stood shoulder to shoulder, their eyes alight with determination and the promise of retribution. As the last light of day vanished from the sky, they knew that the battle that lay before them would test their very souls. But with Lucian to guide them and the knowledge that they fought for something greater than themselves, they would not falter.

"May we stand as one," Lucian whispered, his gaze sweeping over the faces of his comrades, "and may our enemies tremble before the might of Eldoria."

The sun dipped low on the horizon, casting a blood-red hue across the sky as if foreshadowing the conflict that would soon engulf the land. Eldoria's warriors stood within their makeshift encampment, each one lost in their own thoughts and prayers for the battle to come. The air itself seemed to hum with anticipation, the tension palpable as every heart pounded and hands shook with barely restrained adrenaline.

"Brothers and sisters," Lucian called out, his voice slicing through the oppressive atmosphere like the sharpest of blades, "we stand on the precipice of destiny! Tonight, we do not merely fight for our homeland– we fight for our very souls!"

A murmur of assent rippled through the gathered warriors, their eyes locking onto Lucian's commanding presence. Captain Thorne Mallory, her muscular form a beacon of strength beside him, nodded her agreement, her steely gray eyes blazing with determination.

"Remember your pledges!" Lucian continued, his blue eyes sweeping over the determined faces before him. "We are not only warriors but symbols of hope. We must hold fast to our unity, for it is our greatest weapon against the encroaching darkness."

"Lucian is right," Seraphina Vale said softly, her brown eyes full of conviction as she tightened her grip on her bow. "We've trained together, bled together– we know each other's strengths and weaknesses. We can rely on each other when the battle rages on."

"Indeed," Kairos Aeterna agreed, his violet eyes inscrutable yet somehow reassuring. "There is no greater force than a unified front. Let us show our enemies that they cannot break us."

"Let them feel the wrath of Eldoria!" Gideon Blackthorn roared, his green eyes alight with fervor as he raised his sword high, the others following suit with a resounding clash of metal.

"Together, we will write our own prophecy," Lucian declared, his gaze sweeping over the assembled warriors. "No matter what obstacles lie ahead, we shall face them as one."

"Let us stand united and defy the darkness!" Aria Stormborn cried out, her blue eyes shimmering with determination as she raised her staff in solidarity.

"May our enemies tremble before us," Lysander Ashwood added, his light gray eyes icy and unwavering. "For victory lies within our grasp!"

"Tonight, we fight!" Cassia Nightshade shouted, her hazel eyes flashing as she brandished her twin daggers. "And may the heavens themselves bear witness to our valor!"

With a deafening roar, the warriors of Eldoria surged forward, their weapons gleaming as they stormed toward the gathering darkness on the horizon. As one, they moved like a great tidal wave, their unity and determination a force to be reckoned with.

"Remember your training, trust in each other, and never surrender!" Lucian commanded, his voice echoing across the battlefield as the first clash of steel rang out. And so, the warriors of Eldoria began to write their own prophecy– one forged in blood, sacrifice, and an unwavering determination to protect all that they held dear.

The skies above Eldoria darkened, casting an otherworldly shadow over the land as if nature itself was preparing for the cataclysmic showdown between good and evil. Lucian's warriors, hearts pounding and hands shaking, drew strength from their leader's unwavering resolve. The anticipation in the air was electric, as if even the earth itself held its breath.

"Look around you," Lucian commanded, his voice resonating with conviction. "See the faces of your brothers and sisters, each one ready to lay down their lives for our people. Let their courage inspire you, for together, we will defy the darkness that threatens us all!"

His words took root within the hearts of the warriors, igniting a spark that blossomed into a mighty flame. The air, heavy with tension, now seemed to hum with newfound hope and determination.

"Let us remember what we fight for," Aria Stormborn proclaimed, her voice clear and strong like the ringing of a bell. "For our families, our friends, and our future!"

"May the heavens themselves guide our blades!" Lysander Ashwood added, his light gray eyes alight with fervor.

"Tonight, we write the final chapter of this dark tale and usher in a new age of peace!" Cassia Nightshade vowed, her hazel eyes flashing with steely resolve.

Lucian nodded solemnly, his piercing blue eyes surveying the warriors before him. "We stand at the precipice of destiny, my friends. But know this: we are not alone in our struggle. The divine watches over us and lends us their strength."

He raised his sword high, the polished steel gleaming against the brooding sky. "Now, let us march forth and meet our fate head-on! For we are Eldoria, and no darkness can extinguish our light!"

As the warriors echoed his battle cry, Lucian felt the weight of the future resting upon his shoulders. It was a burden he bore willingly, for the love of his people and the burning desire to protect them from the malevolent forces that sought to rip their world asunder.

The thundering footsteps of the Eldorian warriors shook the earth beneath them, drowning out the whispers of doubt that threatened to poison their resolve. Lucian glanced skyward, steeling himself for the trials and tribulations that lay ahead. The heavens seemed to answer with a distant rumble, as if acknowledging the magnitude of the challenges they faced.

"May our courage never falter," Lucian whispered to himself, his gaze fixed on the horizon where darkness loomed like a monstrous wave poised to crash down upon them. "For we are Eldoria, and we shall not be broken."

With a final deep breath, Lucian plunged into the fray, leading his brave warriors into battle against an ancient evil that would test their very souls. And as the first clash of steel rang out, the prophecy of Eldoria began to unfold– a tale of hope, sacrifice, and the indomitable spirit of humanity in the face of apocalyptic darkness.

VII

GATHERING ALLIES

The small village of Eldareth lay nestled within the realm, a hidden gem surrounded by an ethereal mist that seemed to dance with whispers of ancient secrets. The air was heavy with magic and mystery, as if the very essence of the land itself held untold tales of prophecy and wonder. The cobblestone streets were lined with modest dwellings made of aged wood and stone, each seemingly breathing with life and history.

In the heart of the village stood Lucian Valerius, a tall and imposing figure, his muscular frame casting a shadow that seemed to merge with the darkness around him. His short, dark hair contrasted sharply with his piercing blue eyes- eyes that held secrets, wisdom, and pain. The seriousness in his gaze was unwavering, as if the weight of the world rested upon his broad shoulders, and he bore it with fierce determination.

Lucian's fingers traced the hilt of his sword, feeling the familiar grooves and patterns etched into the metal. His entire being was focused on the mission ahead, the prophecy that had guided him since he first understood its significance. This village, this sanctuary of secrets, would be the birthplace of a great battle– one that could seal the fate of mankind for a thousand years.

As the sun dipped below the horizon, casting eerie shadows across the village, Lucian felt the familiar stirrings of unease. The darkness seemed to hold a power all its own, and he knew that it would soon be time to face whatever challenges lay ahead. With a final glance around the village, he steeled himself for what was to come. The end of the thousand years of captivity of Satan was near, and Lucian Valerius would do everything in his power to ensure that the forces of evil did not prevail.

Aria Valerius emerged from the shadows of a nearby hut, her medium-length brown hair dancing in the wind as she moved with the grace of a seasoned warrior. Her blue eyes, so like Lucian's, held a warmth and kindness that belied her fierce determination. She approached her brother with a smile, her supportive nature shining through even in the dim light.

"Are you ready for our training session, Lucian?" she asked, her voice steady and confident.

Lucian nodded, his eyes never leaving her face. "Of course, Aria," he replied, his tone serious but tinged with affection. "We must be prepared for whatever lies ahead."

Together, they walked to the village outskirts, where a small, makeshift training area had been set up. The air was thick with tension, charged with an energy that seemed to whisper of the impending apocalypse. In the distance, a storm brewed, its dark clouds roiling and undulating like a living thing.

As they began their drills, Lucian led Aria through a series of intricate swordplay maneuvers, each one executed with precision and lethal intent. His movements were fluid and powerful, a testament to his unwavering dedication to his mission. Aria mirrored her brother's actions, keeping pace with him despite the complexity of the techniques.

"Remember to keep your guard up, Aria," Lucian cautioned as they crossed blades, his voice barely audible over the clash of steel against steel.

Aria gritted her teeth, adjusting her stance as she parried another blow. "I know, Lucian. I won't let you down," she responded, her eyes focused on her brother's movements.

The two continued to spar, their bodies moving in perfect harmony as they pushed one another to the edge of their abilities. As sweat poured from their brows and their muscles burned with exertion, it was clear that neither would back down from the challenge.

In a quiet moment between strikes, Lucian's eyes met Aria's, and for a brief instant, his stoic facade crumbled. "Aria," he whispered, his voice thick with emotion, "I... I worry about our mission. The prophecy speaks of darkness, of a battle that will shake the foundations of our world. Can we truly stand against such evil?"

Aria's gaze never wavered as she reached out to clasp her brother's hand. "Lucian, I have no doubt in your abilities, and you should have none either. We were chosen for this task for a reason. Together, we can face whatever challenges lie ahead."

With renewed determination, they resumed their training, each strike and parry echoing their unbreakable bond. As the storm drew closer, its thunderous rumble a harbinger of the trials to come, Lucian and Aria stood united, ready to face the end of the thousand years of captivity of Satan- and whatever horrors awaited them in the darkness.

As the sun dipped below the horizon, its fading light cast long shadows across the training ground. Lucian and Aria stood facing each other, their breaths visible in the cold air. The weight of the coming prophecy hung heavy on their shoulders, fueling their determination to prepare for the battle ahead.

"Lucian," Aria said, her voice firm but gentle. "Do you remember the stories Father used to tell us? About how the Creator chose us as His warriors?"

A flicker of warmth crossed Lucian's face as he nodded. "I do. He spoke of our destiny to stand against the darkness, side by side."

"Then trust in that, brother," Aria urged, her eyes shining with conviction. "Our bond is stronger than any weapon forged by man. We have always faced adversity together, and we will continue to do so until the end."

As they resumed their training, Lucian found himself studying his sister's every move. He marveled at her strength and agility, yet a protective instinct welled up within him. Each parry of her blade was met with equal force, ensuring she would not be caught off guard. Every feint was countered, teaching her to anticipate the enemy's next move.

"Be mindful of your surroundings, Aria," Lucian cautioned, his voice laced with concern. "The enemy will not hesitate to exploit any weakness."

"Neither will I," Aria replied, driving her sword forward with a fierce determination. Yet, beneath her steely exterior, Lucian recognized the unspoken fear that gripped her heart. It mirrored his own.

"Promise me something," Lucian said suddenly, halting their dance of steel. Aria looked at him expectantly, her breath coming in shallow gasps. "Promise me that no matter what happens, you will stay close to me. I cannot bear the thought of losing you."

"Lucian, you know I would never leave your side," Aria answered softly, her hand reaching out to grasp his. "We are bound by blood and by destiny. I will be there until the end, whatever that may be."

As their gazes locked, an unspoken vow passed between them. They were more than siblings; they were a united force against the darkness that threatened to consume their world. Together, they would face the end of the thousand years of captivity of Satan and emerge victorious or not at all.

With renewed vigor, Lucian and Aria resumed their training, their movements precise and deadly. The sound of steel on steel rang through the air as they pushed themselves to their limits, knowing that only together could they hope to survive the trials ahead.

Underneath the canopy of a dying sun, its blood-red light casting an eerie glow over the desolate village, Lucian and Aria stood side by side, their breaths labored from hours of training. The weight of the prophecy hung heavy in the air as if the world itself held its breath, waiting for the end of the thousand years of captivity of Satan.

"Sometimes I wonder," Aria began hesitantly, her eyes fixated on the horizon where darkness seemed to seep from unseen crevices, "what life would have been like if we hadn't been chosen for this mission. Do you ever think about it?"

Lucian's grip tightened around his sword, his piercing blue eyes not leaving the treacherous landscape before them. He sighed, considering her question. "Yes, I do. I dream of a simple life, away from all this chaos. But I know that is not our destiny."

"Neither is it mine," Aria replied, her voice soft yet resolute. She looked up at her brother, admiration shining in her eyes. "You've always been so strong, Lucian. How do you keep going when everything seems hopeless?"

"Because I must," he admitted, his gaze never wavering. "It is my duty to protect you and ensure that the prophecy is fulfilled. We cannot let our fears dictate our actions."

"Then let us face those fears together," Aria suggested, determination lacing her words. "Let us conquer them so they do not control us."

"Very well," Lucian agreed, nodding toward the open field before them. "Tell me your fears, and I will share mine."

As they resumed their training, Aria spoke of her fear of failure, of not being able to stand by Lucian's side when he needed her most. Lucian, in turn, confessed his fear of losing his sister, of being unable to protect her from the darkness that threatened their world.

With each admission, their movements grew more fluid and synchronized, their fears fueling them, driving them to push their limits. The clashing of their swords echoed throughout the empty village, a testament to their unwavering determination.

"Enough!" Lucian called out after a particularly fierce exchange, both of them panting with exertion. "We have faced our fears today, but we cannot let them consume us. We must continue our training, for the end is near."

"Agreed," Aria said, wiping the sweat from her brow. She looked into her brother's eyes and saw the fire that burned within him, the unyielding resolve that would see them through the end of days.

"Remember," Lucian cautioned, as they picked up their weapons and prepared for another round, "we are the last hope for this world. Our dreams, our fears– they matter little in the face of what lies ahead. We must stand together, united against the darkness, or all will be lost."

As the sun dipped below the horizon, bathing the world in shadow, Lucian and Aria readied themselves for the coming storm. In the final moments of twilight, their swords danced once more, a promise of defiance against the encroaching darkness and the fulfillment of the prophecy that bound their fates together.

A cold wind swept through the village, carrying with it a foreboding sense of what was to come. The sun had disappeared behind ominous clouds, casting a haunting darkness over the land. Lucian and Aria stood in the center of the training grounds, their breaths visible in the chilling air.

"Something's coming," Lucian muttered, his piercing blue eyes scanning the dark horizon for any sign of trouble. "I can feel it. This mission... it's bigger than anything we've ever faced before."

"Lucian," Aria replied gently, placing a hand on her brother's tense shoulder. "You've been preparing for this your entire life. You're the strongest warrior I know, and you won't face this alone. I'll be by your side, every step of the way."

"Thank you, Aria," Lucian whispered, his eyes glistening with unshed tears. "But the weight of this responsibility... sometimes, it feels like too much to bear."

"Hey, look at me," Aria commanded softly, forcing him to meet her gaze. "We will face this together. We will protect each other, and we will save our people. It's not just about you or me— it's about all of us, fighting as one. I believe in you, Lucian. And I will always be here for you."

"Always?" Lucian asked, his voice cracking under the strain of his emotions.

"Always," Aria confirmed, her blue eyes shining with unwavering conviction.

"Alright," Lucian said, taking a deep breath and steeling himself against the encroaching darkness. "Let's finish this training session then. We need to be ready."

"Together," Aria reminded him, retrieving her sword and falling into position beside him.

"Right. Together," Lucian agreed, his jaw set in determination as he grasped his weapon tightly.

They began to spar once more, their movements fluid and powerful even under the oppressive cloud cover. Lucian's expertise was evident in every swing of his sword, while Aria's determination to keep up with her brother shone through in her fierce counterattacks.

"Remember," Lucian said between strikes, "what we're fighting for."

"Of course," Aria replied, parrying his next blow with a determined look in her eyes. "For our people. For our freedom."

As the wind howled around them and the darkness closed in, Lucian and Aria fought on, united in their purpose and driven by their love for each other. They knew that the end of days was upon them, and they would face it together– bound by blood, by prophecy, and by the unbreakable bond of family.

As the storm gathered above them, Lucian and Aria stood facing each other, swords poised for the final strike. The air was electric, charged with anticipation and fear of the unknown. Yet beneath it all, an unyielding resolve burned within their souls.

"Are you ready, sister?" Lucian asked, his piercing blue eyes locked on hers.

"More than ever," Aria replied, her voice firm and steady.

"Then let us reaffirm our commitment to this mission and to each other," Lucian declared, raising his sword in a symbolic gesture.

"May we stand strong against the darkness that threatens to engulf us," Aria added, mirroring her brother's actions.

"May our love for each other be our guiding light," Lucian continued, lowering his sword slowly.

"May we protect our people, our land, and our freedom," Aria finished, her voice resolute.

Their swords clashed together in a bright spark, signifying the unbreakable bond between them and their unwavering commitment to their cause. As they stepped back, the wind howled around them, swirling leaves and debris in its violent embrace.

"Remember," Lucian whispered, his voice barely audible amidst the tempest, "no matter what happens, I will always be by your side. And you will always be by mine."

"Always," Aria affirmed, her eyes glistening with fierce determination.

Just as their words echoed through the storm, a deafening crack split the sky. A bolt of lightning seared through the heavens, striking the ground mere inches from where they stood. The force of the impact threw them apart, leaving them sprawled across the damp earth.

"Lucian!" Aria cried out, struggling to rise amidst the torrential downpour.

"Stay where you are!" Lucian shouted back, his voice hoarse and strained. "Something's coming!"as his hands moved, looking for something to grab on to, another bolt of lightning strike the sky luminating the entire dark sky across the havens. Lucian struggling to get up, his breath filled the night dark sky.

The air grew heavier by the second, suffocating them with its oppressive weight. The ground trembled beneath their feet, as if warning of the impending doom that lurked just beyond the horizon. All around them, the village seemed to cower in fear, bracing itself for the onslaught of darkness.

"Lucian... what is it?" Aria asked, her voice quivering with a mixture of dread and curiosity.

"Something ancient... something powerful," Lucian replied, his eyes scanning the roiling skies above. "And it's coming for us."

As they stood amidst the chaos, united in their purpose and resolute in their love for each other, Lucian and Aria were suddenly struck with the chilling realization that this was only the beginning. The end of days had arrived, heralding forces more terrifying than they could have ever imagined.

"Ready yourself, sister," Lucian warned, his breath visible in the icy air. "Our greatest challenge lies ahead."

The sun set ablaze the peaceful and idyllic village of Thorne, painting its quaint houses in hues of gold and crimson. Nestled within a lush valley, the village was a sanctuary to those seeking refuge from the chaos of the outside world. It was here that Lucian Valeria had chosen to devote his time and energy, working tirelessly to maintain the harmony that prevailed among the villagers.

Lucian stood tall with a strong, broad-shouldered frame, his dark hair falling in unruly waves around his chiseled face. His piercing blue eyes reflected the steadfast determination that fueled his every action, as he surveyed the progress of the latest community project he had spearheaded. With an air of quiet authority, he directed the villagers in their tasks, ensuring that each stone was laid perfectly for the new bridge that would connect Thorne to the neighboring settlement.

"Great job, everyone! We're making excellent progress," Lucian called out, his voice resonating with sincerity and encouragement. The villagers responded with smiles and nods, feeling inspired by the young man's unwavering commitment to the welfare of their community.

Just beyond the bustling construction site, a figure emerged from the edge of the woods, her delicate steps hesitant yet purposeful. Aria Everhart took in the scene before her with a mixture of awe and curiosity. Her long, auburn hair cascaded down her back, framing her porcelain skin and bright green eyes that sparkled with intelligence. She had arrived in Thorne only days prior, drawn to the village by an inexplicable yearning for a simpler life, where she could use her innate compassion and knowledge to make a meaningful impact on the world.

Aria's gaze fell upon Lucian, and even from a distance, she could sense the strength and determination that radiated from him. As if sensing her presence, Lucian turned and met her gaze, momentarily transfixed by the ethereal beauty that stood before him.

"Can I help?" Aria ventured, her voice soft yet resolute, as she approached the group of workers.

"Of course," Lucian replied, his eyes never leaving hers. "We could always use more hands."

With a grateful smile, Aria joined the villagers in their labor, guided by Lucian's gentle instructions and unwavering support. As they worked side by side, an unspoken bond began to form between them, forged from their shared love for humanity and their desire to make a difference in this fractured world.

In the waning light of day, the sun cast its final golden beams on the village of Thorne, illuminating the faces of Lucian Valeria and Aria Everhart, two souls united by fate and bound together by a shared purpose—to face the darkness of the world hand in hand and bring forth a new era of hope and redemption.

The sun dipped low in the sky, casting an eerie blood-red hue over the peaceful and idyllic village of Thorne. Shadows danced upon the cobblestone streets, as if whispering secrets of the impending darkness that would soon engulf the world. Yet amidst this foreboding atmosphere, life continued to thrive, a testament to the resilience and determination of the human spirit.

Lucian Valeria stood on the outskirts of the village square, his piercing blue eyes scanning the horizon for any signs of danger. The fiery light played off his dark hair, giving him an almost otherworldly appearance. As he turned to survey the villagers going about their daily tasks, his gaze fell upon a figure he had not seen before.

Aria Everhart stood at the edge of a bountiful garden, her long auburn hair cascading down her back like a waterfall of flame illuminated by the setting sun. Her bright green eyes sparkled with intelligence and curiosity as she studied the vibrant petals of a blooming rose. The beauty of the scene was striking, yet it was not its aesthetic allure that drew Lucian's attention; it was something deeper, an inexplicable connection that seemed to tug at the very core of his being.

"Hello," Lucian ventured, approaching Aria with caution, as if testing the waters of this newfound bond. "I don't believe we've met."

"Hi," Aria replied, her voice lilting and melodic like birdsong. "My name is Aria. I just arrived in Thorne yesterday. And you are?"

"Lucian. Welcome to our village," he said, offering her a warm smile that seemed to chase away the encroaching shadows. "What brings you here?"

"I wanted to make a difference," she confessed, her fingers brushing against the delicate petals of the rose. "To use my gifts to help others and bring some light into this world."

"Ah, a noble aspiration," Lucian mused, his eyes never leaving her face. "You know, I've always felt that same calling– the desire to protect and serve our world, especially in these dire times."

"Sometimes it feels like an overwhelming responsibility," Aria admitted, her gaze meeting his as a shared understanding passed between them.

"It can be," Lucian agreed, nodding solemnly. "But if we face it together, perhaps the burden will be lighter."

Their conversation continued, flowing effortlessly like a river merging with the sea. As they spoke of their dreams and aspirations, their love for nature, and their deep-seated desire to make a difference, it became increasingly apparent that their connection was not merely a fleeting fancy, but rather the beginning of something enduring and profound.

And so, as the sun dipped below the horizon and twilight descended upon Thorne, Lucian Valeria and Aria Everhart stood together amidst the fading beauty of the garden– two souls whose fates had become intertwined, poised on the precipice of a new chapter in the epic struggle between light and darkness.

The first light of dawn cast a warm, golden hue over the peaceful and idyllic village of Thorne. Lucian and Aria walked hand in hand along a cobblestone path, surrounded by quaint cottages adorned with blooming window boxes. The scent of freshly baked bread wafted through the air as they strolled past the village bakery, a testament to the hardworking hands that shaped the community.

"Isn't it marvelous how everyone here works together for the greater good?" Aria mused, her bright green eyes taking in the sights around them.

"Indeed," Lucian agreed, his piercing blue eyes reflecting the warmth of the morning sun. "It's a rare and precious thing to find such unity, especially in these times."

As they continued their exploration, they encountered several villagers going about their daily routines. Old Mr. Hawkins, the village blacksmith, waved from his forge, his skilled hands shaping metal into tools and implements essential to the community. Nearby, young Timothy dashed about, delivering messages and parcels with a beaming smile on his face.

"Morning, Lucian! Aria!" he called out, pausing just long enough to catch his breath before continuing on his way.

"Good morning, Timothy!" Aria replied, her melodic voice carrying a genuine warmth that seemed to touch every soul she encountered.

"Seems like you two are becoming quite the pair," Mr. Hawkins observed, wiping soot-streaked hands on his leather apron. "In all my years, I've never seen Lucian so taken by anyone. You must be something special, Miss Everhart."

Lucian felt a flush rise to his cheeks, but he couldn't deny the truth in the blacksmith's words. The connection he shared with Aria was unlike anything he'd experienced before, and it had only grown stronger since their chance encounter in the garden.

"Mr. Hawkins, Aria is indeed special," Lucian said, his voice filled with conviction. "She has a rare gift– not only for understanding the world around her but also for seeing the potential in everything and everyone."

Aria squeezed his hand, a silent acknowledgement of their shared purpose and growing bond. They continued their walk, exchanging pleasantries with more villagers along the way: Mrs. Caldwell, tending to her flock of chickens, and young Sarah, who proudly showed off her latest sewing project. Each interaction reinforced their sense of belonging and the knowledge that they were part of something greater than themselves.

"Lucian," Aria whispered as they paused beneath the shade of an ancient oak, "I can't help but feel that we were brought together for a reason. The village, the people, our connection… it's all so much bigger than us."

He looked deep into her eyes, sensing the truth of her words. "Yes, Aria, I believe you're right. We have a purpose here, one that transcends the ordinary– and together, we will face whatever challenges lie ahead."

As they stood beneath the sprawling canopy of the oak, Lucian Valeria and Aria Everhart felt the weight of their destiny settle upon their shoulders. Yet, even as the shadows of impending darkness began to gather at the edges of their awareness, the love and support of their community shone like a beacon, guiding them ever forward towards their fateful journey.

The afternoon sun cast a warm, golden light over the peaceful and idyllic village of Thorne as Lucian and Aria ventured towards the outskirts of town. The air was filled with the scent of freshly bloomed wildflowers, and the distant murmur of a flowing stream could be heard in the background. As they walked hand in hand, they couldn't help but admire the picturesque landscape that enveloped them– a testament to the enduring power of nature even in uncertain times.

"Look, Lucian!" Aria exclaimed, pointing towards a small group of villagers gathered around a frail old man seated on a rickety wooden chair. They watched as one by one, the villagers approached the elder, offering him baskets filled with fruits, vegetables, and other provisions.

"Ah, that's Old Man Thomas," Lucian explained, his voice tinged with warmth and admiration. "He's been living alone ever since his wife passed away last year. The villagers take turns helping him out with food and chores. It warms my heart to see people come together like this."

Aria's eyes shimmered with unshed tears as she squeezed Lucian's hand tighter. "It's beautiful, isn't it? In the face of darkness, humanity still finds a way to shine through."

As they continued their walk, Lucian guided Aria towards a lush and verdant community garden nestled along the banks of the babbling stream. Rows of healthy vegetables swayed gently in the breeze, while bees buzzed lazily among vibrant blossoms.

"Here we are," Lucian announced proudly. "This is our village's pride and joy– a place where everyone comes together to nurture life and provide sustenance for all."

"Lucian, it's absolutely breathtaking," Aria breathed, her green eyes wide with wonder. "I would love to help tend to this garden and contribute to something so meaningful."

"Then let's get started," Lucian replied with a smile, grabbing a pair of gloves and handing them to Aria. They knelt side by side, tending to the earth and nurturing the growth of the plants that would one day feed their community.

As they worked together in harmony with nature, their thoughts echoed one another:

"Even as darkness threatens to consume the world, this garden serves as a reminder that life will always find a way."

"Through our love for each other and the shared purpose we have found in this village, we can face whatever challenges lie ahead."

"May the light of humanity continue to shine bright amidst the shadows."

The sun dipped towards the horizon, casting long shadows over the land. Lucian and Aria paused in their labor, gazing up at the vibrant hues of the sky– a reminder that even in the most trying times, beauty could still be found in the world around them.

"Remember this moment, Aria," Lucian whispered, his blue eyes reflecting the fiery colors of the sunset. "This is what we're fighting for– not just for ourselves, but for everyone who finds solace and hope in the goodness of humanity."

And as they stood hand in hand, hearts swelling with love and determination, Lucian Valeria and Aria Everhart were ready to face the challenges that lay ahead, guided by the unwavering belief in the power of human kindness and the enduring strength of the natural world.

In the dimming twilight, as the day's labor drew to an end, Lucian and Aria found themselves seated upon an ancient wooden bench at the edge of the village square. The air was thick with the scent of freshly turned earth and the sweet perfume of wildflowers– a testament to the life that thrived within Thorne's borders.

"Sometimes I wonder," Lucian mused, his voice low and contemplative, "if our efforts will truly make a difference in the grand scheme of things."

Aria turned her bright green eyes toward him, her brow furrowing in concern. "What do you mean?"

"Look around us," he gestured to the peaceful scene before them. "This village is a sanctuary amidst the chaos that threatens to overtake the world, but it's just one small corner of a vast, complex tapestry. Can we honestly hope to change the course of events beyond these walls?"

Aria reached for his hand, giving it a reassuring squeeze. "Perhaps not on our own, but every act of kindness, every moment of connection, has the power to create ripples that extend far beyond what we can see."

"Listen," she continued, her voice soft yet unwavering, "I know the weight of responsibility you carry, but you don't have to bear it alone. I'm here with you, and together, we can face whatever comes our way."

Lucian allowed himself a faint smile, touched by her unwavering faith in him. But even as they shared this moment of vulnerability, the shadows of uncertainty loomed ever closer.

"Did you hear the rumors?" a hushed voice whispered nearby, shattering the stillness of their conversation. They turned to find an older woman, her eyes wide with fear, speaking to a group of villagers. "They say the darkness grows stronger, reaching out its tendrils to claim more territory with each passing day."

"Surely it won't reach us here," a man replied, his voice wavering with uncertainty. "We're protected by the ancient wards and the purity of our hearts."

"Alas, my friends," the old woman sighed, "no place is truly immune to the encroaching shadows. We must prepare ourselves for the trials and tribulations that lie ahead."

As Aria and Lucian exchanged glances filled with trepidation, they knew that their peaceful haven could not remain untouched forever. The darkness was relentless in its pursuit, and soon, they would be called upon to face its challenges head-on.

"Remember what we've built here, Lucian," Aria whispered, her eyes shining with determination. "No matter what comes, we'll stand together, united by our love for this village and for one another."

And as night descended upon Thorne, casting its cloak of shadows over the world, Lucian Valeria and Aria Everhart steeled themselves for the battles to come, fueled by their conviction in the light of humanity and the strength of their unwavering bond.

The sun dipped below the horizon, painting the sky above Thorne in a vibrant tapestry of reds and oranges. Lucian Valeria stood at the edge of the village, gazing upon the breathtaking scene with appreciation. One could almost forget the rumors of encroaching darkness when faced with such beauty.

"Lucian," Aria Everhart's voice broke through his reverie. As he turned to face her, her green eyes shone with intensity that matched his own, and their gazes locked for a moment– both acknowledging the weight of responsibility they felt.

"Are you ready?" she asked quietly, her fingers playing nervously with the hem of her dress.

"Ready as I'll ever be," he replied, swallowing hard. "But are we enough, Aria? Can we truly protect this village from whatever lies ahead?"

"Only time will tell," Aria answered, her voice steady despite the fear that lurked beneath the surface. "But we must try, Lucian. We owe it to these people– to ourselves."

As the last rays of sunlight vanished, casting the world into twilight, a sudden gust of wind tore through the village. Lucian and Aria exchanged apprehensive glances, their shared unease palpable in the air.

"Did you feel that?" Aria whispered, her eyes widening.

"Something's coming," Lucian murmured, his hand instinctively reaching for the hilt of the sword at his side.

Just then, an eerie wail echoed through the streets of Thorne, sending a shiver down the spines of all who heard it. The villagers emerged from their homes, their faces etched with concern as they gathered around Lucian and Aria.

"What was that sound?" one man demanded, his eyes darting nervously toward the surrounding forest.

"Could it be...the darkness?" another woman asked, her voice trembling.

"Enough!" Lucian raised his hand, silencing the murmurs. "We don't know what we're dealing with yet, but we must remain calm. Panic will only make things worse."

Aria nodded in agreement, her gaze sweeping over the gathered villagers. "We'll investigate the source of that sound," she assured them. "In the meantime, stay vigilant and protect one another."

As they moved toward the edge of the village, Lucian's mind raced with a torrent of thoughts and fears. The weight of responsibility bore down on him, threatening to crush him beneath its relentless pressure.

"Lucian," Aria whispered, her fingers brushing against his as they walked side by side, "whatever happens, I'll be right here. We'll face this together."

"Thank you, Aria," he replied, his voice thick with emotion. "I don't know what I'd do without you."

As they reached the outskirts of Thorne, the sounds of the villagers' anxious whispers fading behind them, Lucian and Aria were met with a sight that sent ice coursing through their veins. A great darkness loomed at the edge of the forest, a swirling mass of shadows that seemed to consume all light in its path.

"Is this the beginning?" Aria breathed; her eyes wide with horror.

"Only one thing is certain," Lucian replied, gripping his sword tightly as they stared into the abyss before them. "Our fight has just begun."

And with those words, the darkness surged forward, engulfing everything in its path– and leaving the fate of Thorne, and its two protectors, shrouded in uncertainty.

VIII

FIRST CHALLENGE

The land of Elyria stretched far and wide, a breathtaking vista of lush green fields swaying gently in the wind, kissed by golden sunlight. Towering mountains stood sentinel on the horizon, their snow-capped peaks gleaming like jewels against a backdrop of azure skies. At the heart of this Eden lay a bustling city, its cobblestone streets teeming with life as merchants hawked their wares, children played, and laughter filled the air. It was a place of prosperity and hope, but all that was about to change.

Arlen Thorne stood at the crest of a hill overlooking the panorama below, his piercing green eyes reflecting the verdant landscape before him. He breathed in deeply, savoring the scent of freshly cut grass and blooming flowers that perfumed the air. For a moment, he felt at peace, but such moments were fleeting these days.

"Look!" cried a voice from behind him, shattering the stillness. "In the sky!"

Arlen turned to see a group of people pointing upwards, their faces contorted with fear and awe. He followed their gaze, his breath catching in his throat as he beheld an unnerving sight. The sun had vanished, swallowed by a sudden eclipse that cast an eerie darkness over the land. Shadows deepened, and a chill crept into the air, sending a shiver down Arlen's spine.

"Is it… the prophecy?" whispered a woman beside him, her voice trembling. "The end of the thousand years?"

Arlen glanced at her, then back toward the darkened sun. His heart pounded in his chest, a sense of foreboding gnawing at him. He'd heard tales of the ancient prophecy– whispers of a time when darkness would fall upon Elyria again, signaling the release of the dread lord Satan from his millennia-long captivity. But he'd never truly believed them. Until now.

"By the gods…" breathed a man, his face ashen with terror. "We must do something! We can't just stand here and let this happen!"

Arlen clenched his fists, determination flaring within him. He couldn't ignore the signs any longer. The end of times was upon them, and he needed to act. But what could one man do against the forces of darkness?

"Listen to me!" he shouted, his voice carrying across the crowd. "We can't give in to fear! We have to fight back, protect our homes and our families! Together, we can overcome this darkness and save Elyria!"

The people stared at him, their expressions uncertain and frightened. Arlen knew he had a long road ahead if he was going to convince them to join him in this battle. But he would not waver. With every fiber of his being, he vowed to see this through and defend the land he loved.

As the eclipse slowly faded and light began to return to the world, Arlen knew that it was only the beginning. A dark storm was coming, and he would be the beacon to guide his people through it. No matter the cost.

The air in the city of Elyria felt heavy with tension, as though it were charged with an unseen force that sent a shiver down one's spine. The citizens had gathered in the city square, their faces a mix of curiosity and unease. The mysterious event of the sudden eclipse had left them puzzled and fearful, unsure what to make of such a strange phenomenon.

"Prophecy? Bah, it's just a natural occurrence," scoffed a burly blacksmith, crossing his arms over his broad chest. "Superstitious nonsense if you ask me."

"Indeed," chimed in a woman, her once-youthful face lined with worry. "We've had eclipses before, and nothing ever came of them. This is no different."

Murmurs of agreement rippled through the crowd, like waves crashing against the shore but then receding back into the vast ocean of uncertainty. Their skepticism was palpable, their dismissive attitudes a shield against the fear that tried to take root in their hearts.

Amidst the whispers and hushed conversations, a tall, strong figure emerged from the throng of people. His short brown hair framed a face that exuded determination, while his piercing green eyes seemed to see beyond the present moment, as if gazing upon a vision only he could perceive. This man was Arlen Thorne, a young warrior whose sense of duty was matched only by his unyielding courage.

"Perhaps we should not be so quick to dismiss this prophecy," Arlen said, his voice steady despite the weight of his words. "We must at least consider the possibility that we are being warned of a coming danger."

"Are you suggesting we give in to panic and superstition, boy?" sneered an elderly merchant, his disdain evident in the curl of his lips.

"No," Arlen replied calmly. "I am merely suggesting that we remain vigilant. If there is even a shred of truth to the prophecy, we must be prepared to face whatever darkness may come."

The crowd exchanged uneasy glances, their skepticism warring with an instinctive desire to protect themselves and their loved ones from harm. Arlen's words had sown seeds of doubt in their minds, but it remained to be seen whether those seeds would take root and blossom into action.

"Prove it then," challenged a young mother, her arms wrapped protectively around her child. "Show us that this prophecy holds any weight at all."

Arlen met her gaze, understanding the fear that lay beneath her defiance. He knew it would not be easy to sway the hearts of the people, but he also knew that he could not stand idly by while the shadows closed in on Elyria. With a determined nod, he replied, "I will do my best to uncover the truth of this prophecy. And should I find evidence of its validity, I will return to share that knowledge with you all."

As Arlen turned to leave, his thoughts raced with the enormity of the task before him. Yet, despite the daunting road ahead, there was no trace of doubt or hesitation in his stride. For Arlen Thorne, the fate of Elyria rested upon his shoulders, and he would bear that burden with unwavering resolve.

The sun dipped low in the sky, casting long shadows across the land of Elyria as Arlen Thorne made his way through the bustling marketplace. The scent of freshly baked bread and spiced meats filled the air, mingling with the earthy aroma of leather and wood. Vendors called out to passersby, their voices blending into a cacophony of sound that echoed off the city's ancient stone walls.

"Fresh fruit, ripe and sweet!" cried a stout man with a bushy beard, thrusting a basket of plump peaches towards Arlen.

"Finest blades in all the land!" boasted another, brandishing a gleaming sword that caught the dying sunlight.

Arlen nodded politely at each vendor but continued on his path. His mind was focused on the prophecy, an ever-present whisper in the back of his mind that refused to be silenced.

As he walked, Arlen's eyes were drawn to a small, shadowed alcove tucked away between two large stalls. An old sage stood there, his back hunched and his hands gnarled like the twisted roots of an ancient tree. Intrigued, Arlen approached the elderly man who studied him with pale, watery eyes.

"Young man," the sage rasped, "I see a heavy burden upon your heart."

Arlen hesitated before responding, his voice barely audible above the clamor of the market. "Indeed, I have recently come across a prophecy that speaks of darkness and doom for our homeland."

"Ah, yes," the sage nodded. "I am familiar with this prophecy. It has haunted my dreams for many nights now."

"Then you believe it to be true?" Arlen asked, hope and dread warring within him.

"Belief is a powerful thing, young one," the sage murmured. "It can make or break nations. But it is not my place to determine the truth of such matters. That responsibility, I fear, falls upon your shoulders."

swallowed hard, his throat suddenly dry. "But how am I to know if this prophecy is nothing more than the ramblings of a madman or the divine warning of impending doom?"

The sage's eyes bored into Arlen's, seeming to peer into the very depths of his soul. "Trust your instincts, young one. They will guide you on the path you must take."

As Arlen stumbled away from the old sage, he felt the weight of responsibility settle upon him like a heavy cloak. He knew that the fate of Elyria rested in his hands, and with each step, the burden grew heavier.

"Can I really do this?" he asked himself, his piercing green eyes scanning the horizon for any sign of hope. "Can I save my homeland from darkness?"

Arlen's heart pounded in his chest, his thoughts racing. The decision was his alone, and with it came the knowledge that the lives of countless men, women, and children hung in the balance.

"Perhaps," he whispered to himself, "I can find a way to prove the validity of the prophecy. Then the people will have no choice but to believe."

And so, with renewed determination, Arlen Thorne set forth on his quest to uncover the truth behind the ominous prophecy that threatened to engulf Elyria in darkness. For the sake of his beloved homeland, he would shoulder the weight of the world and face whatever trials lay ahead.

With a steely resolve, Arlen sought out the knowledge of Elyria's oldest and wisest inhabitants, hoping to find answers in their ancient texts and whispered secrets. He spent days upon days in the hallowed halls of libraries and temples, poring over dusty scrolls and faded manuscripts with trembling hands. His piercing green eyes scanned the pages, searching for any hint of information that could validate the prophecy.

"Is there truth in these words?" Arlen asked an elder, his voice echoing through the dimly lit chamber. The man, hunched and frail, stroked his long white beard as he considered the question.

"Truth, young one, is often obscured by time and the hearts of men," the elder replied cryptically. "But I sense a great conviction within you. Follow your heart, and the truth shall reveal itself."

Arlen nodded, his heart heavy with the gravity of the task before him. As he continued his research, he uncovered evidence of ancient prophecies foretelling great calamities– wars, famines, and cataclysms that had befallen Elyria in the past. Each passage resonated with an eerie familiarity, stirring a growing sense of urgency within him.

"Could this be it?" he wondered, his thoughts consumed by the possibility of impending doom. "I must convince them. I must make them see."

Determined to spread the word, Arlen organized town meetings and delivered impassioned speeches, his voice carrying throughout the city streets with fervent intensity. He preached of the prophecy's dire warnings, imploring his fellow citizens to heed its message and prepare for the coming darkness.

"Brothers and sisters of Elyria!" he called out, standing atop a makeshift stage in the bustling city square. "Hear my words and take them to heart! A great evil approaches, and we must stand united against it. We cannot sit idly by, waiting for our doom. We must act– now!"

As he spoke, Arlen could feel the eyes of the crowd upon him– some filled with fear and uncertainty, others with skepticism and doubt. He knew that his words alone might not be enough to sway their hearts, but he also knew that he could not give up. Elyria's fate depended on it.

"Will you stand beside me?" he implored, his voice breaking as emotion threatened to overwhelm him. "Will you fight for the future of our land and our people?"

With every fiber of his being, Arlen hoped and prayed that his message would reach those who were willing to listen, those who would join him in his quest to save Elyria from the impending darkness. And as he looked out at the sea of faces before him, he saw the first flickers of hope begin to ignite, like a tiny flame slowly growing into a roaring fire.

Arlen stood in the dimly lit town hall, his heart pounding with anticipation and urgency as he prepared to address the gathered citizens. Shadows danced around the edges of the room, cast by flickering candlelight, creating an eerie atmosphere that seemed to mirror the dark times ahead.

"Good people of Elyria," Arlen began, his voice steady despite the quivering in his chest. "The end of days draws near, and we must band together to face the coming darkness."

His words were met with a mix of hushed whispers and uncomfortable shuffling. Arlen could feel the skepticism in the air, like a thick fog suffocating him. He steeled himself, determined not to let their doubts deter him from his mission.

"Silence!" boomed a voice from the back of the room, cutting through the murmurings like a knife. A man stepped forward, his broad shoulders and imposing stature standing out amongst the crowd. His eyes were cold, devoid of empathy or concern. This was Councilman Gravus, a powerful figure within Elyria's government and a known adversary of any who challenged the status quo.

"Tell me, young man," Gravus sneered, addressing Arlen with disdain. "What makes you think that your words are anything more than the ramblings of a madman? You speak of prophecies and doom, yet I see no evidence to support your claims."

Arlen fought the urge to clench his fists, his frustration growing as he faced this unexpected opposition. He had anticipated skepticism but had not expected it to be so forcefully presented.

"Sir, I have consulted ancient texts and spoken with wise elders," Arlen replied, trying to keep his voice calm and controlled. "The signs are clear—darkness is coming, and we must prepare for it."

"Ha!" laughed Gravus, his mocking tone echoing throughout the hall. "Superstition and fear-mongering, that's all this is."

The crowd murmured in agreement, their doubts seemingly solidified by Gravus' scathing words. Arlen felt his heart sink as he realized the magnitude of the challenge before him. He had to find a way to overcome the resistance, to convince them of the truth.

"Please, you must believe me," Arlen pleaded, desperation creeping into his voice. "Our world is in grave danger, and we have a responsibility to protect it!"

But with each impassioned plea, it seemed as though the door to their hearts closed further, their skepticism only growing stronger. Yet, despite the mounting obstacles and the suffocating weight of doubt, Arlen could not– would not– give up. His eyes blazed with determination, his spirit unyielding in the face of adversity.

"Mark my words, Councilman Gravus," he vowed, his voice resolute. "I will not be silenced, and I will not stand idly by while our people are led blindly toward destruction. The truth will be revealed, and Elyria will rise against the darkness."

As the town hall emptied, leaving Arlen standing alone amidst the flickering shadows, he knew that his greatest battle had just begun. And though the path ahead was fraught with uncertainty and opposition, Arlen Thorne would not waver in his quest to save his beloved homeland.

As the sun dipped below the horizon, casting an eerie twilight upon the land, Arlen Thorne stood at the edge of Elyria's bustling market square. He observed the crowds with a keen eye, his heart heavy yet unyielding in its resolve. Dusk settled on the city like a shroud, and the air was thick with tension, the very atmosphere seemingly resonating with the urgency of his mission.

"Listen, my fellow citizens!" he called out, raising his voice above the din of the marketplace. "A great danger looms before us, and we must act now to save our beloved Elyria!"

His words were met with dismissive scoffs and sneers, and his pleas seemed to fall upon deaf ears. But Arlen would not give up. With determination burning in his green eyes, he resorted to other means to reach the people. Unfurling a stack of hastily crafted pamphlets, he began to distribute them among the throngs of passersby, each piece of parchment containing a dire warning of the impending darkness.

"Please, take these and read," he implored, extending the pamphlets toward indifferent hands. "Our future depends on it."

Though many snatched the papers away with disdain or refused them outright, Arlen pressed on undeterred. His passion for his cause was evident in every word he spoke, in every action he took. He could feel the scornful glances and hear the whispered ridicule around him, but he refused to let it stifle his determination.

"Darkness is coming! We cannot stand idly by!" he cried, his voice hoarse from hours of relentless speech. It was then that he noticed a small group of citizens gathered nearby, their expressions curious rather than contemptuous. As they listened intently to his warnings, Arlen felt a spark of hope ignite within him— perhaps he was not alone in this fight after all.

"Tell us more," urged one of the listeners, a middle-aged woman with a hard, weathered face. "What can we do to protect our families and our homes?"

Arlen's heart swelled with gratitude at her words, his resolve fortified by the knowledge that there were others who shared his concerns. He addressed the group directly, detailing the prophecy, the signs of its imminent fulfillment, and the steps they could take to prepare for the trials ahead.

"Join me," he implored them, his voice filled with conviction. "Together, we can stand against the darkness and ensure the preservation of Elyria."

As the gathering dispersed, many took Arlen's message to heart, their eyes reflecting a newfound sense of purpose. It was a small victory, but a vital one— a beacon of hope amidst the encroaching shadows. With renewed determination, Arlen Thorne vowed to continue his mission, driven by an unwavering commitment to safeguard his homeland from the prophesied apocalypse.

The sun dipped below the horizon, casting a blood-red glow over the land of Elyria. Arlen stood at the edge of a cliff, gazing out across the vast landscape before him. The wind whipped around him, tugging at his worn cloak, stirring an inner fire that burned with determination. He kneel before the gods and slowly put his head down, with tears trickling slowly down his face. As darkness fell, he knew that time was running out; he must gather a group of brave individuals, those willing to stand by his side in the face of impending doom.

"Tomorrow," he whispered to himself, "the battle begins."

Arlen's green eyes scanned the bustling city below, searching for signs of hope amidst the chaos. He could see people hurrying about their daily routines, oblivious to the danger that loomed on the horizon. His heart ached for his fellow countrymen- how many would perish if they refused to heed his warnings?

"Such ignorance," he muttered under his breath. "I must find those who will listen, who will fight."

As the first stars appeared in the night sky, Arlen descended the rocky path to the city, his resolve unwavering. He walked the streets, observing the faces of those he passed, searching for any hint of courage or conviction.

"Join me!" he called out, his voice echoing through the dimly lit alleys. "Together we can protect Elyria from the darkness that threatens us all!"

Some turned away, shaking their heads in disbelief or fear. Others laughed and mocked him. But there were a few- a precious few- whose eyes met his with a spark of defiance, a glimmer of recognition.

"Are you willing to risk everything for our homeland?" he asked these brave souls, his gaze never faltering. "Will you stand beside me, and Lucian as we confront the forces of evil?"

One by one, they agreed, their voices resolute. A ragtag band of warriors formed around Arlen: a blacksmith with arms like iron, a cunning thief with quick hands and quicker wit, a healer whose compassionate touch could mend both body and soul. Each brought their unique skills and strengths to the cause, bound together by a shared purpose.

"Tomorrow, we will gather in secret," Arlen instructed them, his voice hushed yet urgent. "Bring any who are willing to fight, who are not blinded by fear or doubt. Together, we will stand against the darkness."

As the group dispersed, Arlen watched them vanish into the night, his heart swelling with pride and hope. Though they were few, he knew that their determination was fierce, their spirits unbreakable. They were Elyria's last hope- the only barrier between the land they loved and the nightmare that threatened to engulf it.

And as the cold wind howled around him, Arlen Thorne vowed once more to do whatever it took to save his homeland from the prophesied destruction. He would lead these brave souls through the fires of hell if necessary, for in their unity lay the salvation of all Elyria.

"Let the darkness come," he whispered to the wind. "We are ready."

In a land called Elyria, danger looms on the horizon. Arlen Thorne, a brave and determined leader, seeks to protect his homeland from the forces of evil that threaten to destroy it. He rallies a group of unlikely warriors, each with their own unique skills and strengths, to join him in the fight. Among them is a blacksmith with arms like iron, a cunning thief with quick hands and wit, and a compassionate healer who can mend both body and soul.

Together, this ragtag band of warriors forms Elyria's last hope against the impending destruction. Arlen leads them with pride and hope, knowing that their determination and unity are the only things standing between their land and the darkness that threatens to engulf it.

As they gather in secret, Arlen instructs them to bring any who are willing to fight, those who are not blinded by fear or doubt. They prepare for battle, ready to confront the forces of evil and risk everything for their homeland.

The conflict rises as the group faces insurmountable odds, with the forces of evil growing stronger every day. The cause seems hopeless at times, but Arlen and his warriors refuse to give up. They fight with all their might, facing challenges that test their strength and resolve.

In the midst of it all, a betrayal threatens to tear the group apart. One of their own turns against them, revealing secrets that threaten to unravel everything they've worked for. But Arlen and his warriors stand strong, refusing to let this setback defeat them.

As the final battle approaches, Arlen and his warriors face their greatest challenge yet. They must confront the darkness head-on, risking everything to save their homeland. In a climactic scene full of action and suspense, they face off against the forces of evil in a battle that will determine the fate of Elyria.

Elyria, a land of unparalleled peace and beauty, stretched out beneath the warm embrace of the sun. The verdant rolling hills seemed to dance under the gentle sway of the breeze, while lush forests whispered ancient secrets as their leaves rustled in harmony. Sparkling rivers meandered through the landscape like veins of liquid silver, nourishing the fertile soil and bringing life to all they touched.

Standing at the edge of a cliff, overlooking this tranquil paradise, was Arlen Thorne. A tall, broad-shouldered man with a strong jawline that spoke of resilience, his intense green eyes mirrored the vibrant hues of Elyria's boundless foliage. As the sun cast its golden rays upon him, it only served to accentuate his air of authority and poise.

With every fiber of his being, Arlen was a testament to the virtues of bravery, determination, and loyalty. His love for his homeland ran as deep as the roots of the great trees that adorned the land, and he considered himself the guardian of all who called Elyria home. He knew that his role came with the weight of responsibility, but it was one that he carried with grace and unwavering commitment.

"Beautiful, isn't it?" he murmured to himself, his voice filled with reverence for the land before him. "I would do anything to preserve this peace."

As if in response to his words, a cool gust of wind brushed against his face, carrying with it the scent of the distant forests and the promise of challenges to come. Arlen closed his eyes, taking a moment to draw strength from the land that he so dearly loved. His heart swelled with determination, and he knew that whatever trials lay ahead, he would face them with the courage and tenacity that had always defined him.

"May the divine watch over you, Elyria," he whispered, opening his eyes once more to drink in the sight of his beloved homeland. "For I will always stand by your side, ready to defend your beauty and tranquility until my dying breath."

Arlen's contemplation was interrupted by the hurried approach of Nadira, her raven black hair flying behind her as she sprinted towards him. Her usually composed face was etched with deep concern, and her dark eyes held a foreboding that sent a shiver down Arlen's spine.

"Lord Thorne," she gasped, her breath ragged from the urgent run. "I bring dire news."

"Speak, Nadira," Arlen urged, his voice steady despite the trepidation that gripped his heart. "What has befallen Elyria?"

"Darkness gathers beyond our borders," she said, her gaze never leaving his. "Whispers of unnatural creatures in the shadows, and whispers of the prophecy being fulfilled."

"May the divine protect us," Arlen breathed, feeling the weight of responsibility settle heavily upon his broad shoulders. His intense green eyes hardened with resolve as he considered the implications of Nadira's words.

"You've always been swift and precise in your assessments, Nadira," he said, his tone betraying his concern for their homeland. "Tell me, what can we do to counter this growing threat?"

"Information is scarce, my lord," she admitted, visibly frustrated. "But I have heard rumors of an ancient artifact that may hold the key to our salvation. It is said to possess immense power, capable of banishing darkness and restoring the light."

"Then we must find it," Arlen declared without hesitation. "Elyria's fate may well depend on our ability to locate this artifact and wield its power against the encroaching darkness."

"Indeed, my lord," Nadira nodded solemnly. "But we must tread cautiously. The path before us will be treacherous, and we cannot afford to be careless."

"True enough," Arlen murmured, his mind racing with thoughts of strategy and potential allies. "We'll need to gather our resources and assemble a team of skilled warriors to aid us in this quest. Time is of the essence, and we must be prepared for whatever challenges lie ahead."

"Very well, my lord," Nadira agreed, determination flashing in her eyes. "I shall begin making the necessary arrangements at once."

"Thank you, Nadira," Arlen said sincerely, placing a hand on her shoulder. "Together, we will ensure the safety of Elyria and its people. The darkness may be relentless, but so are we."

They stood there for a moment, united in their resolve to protect their homeland from the impending apocalypse. The tranquility that had once graced Elyria hung by a thread, but they would fight to preserve it until their final breaths. And as they turned to face the uncertain future, Arlen couldn't help but feel a flicker of hope amidst the gathering storm.

As Arlen's thoughts raced, he sought the counsel of his most trusted advisor, Gideon Ashford. The man stood like a statue at the edge of the room, his sharp features and piercing blue eyes focused on the task at hand. Gideon had been by Arlen's side for as long as he could remember; their bond was unbreakable, forged in the fires of countless battles and hardships. Arlen knew that Gideon's unwavering loyalty would be invaluable in the trials to come.

"Send word to the others," Arlen commanded, his voice heavy with the weight of responsibility. "We must gather our closest advisors immediately. Time is not on our side."

"Of course, my lord," Gideon replied, nodding solemnly. He wasted no time in carrying out the order, dispatching messengers with swift efficiency. Despite the urgency of the situation, Arlen couldn't help but admire Gideon's ability to remain calm under pressure.

Soon enough, the private meeting hall filled with a tense energy as Arlen's closest advisors trickled in. Each one bore expressions of concern and determination, their eyes revealing the gravity of the growing threat. As they gathered around the large, wooden table, Arlen took a deep breath, preparing himself for the difficult conversation ahead.

"Thank you all for coming so quickly," Arlen began, his green eyes scanning the faces of his allies. "As I'm sure you've heard, we face a darkness unlike any other– a force that threatens to consume Elyria and all we hold dear."

The room fell silent, the air thick with tension. It was clear that everyone understood the severity of the situation, and they looked to Arlen for guidance.

"Time is our enemy, and we must act swiftly," Arlen continued, his voice resolute. "We need to find a solution to this growing threat, and we must do so as a united front. I trust each of you to bring your unique skills and expertise to the table."

"Of course, my lord," Gideon said, his voice steady and strong. "We will stand by you, no matter the cost."

"Indeed," another advisor agreed, nodding fervently. "We are all in this together, and we will fight to protect Elyria and its people."

Arlen couldn't help but feel a surge of pride at the unwavering loyalty displayed by his advisors. They understood the stakes, and they were willing to put everything on the line for the sake of their homeland.

"Then let us begin," Arlen declared, determination burning in his eyes. "We will face this darkness head-on, and we will triumph. Together, we are Elyria's last hope."

As the meeting commenced, Arlen's thoughts swirled with strategies and contingencies. He knew that the road ahead would be fraught with peril, but he was steadfast in his resolve. With his trusted advisors by his side, he would face the apocalypse and fight to save his people from the clutches of darkness.

The meeting took place in a secluded chamber deep within the fortress walls, far from the prying eyes of outsiders. Torches flickered along the stone walls, casting eerie shadows that seemed to dance to the rhythm of some ancient, ominous melody. The scent of burning wood and aged parchment filled the air, mingling with the faint aroma of cold iron that clung to the weapons adorning the walls.

At the center of the room stood a heavy oak table, its dark surface scarred by the passage of time and countless strategizing sessions. Arlen Thorne, his green eyes alight with determination, presided over the gathering of his most trusted advisors. He studied the map before him, his fingers tracing the lines that marked the boundaries of Elyria and the surrounding lands.

"Reports have been coming in from all corners," Arlen said, his voice commanding their attention. "The darkness has spread further than we could've ever imagined. We must prepare for what lies ahead."

His advisors listened intently, each weighed down by the gravity of the situation. Nadira "The Shadow" Kadir, her raven-black hair falling like a curtain around her dark, calculating eyes, was the first to break the silence. "We should fortify our defenses, strengthen our borders. They must not breach our walls."

"Agreed," Gideon Ashford interjected, his piercing blue eyes fixed on his friend and leader. "But we also need to gather allies, those who still resist the darkness. United, we stand a better chance."

Arlen considered both suggestions thoughtfully, his mind working through potential scenarios and their consequences. Every decision held the weight of countless lives, and he knew he could not afford any missteps.

"Both strategies have merit," he finally said, looking up from the map. "We will begin by reinforcing our defenses and securing our homeland. Gideon, I need you to reach out to our potential allies and ensure their support. Nadira, work with our scouts to gather intelligence on the enemy's movements and capabilities."

The room filled with a renewed sense of purpose as Arlen's advisors acknowledged his orders, eager to take action. The stakes were higher than ever, but under Arlen's guidance, they remained steadfast in their determination to protect Elyria from the encroaching darkness.

"Remember," Arlen continued, his voice filled with resolve, "we are fighting not only for ourselves but for the generations to come. We must preserve the light of Elyria against this darkness. Together, we will overcome this threat and secure our future."

Heads nodded in agreement, eyes blazing with conviction. Arlen knew that the road ahead would be fraught with danger and sacrifice, but he also knew that he had the finest warriors and strategists by his side. And with them, he would face the end of days, standing firm against the forces of evil, ready to defend his people and his homeland until his last breath.

The air was thick with tension, the weight of responsibility hanging heavily over the room. Arlen Thorne studied the faces of his advisors, each one a reflection of the dire nature of their situation. The low hum of whispered conversations filled the space, punctuated by the occasional crackle from the fireplace.

"Friends," Arlen began, "our enemy grows stronger every day. We must remain vigilant and united in our efforts to protect Elyria and her people." His intense green eyes swept across the room, ensuring that he had every person's attention.

"Indeed," Nadira Kadir, the skilled archer known as "The Shadow" for her stealth and concealment abilities, spoke up. "I have seen firsthand how cunning these forces can be. We must not underestimate them."

"True," Gideon Ashford agreed, his piercing blue eyes reflecting the firelight as he leaned forward. "But we also cannot afford to spread ourselves too thin. Our focus should be on fortifying our defenses and preparing for the battles to come."

Arlen considered Gideon's words, knowing that they held wisdom. He then turned to Nadira, seeking her input. "What do your scouts say about the enemy's movements?"

"From what we've gathered, it seems they prefer to strike when least expected," Nadira replied, her dark eyes narrowing as she recalled the reports she had received. "Their purpose is to sow fear and chaos, breaking the spirit of the people before attempting to conquer them outright."

"Then we must be prepared for anything," Arlen declared, his voice firm with resolve. He looked around at his advisors, taking note of their individual strengths and skills. "Our unity will be our greatest weapon against this threat. Each of you brings something unique to our cause, and together, we will face the darkness and prevail."

"Your faith in us is inspiring, Arlen," Gideon said, his voice filled with loyalty and determination. "We will not let you down."

"Nor will I let any of you down," Arlen replied, locking eyes with each member of his council. "Our fates are intertwined, and we must rely on one another in order to survive what is coming."

"Let us pledge ourselves to this cause, then," Nadira suggested, her tone solemn but resolute. "Together, we will stand against the darkness, no matter what form it takes."

"Agreed," Arlen said, his heart swelling with pride as he watched his advisors join hands, a symbol of their unity and commitment. He knew that the battle ahead would be unlike any they had ever faced, but with these warriors by his side, he believed that they could defy the odds and protect Elyria from the end of days.

"May the light of Elyria guide us through the darkness," Arlen intoned, feeling the weight of his responsibility as the leader of such a diverse and powerful group. "Together, we shall forge a new dawn for our people." And with those words, they solidified their pact, ready to face the apocalyptic storm that loomed on the horizon.

In the dimly lit council chamber, a sense of urgency filled the air as Arlen and his advisors huddled around an ancient, worn map of Elyria spread across the oak table. The flickering candlelight cast eerie shadows on their faces, highlighting their determination to protect their homeland.

"First, we must bolster our defenses," Arlen declared, his green eyes alive with resolve. "We cannot risk being caught unprepared."

"Agreed," Gideon chimed in, his piercing blue eyes scanning the map as his mind worked through various strategic possibilities. "We should send scouts to gather information on any approaching forces, as well as rally our allies to our cause."

"An excellent plan," Nadira added, her dark eyes glinting in the candlelight. "I can lead a team of archers to reinforce key locations and provide cover for our troops."

"Good," Arlen nodded, approving of their contributions. "But we must also prepare for the worst. If the darkness manages to breach our defenses, we will need to have a fallback plan in place."

"Perhaps we could embark on a quest to seek out ancient relics or forgotten knowledge that may aid us in our struggle against the encroaching evil," suggested Gideon thoughtfully, tracing a finger along an intricate web of symbols on the map.

Arlen considered the idea, his thoughts racing with potential outcomes and consequences. "It is risky, but it could be the key to our survival. We should assemble a small group of our finest warriors for this task– those who possess unique skills and strengths."

"Count me in," Nadira said without hesitation, her voice steady and resolute. "I will do whatever it takes to ensure the safety of Elyria."

"Thank you, Nadira," Arlen replied, his heart swelling with gratitude for her unwavering loyalty. "Together, we shall face the end of days and emerge victorious."

As the council continued to devise their plan, Arlen's mind was consumed by a growing sense of anticipation. With each decision made, the fate of Elyria hung in the balance, and he felt the weight of his responsibility as never before.

"Time is of the essence," he reminded his advisors, his voice heavy with the gravity of their situation. "We must act quickly, for we know not when the darkness will strike."

As they finalized their plans, an uneasy silence fell over the chamber. The air grew thick with tension, as if an invisible hand tightened its grip on the very atmosphere around them. It was then that Arlen noticed something strange on the ancient map– a small symbol hidden in the corner, partially obscured by years of wear and tear.

"Wait," he whispered, his heart pounding in his chest. "What is this?"

His advisors leaned in closer, their eyes narrowing as they examined the mysterious marking. The room seemed to grow colder, as if the shadow of impending doom had settled upon them.

"By the heavens…" Gideon breathed, his voice faltering. "Could it be…?"

"Is it possible?" Nadira murmured, her face pale with shock.

"Impossible!" Arlen declared, his voice trembling with disbelief. "I thought it was just a legend! How can it be real?"

The revelation sent a shudder through the room, as if the world around them had shifted on its axis. Their carefully laid plans now seemed to hang by a thread, their hopes of victory overshadowed by a monstrous new threat.

"Then we truly are facing the end of days," Gideon whispered, his eyes locked on the fateful symbol. "And our battle has only just begun."

As the magnitude of their discovery began to sink in, Arlen clenched his fists, steeling himself for the trials ahead. The darkness had thrown down its gauntlet, and now it was up to him and his advisors to determine the fate of Elyria. United in purpose, they faced the coming storm with courage, ready to confront the ultimate evil that threatened to consume their world.

IX

BETRAYAL

The first light of dawn cast a feeble glow over the small village, revealing the haggard faces of its inhabitants as they emerged from their modest homes. Fear and oppression clung to the air like a bitter fog, settling over each person like an unwanted burden. It was in this atmosphere that Valthor Malgath's rule held them captive, his iron grip tightening with each passing day. The villagers' eyes darted nervously from side to side, their voices hushed, as if even the act of speaking would draw the ire of their ruthless leader.

As the sun rose higher, a figure appeared on the outskirts of the village– a stooped, elderly man shrouded in tattered robes. His face was lined with age, but beneath the wrinkles and the silver-white hair that framed his face, there lay the piercing eyes of a man who had seen much and understood more. He moved through the crowd with a grace that belied his years, carrying himself with a quiet dignity that seemed to part the sea of nervous villagers before him.

"Make way for the seer," whispered one woman to her neighbor, her voice trembling with both awe and trepidation.

"Is it true what they say about him?" asked the other, her eyes wide with curiosity.

"Indeed," replied the first. "He has spoken prophecies that have come to pass, and his wisdom is said to be unmatched."

As the old seer approached the center of the village square, he paused, raising his head to survey the crowd. His gaze was steady, unflinching, and seemed to pierce the hearts of those who met it. In his presence, the villagers found themselves torn between the comfort of his wisdom and the fear that any association with him would only serve to draw Valthor's wrath down upon them.

"Children of the Earth," the seer began, his voice strong and clear despite the age that weighed upon him, "I come bearing a message of hope."

The villagers huddled together, their faces etched with deep lines of worry and fear as they awaited the words of the old seer. Lucian Thorne's piercing blue eyes surveyed the crowd, taking in the desperation that hung heavy in the air. It was said that the seer had once prophesied the great flood that had ravaged the land years ago, leaving only devastation in its wake, and he had also foretold the rise of Valthor Malgath, the tyrant whose iron grip on the village now choked the life from its people.

"Listen well, for I have seen a vision," the old seer declared, his voice resonating with the weight of ages. "A time of reckoning approaches, when the chains that bind us shall be broken, and the scales shall tip in favor of justice."

As the gathering leaned in closer, straining to hear every word, Lucian could not help but feel a flicker of hope stirring within him. The seer's past prophecies had come to pass, and his wisdom held a power that could not be denied.

"From ancient slumber shall awaken the Serpent, its fiery breath scorching the heavens, and its venomous fangs sinking deep into the heart of darkness," the seer continued, his voice gaining strength as he painted a vivid picture of apocalyptic destruction. "But fear not, for amid the ashes of the fallen world a new dawn shall arise, heralded by those who were chosen to bear the fire of change."

Lucian's heart raced as he listened to the prophecy, feeling the words sear into his soul like a branding iron. He could see, in his mind's eye, the cataclysmic battles that would rage between good and evil, the countless lives sacrificed in pursuit of freedom from Valthor's tyranny.

"Mark my words," the seer warned, his gaze sweeping over the villagers like a storm-tossed wave. "The time draws near when the Serpent's wrath shall be unleashed, and only those who stand united in defiance of darkness shall prevail. The path will be fraught with peril, but together we shall forge a new destiny for our people."

As the seer's words rang through the village square, Lucian felt the stirrings of a long-dormant fire within him. It was as if the prophecy had awakened something primal in his soul, a ferocious determination to fight for the freedom of his people and bring an end to Valthor's rule.

"Take heed of this prophecy," the old seer intoned, his voice echoing with the authority of one who speaks with the voice of the divine. "For it is our last hope, the final spark that may yet kindle the flame of rebellion and burn away the shadow that has fallen upon us all."

As the villagers absorbed the gravity of the seer's words, Lucian knew that the time for action was at hand. The prophecy had been delivered, and its message was clear: they must rise up against Valthor Malgath or be forever lost to the darkness.

The villagers stood transfixed, as if the very air around them had become charged with the weight of the seer's words. Uncertainty and hope flickered across their faces, like the dancing shadows cast by a flickering candle.

"Can it be true?" an elderly woman whispered, her gnarled hands trembling as she clutched the worn shawl around her shoulders. "Is there really hope for us?"

"Quiet, Muriel," hissed another villager, a tall man with a scarred face and wary eyes. He glanced nervously over his shoulder, as if expecting Valthor's guards to emerge from the shadows at any moment. "We must not speak of this too loudly."

Lucian could hear the murmurings of doubt and disbelief spreading through the crowd, but he could also sense the undercurrent of hope that pulsed beneath the surface. Some dared to believe that the prophecy held the key to their salvation, while others feared it was nothing more than the ramblings of a madman. But amidst the chaos of conflicting emotions, one thing was certain: the seeds of rebellion had been planted.

"Listen well, friends," Lucian urged, raising his voice above the whispers that swirled around him like a gathering storm. "The time has come for us to make a choice. Will we cower in fear, allowing Valthor to tighten his grip upon our throats? Or will we stand together, united by the fire of hope that burns within our hearts?"

"Easy for you to say," scoffed a middle-aged woman with a stern expression, her arms crossed over her chest. "You haven't suffered as we have. What guarantee do we have that this prophecy is not just another of Valthor's tricks?"

"Would that I could offer you certainty," Lucian admitted, his blue eyes filled with a solemn resolve. "But all I can offer is my faith in the seer's words, and my unwavering determination to see this through to the end. Will you stand with me?"

"Lucian speaks the truth," Lilith interjected, her violet eyes glowing with a fierce intensity. "We have nothing to lose by placing our trust in the prophecy. If we do not act now, we condemn ourselves to eternal darkness."

The crowd stirred, the tide of hope beginning to rise above the waves of doubt and fear. For every skeptical glance, there was a nod of agreement. For every hushed whisper of doubt, there was a murmured prayer for deliverance.

"Very well," the stern-faced woman said at last, her voice wavering with emotion. "I… I will stand with you, Lucian Thorne. May the heavens help us all."

As the villagers pledged their allegiance one by one, their voices growing stronger with each declaration, Lucian knew that the battle had only just begun. The path before them would be fraught with danger and despair, but he could not allow himself to falter. The prophecy had spoken, and it was his duty to ensure that its promise was fulfilled.

"Then let us begin," he said quietly, his gaze sweeping over the sea of determined faces before him. "For the darkness shall not claim us without a fight."

The sun dipped low on the horizon, casting long shadows across the dusty streets of the village. Lucian Thorne gazed upon his people– their eyes alight with a mixture of fear and hope, and he knew that beneath it all, lay a deep longing for freedom. Their whispers were filled with dreams of a better tomorrow, one where they could live in peace, free from Valthor's brutal regime.

"Lucian," whispered a young woman, her voice trembling with emotion. "Do you believe we can really be free? Can this prophecy truly save us?"

"Shh!" A middle-aged man hushed her sharply, glancing around nervously. "Not so loud, child! If Valthor's guards hear you…"

"Look at them," Lucian murmured, his gaze following the guard patrol as they marched through the narrow streets, their boots thudding against the cobblestones. The villagers instinctively shied away from them, pressing themselves against the crumbling walls of their homes. "Their presence is a constant reminder of our bondage. But I have faith in the prophecy, my friends. We must cling to that hope, especially now."

"Valthor's rule is tightening its grip on us," an elderly man lamented, pulling his worn cloak tighter around his frail frame. "His restrictions are suffocating us, and we are slowly losing any sense of freedom we once had. His curfews force us into hiding long before nightfall, and the heavy taxes drain us of what little we have left."

"Curfew will soon be upon us," Lucian said, casting a wary glance toward the darkening sky. "We should disperse. Gather your loved ones close. Tonight, let us dream of a brighter future, where Valthor's shadow no longer looms over our heads."

As the villagers nodded in agreement, each offering a quiet word of encouragement, Lucian felt the weight of responsibility settle upon his shoulders. Their fear was palpable, their hope fragile, and it rested upon him to guide them through the darkness that threatened to engulf them all.

"Freedom," he whispered, his voice barely audible as he watched the villagers scatter to their homes, their eyes filled with longing for a life without Valthor's iron fist. "We shall have our freedom."

As the final rays of sunlight disappeared behind the horizon, and the ominous tolling of the curfew bell echoed through the village, Lucian knew that the days ahead would test them in ways they never could have imagined. But he also knew, deep within his heart, that the fire of hope had been kindled– and so long as it burned, they would fight for their freedom until the very end.

The moon hung low in the sky, casting a dim and eerie glow of orange, red colors over the village. The oppressive silence that blanketed the night was only occasionally broken by the muted whispers of the villagers. As they crept through the narrow streets, their shadows flitted across the crumbling facades of buildings that had long since lost their former glory.

Lucian Thorne stood at the heart of the village square, his piercing blue eyes scanning the faces of those who had gathered before him. He knew each of them well, for they were his people– the ones he had sworn to protect from Valthor's brutal regime.

"Brothers and sisters," Lucian began, his voice low and steady. "We have come together tonight, united by our shared desire for freedom and peace. Let us not be swayed by doubt or fear, for we have been given a prophecy– a glimmer of hope amidst these dark times."

Among the villagers, three key figures shifted uneasily, embodying the different perspectives on the prophecy. There was Gideon, an old and weathered man who had seen countless prophecies come and go, yet still clung to the hope that one day, change would come. Beside him stood Maris, a young mother whose skepticism shone in her wary eyes, her arms cradling her infant child protectively. And finally, there was Elijah, a fiery-eyed youth who burned with passion for the cause, his every word a rallying cry for rebellion against Valthor's rule.

"Hope is a dangerous thing," Maris whispered, her voice trembling with uncertainty. "What if this prophecy leads us astray? We have already suffered so much, and I fear for what will become of my child if we place our faith in something that may never come to pass."

Gideon placed a gnarled hand on her shoulder, attempting to reassure her. "I have lived through many a prophecy, my dear. Some have come true, others not. But we must hold onto hope, for it is the only thing that keeps us going in these dark times."

Elijah, however, was brimming with fervor. "We can't stand idly by while Valthor continues to oppress us!" he exclaimed. "This prophecy is a sign— a message from the heavens that our time has come! We must rise up and fight for our freedom!"

As the villagers listened intently, Lucian weighed their words carefully. He understood the fear that gripped Maris's heart, the weary hope in Gideon's eyes, and the burning passion of Elijah. These emotions churned within him as well, but he knew that he must remain strong for his people.

"Each of you speaks truth," Lucian said solemnly. "But we cannot let doubt consume us. We must be vigilant, and prepare for the days ahead."

The village itself seemed to echo the despair that hung heavy over its inhabitants. Dilapidated buildings sagged under the weight of years of neglect, their once-bright colors faded into a dreary gray. Weary souls trudged through the muddy streets, their shoulders stooped beneath the burden of oppression. And yet, amidst the sorrowful landscape, there were small signs of defiance: windows adorned with wilting flowers, walls covered in hastily scrawled messages of hope and rebellion, and the quiet resolve in the eyes of those who refused to be broken.

"Let us come together," Lucian continued, "and unite our strengths so that we may face whatever challenges lie before us. For it is only through unity and determination that we may finally break the chains that bind us."

His words hung in the air, a silent call to action that stirred the hearts of all who heard it. As they dispersed into the night, each carrying the weight of the prophecy and their own fears and hopes, Lucian knew that they were on the cusp of something monumental— a turning point that would either lead them to freedom or plunge them deeper into darkness.

"May we find the strength to face what lies ahead," he murmured, his gaze fixed on the flickering candlelight that danced in the windows of the village homes. "For the sake of us all."

The sun rose weakly over the horizon, casting a feeble light on the decrepit village. Lucian walked through the streets, observing the toil of his fellow villagers as they carried out their daily tasks. The once-vibrant marketplace now stood nearly empty, its merchants hawking meager wares while children scrounged for scraps in alleyways. Their struggle seemed insurmountable, and yet, the prophecy had ignited a spark within them.

"Lucian," called Nadia, her green eyes shining with determination. "I've been practicing all night. When the time comes, I'll be ready."

"Good," Lucian replied, nodding at her. "We need every able hand we can muster."

Hushed conversations filled the air as villagers shared their thoughts on the prophecy. Some were hopeful, daring to believe that change was possible, while others remained skeptical, their faith eroded by years of suffering.

"Can you really save us?" an old woman asked Lucian, her voice cracking with age. "I have seen so much pain... it is difficult to believe."

"Trust in the prophecy," he answered, his blue eyes radiating conviction. "And trust in our resolve. Together, we will overcome this darkness."

In every corner of the village, the prophecy stirred something deep within its inhabitants. For some, like Elias, it manifested as a quiet determination. For others, like Dorian, it was a burning rage against the injustice they had endured. And for a few, like Lilith and Cassia, it was a cautious hope that dared not speak its name.

"Lucian," whispered Cassia, her gray eyes clouded with worry. "What if we fail? What if the prophecy leads us astray?"

"Then we will regroup and find another way," Lucian replied firmly. "But we must try. We owe it to ourselves and to those who have suffered under Valthor's rule."

As the day wore on, the village continued its laborious existence. Yet despite their hardship, the villagers moved with a newfound purpose. The prophecy had rekindled the flames of hope that had long been extinguished in their hearts.

"Tonight, we gather in secret," Lucian told his closest allies. "We must discuss our plans for when the prophecy comes to pass. We will be ready for whatever challenges lie ahead."

"May the gods guide us," murmured Elias, his expression solemn yet resolute.

The sun dipped below the horizon, leaving the village shrouded in darkness. As the villagers retreated to their homes, the weight of anticipation hung heavily in the air. The prophecy had set them on a path toward an uncertain future, but it was a path they would walk together, united in their struggle against tyranny.

"Tomorrow, we begin anew," Lucian whispered to himself as he gazed upon the night sky. "For the sake of us all, we must succeed."

And so, with the world teetering on the brink of chaos, the villagers prepared themselves for the trials that lay ahead. Fueled by the promise of the prophecy, they faced the dawn with renewed strength and unwavering resolve, determined to reclaim their freedom or die trying.

In a world on the brink of chaos, the villagers of an unnamed village gather in secret to discuss their plans for the prophecy that will soon come to pass. Lucian, the leader of the group, is resolute as he addresses his closest allies, declaring that they must be ready for whatever challenges lie ahead. Elias, one of the members of the group, murmurs a prayer to the gods, his expression solemn yet determined.

As the sun sets, the villagers retreat to their homes, the weight of anticipation heavy in the air. The prophecy has set them on a path towards an uncertain future, but they are united in their struggle against tyranny. Lucian gazes upon the night sky and whispers to himself that tomorrow they will begin anew. For the sake of all, they must succeed.

The dawn brings renewed strength and unwavering resolve as the villagers prepare themselves for the trials that lay ahead. They are fueled by the promise of the prophecy and determined to reclaim their freedom or die trying. As they set out on their journey, they encounter many obstacles and challenges. The journey is long and treacherous, but their determination never falters.

Lucian and his allies face many trials along the way, but they are steadfast in their resolve to succeed. They encounter dangerous creatures, treacherous terrain, and hostile enemies, but they never lose sight of their goal. As they journey closer to their destination, they discover that there are other groups who also seek to fulfill the prophecy. Some are willing to help them, while others are determined to stop them at any cost.

As they near their destination, Lucian and his allies face their greatest challenge yet. The forces of tyranny have gathered to stop them from fulfilling the prophecy. A fierce battle ensues, and it seems that all is lost. But just when it seems that all hope is gone, a twist occurs that changes everything.

The village of Larsa lay nestled within the embrace of a secluded valley, its humble dwellings hidden from the eyes of the world by a dense canopy of ancient trees. Here, time seemed to stand still, as if the very air was charged with anticipation. The villagers went about their daily tasks with hushed voices and furtive glances, each one keenly aware that they stood on the precipice of something monumental.

As the sun dipped below the horizon, painting the sky in hues of crimson and gold, the villagers congregated in the village square, their faces lit by the flickering glow of torchlight. In the midst of this gathering stood a man whose mere presence commanded the undivided attention of all who beheld him. This was Lucian Valeria, a figure both revered and feared for his unwavering determination and iron resolve.

Lucian's piercing blue eyes seemed to bore into the souls of those assembled before him, his gaze unyielding yet compassionate. His dark hair, streaked with strands of silver, framed an expression that spoke volumes of the weight he carried upon his shoulders. He surveyed the crowd, each face familiar to him, each one bearing the marks of hardship and suffering that had become their common lot.

"Brothers and sisters," Lucian began, his voice resonating with quiet authority, "tonight we stand at the crossroads of destiny. For too long, we have endured oppression, our spirits shackled by tyranny and deceit. But no more! Our time has come– the prophecy foretold is at hand!"

As he spoke, the murmurs of the villagers rose like a tide, the currents of hope, fear, and desperation intermingling in the twilight air. Sensing the building tension, Lucian raised his hands, beseeching calm. "We must be vigilant, my friends, for the path we tread is fraught with peril. The forces arrayed against us are cunning and ruthless, but we shall not falter! For we are united in our struggle, bound by our shared desire for freedom!"

With these stirring words, Lucian ignited a fire within the hearts of his people, a flame that burned with fierce resolve and unwavering determination. As they dispersed to their homes, each villager carried the promise of the prophecy close to their hearts, bolstered by the knowledge that their champion stood beside them, ready to lead them into the coming storm.

The sun dipped below the horizon, casting an eerie glow upon the obscure village of Larsa, nestled between the craggy cliffs and dense foliage that shielded it from prying eyes. The air was thick with anticipation, as if the very clouds above were holding their breath in anxious wait.

Lucian Valeria stood at the edge of a clearing, his piercing blue eyes scanning the shadows for his trusted allies. Dark hair framed a determined expression, etched with both resolve and compassion. As the last vestiges of daylight retreated, familiar figures emerged from the gloom, drawn to Lucian's commanding presence like moths to a flame.

They converged upon an ancient oak tree, gnarled roots snaking across the ground, providing both seclusion and solace for this clandestine gathering. This would be their council, where they would forge the path to mankind's salvation or damnation– the stakes had never been higher.

"Friends," Lucian began, friends, i have traveled far, with no food or water to eat or to drink. But the gods have spared my life of and my old horse, to bring you a message of distress. his voice steady and filled with determination. "We stand on the precipice of a great conflict, one that will test our strength, our cunning, and our faith. But I have no doubt that together, we shall emerge victorious."

His words echoed through the hearts of those assembled, each bearing the scars of past battles and the weight of their loyalty to Lucian and the cause. Their collective gaze held the fierce light of conviction, as they prepared themselves for the trials that lay ahead.

"Before us lies a challenge unlike any we've faced before," Lucian continued, his tone equal parts warning and encouragement. "The enemy is relentless, but so too are we. We must steel ourselves for the days to come, for only then can we break the chains of tyranny and usher in a new era— one free from darkness and despair."

As his allies listened intently, thoughts raced within their minds, conjuring images of potential foes, hidden dangers, and the promise of victory. Each warrior's heart swelled with equal parts trepidation and determination.

"Know this," Lucian concluded, his voice unwavering as it rose above the whispering wind that rustled the leaves around them. "Whatever may come, I stand beside you— not as your leader, but as your brother-in-arms. Together, we shall face the end of days, and when the dust settles, we will rise triumphant!"

With renewed vigor, the assembly dispersed into the shadows once more, their spirits buoyed by Lucian's impassioned words. They knew all too well the hardships that lay ahead, but there was no turning back now. The fate of mankind rested upon their shoulders, and they would either see it to salvation or die trying.

The wind whispered through the trees, carrying with it the faint scent of impending rain as Lucian and his allies gathered in a circle beneath the canopy. The flickering light of a single torch illuminated their faces, casting shadows that danced and intertwined with the darkness beyond.

"Time is short," Lucian began, his blue eyes alight with purpose. "We must finalize our plans and prepare for the fulfillment of the prophecy. Each of you brings unique strengths and insights, and together, we will overcome the darkness."

"Lucian, I have been studying the ancient texts and consulting with the village elders," said Elias llow, his warm brown eyes reflecting the wisdom of years spent seeking knowledge. His voice was gentle, yet carried an authority born from deep spiritual connection. "It is said that at the end of the thousand-year captivity of Satan, a great battle will be fought on the shores of the sea. We must ensure that we are there to stand against him."

"Agreed," Lucian nodded, his thoughts turning to strategies and tactics. "We need to position ourselves carefully and choose the right moment to strike. Timing will be crucial if we are to succeed."

"Indeed," murmured Elias, his expression solemn yet determined. He closed his eyes and whispered a prayer to the gods, asking for their guidance and protection in the trials ahead. As he finished, the wind seemed to carry his words away, as if delivering them straight to the heavens.

"Let us split into groups," suggested Lucian, turning to the others. "Each group will have specific tasks to complete in preparation for the great battle. We'll reconvene here in three days' time to discuss our progress and make any necessary adjustments."

"Three days should be enough time for my team to gather supplies and weapons," offered one ally, a tall woman with fiery red hair and a steely determination etched across her face.

"Meanwhile, my group will scout the coastline and find the most advantageous position for us to strike from," added another, his dark eyes gleaming with cunning.

"Very well," Lucian agreed, his gaze sweeping across each face in turn. "We must all be prepared to do whatever it takes to fulfill our destiny. Remember, united we stand, divided we fall."

With a chorus of affirmative murmurs, the allies dispersed to their respective tasks, their minds filled with plans and strategies as they set forth into the night. As the torchlight flickered and dimmed, Lucian stood alone beneath the trees, his thoughts a mix of anticipation and concern.

"May the gods guide our path," he whispered into the darkness, his breath mingling with the cool night air. And with that, he too vanished into the shadows, driven by an unwavering resolve to see the prophecy fulfilled and the end of Satan's reign at hand.

The sun had dipped below the horizon, casting long shadows over Larsa's village square. The hushed whispers of the villagers seemed to echo the anticipation that hung heavy in the air. They knew their lives were about to change, and that change was a double-edged sword- it could bring freedom or death. Lucian Valeria stood at the center of it all, his piercing blue eyes surveying the gathered crowd with a mix of concern and determination.

"Friends," he began, his voice commanding yet gentle, "the time has come to put our plans into action. The prophecy speaks of a great battle that will determine our fate, and we must be prepared to face whatever challenges lie ahead."

Mara Valis stepped forward, her fiery spirit blazing like a beacon in the dimming light. Her green eyes, which seemed to pierce through one's very soul, locked onto Lucian's as she spoke with unwavering conviction. "We have suffered for too long under the yoke of tyranny," she declared, her voice strong and clear. "It is our duty to challenge the authority that oppresses us, and I am committed to this cause with every fiber of my being."

Lucian nodded solemnly, acknowledging Mara's passion and resolve. He then turned his attention to Cassius Ay, who wore a cunning smile as he approached the gathering. His dark hair framed a pair of sharp gray eyes that belied a mind always calculating and strategizing.

"Indeed, our enemy is formidable," Cassius agreed, his silver tongue weaving a web of words that captivated his listeners. "But we can exploit their weaknesses if we play our cards right. We must strike swiftly and unexpectedly, like a viper in the grass. Our forces may be smaller, but we have the advantage of knowing the land and its secrets."

As Cassius shared his strategic suggestions, Lucian's thoughts raced, evaluating the potential obstacles they might face. He weighed the risks against the rewards, his mind honing in on each detail until a plan began to take shape. Yet, even as he considered their chances of success, he knew that the outcome would ultimately be decided by forces beyond their control.

"Your wisdom is invaluable, Cassius," Lucian acknowledged, his voice filled with gratitude. "We will heed your counsel and act accordingly."

But even as they spoke of strategy and determination, Lucian could not shake the feeling that the true battle had only just begun. The end of

Satan's thousand-year reign was drawing near, but its conclusion remained uncertain. As the villagers dispersed into the dusk, preparing themselves for the trials ahead, Lucian took one last look at the darkening sky.

"May the gods guide us," he whispered, his voice barely audible above the rustling of leaves. And with that, he retreated into the shadows, his heart heavy with responsibility, yet buoyed by the hope that burned within him like an eternal flame.

The dying embers of the fire cast a dim glow upon the faces of Lucian's allies, flickering shadows painting their expressions with an eerie intensity. As the discussions continued, Livia Thorne's dark eyes glided from one speaker to the next, her slender fingers playing absently with the frayed edge of her cloak. She appeared almost fragile in the wavering firelight, a raven-haired wraith haunting the periphery of the gathering.

"Lucian," she said softly as a lull fell upon the group, her voice lilting like the wind whispering through the trees. "I have been watching the reactions of our people, listening to their concerns and fears. They are loyal, but many feel uncertain. They need reassurance that we stand by them, that our cause is just."

Her words carried weight, for Livia had always possessed a keen insight into the human heart, an ability to see beyond masks and facades and into the very souls of those around her. Lucian met her gaze, his piercing blue eyes reflecting the sincerity of her counsel.

"Thank you, Livia," he said, his voice firm yet gentle. "Your observations are astute, as always. We must ensure that our people understand the gravity of our struggle and the unity that binds us together."

With a nod, he turned back to his allies, his broad shoulders squared against the encroaching darkness. "My friends," he began, his voice resolute, "we are bound by a common purpose, united in our determination to end the tyranny that has held us captive for a thousand years. Now, more than ever, we must stand together, shoulder to shoulder, each of us lending our strength to the other."

He paused, scanning the faces before him, each etched with varying degrees of hope and fear. "Know this: I would gladly lay down my life for any one of you, for the cause we serve is greater than any single life. We fight not just for ourselves, but for the generations that will follow, and for the countless souls who have suffered under this cruel reign."

As Lucian spoke, his allies exchanged glances, their spirits buoyed by his unwavering determination. Mara's green eyes sparkled with renewed fire, and Cassius' cunning smile returned, his silver tongue ready to weave words of inspiration.

"Let us remember," Lucian continued, "that our actions today will echo throughout history. Our struggle may be fraught with danger, but it is also filled with hope– the hope that we may reclaim our freedom and restore the light of justice to this darkened world."

With these words, a renewed sense of purpose settled over the group, each ally drawing strength from the others. Livia smiled softly at Lucian, her eyes brimming with gratitude and admiration. For they knew that, under his guidance, they would face the coming trials with resolve, united in their quest to fulfill the prophecy and break the chains that bound them.

As the meeting drew to a close, Lucian stepped away from the gathering, his heart heavy with the weight of responsibility. The cool night air brushed against his face, and he lifted his gaze to the heavens, seeking solace in the vast expanse of the sky. Stars shimmered like distant beacons, guiding him toward an uncertain future.

"Tomorrow," he whispered, his breath condensing in the darkness, "we shall begin anew. With each dawn comes a chance to change our fate, and I swear that we will rise to meet this challenge with unwavering resolve."

Lucian's thoughts turned inward, mingling with the whispers of his allies as they dispersed into the shadows. Their loyalty and courage bolstered his spirit, filling him with a determination that burned like the embers of a dying flame. He knew that the days ahead would test their mettle, and the prophecy that had once seemed so distant now loomed over them like an approaching storm.

As the first light of dawn crept across the village, the faintest touch of pink staining the horizon, Larsa stirred to life. The villagers emerged from their homes, their faces etched with the lines of hardship but also alight with the fire of rebellion. They gathered in hushed groups, murmuring prayers to the gods and steeling themselves for the trials that lay ahead.

Lucian watched them, his piercing blue eyes filled with pride and compassion. He knew that the road before them was fraught with danger, but he also understood the power of hope– the hope that their sacrifices might one day bring about the end of tyranny and restore freedom to their people.

"Today we fight not just for ourselves, but for all who have suffered under the yoke of oppression," he said softly, his words echoing through the hearts of those who stood by his side. "Let us stand tall, united by our purpose and bound by our determination to reclaim what has been stolen from us. We shall either find victory or embrace death, but we will never yield."

The villagers exchanged determined glances; their spirits buoyed by Lucian's unwavering conviction. As the sun crept higher, casting its golden light upon the village, they felt the stirrings of something greater than themselves– a force that would drive them forward in their quest for freedom, no matter the cost.

"Are you ready?" Lucian asked them, his voice steady and resolute.

"We are," they replied as one, their voices ringing through the crisp morning air, echoing the promise of the prophecy that had brought them together.

"Then let us begin."

X

CONFLICT
ESCALATES: QUEST OR MISSION

The city of Lysoria stretched out beneath a sky painted with the colors of impending doom. A cacophony of voices filled the air, merchants hawking their wares in the bustling marketplaces and people bartering like there was no tomorrow. Towering buildings of stone and wood stood sentinel over the streets below, casting long shadows that seemed to foretell the darkness that loomed on the horizon.

Atop one such tower, Lucian Valerius stood watch over his city. The wind whipped around him, tugging at his short-cropped hair as he surveyed the metropolis below. He was a skilled and courageous warrior, forged by years of battle and sacrifice– and he would need every ounce of that strength and courage for the trials that awaited him.

"Look at them," he muttered under his breath, "so unaware of the danger that draws near." His piercing blue eyes narrowed as he took in the scene below, a storm of determination brewing within them. He knew all too well the forces of darkness that threatened his world, and the fear they instilled in the hearts of those who knew the truth.

"Lucian." The voice came from behind him, causing the warrior to stiffen slightly before relaxing once more. He knew that voice, knew the person who spoke it, and trusted her with his life.

"Speak your mind, Cassia," Lucian replied, not tearing his gaze away from the city below.

"Rumors have spread through the city," she said, her words measured and careful. "They say there is an artifact, one that may hold the power to turn the tide against the darkness."

"Rumors are just that- rumors," Lucian answered dismissively, though even as he spoke, he couldn't deny the flicker of hope that stirred within him. Could it be true? Could there be something out there that could save his people from certain doom?

"Perhaps," Cassia agreed, her warm brown eyes meeting his for a moment before returning to the city below. "But if there's even a chance that it's true, we have to try."

"Indeed," Lucian murmured, his thoughts churning like a tempest as he considered the implications. If there was an artifact, one that could grant them the power to stand against the darkness, then he would find it– and he would use it to save his people, no matter the cost.

"Prepare the horses," he commanded, turning away from the vista and locking eyes with Cassia. "We ride at dawn."

Lucian's piercing blue eyes, like two gleaming sapphires, stood out against his sun-kissed skin and framed by his chiseled features. He blinked away a bead of sweat that threatened to roll down his forehead as he descended the tower's steps, his muscular build and warrior's grace evident with each controlled movement.

"Commander Valerius," a merchant called out, bowing low in respect. Lucian acknowledged him with a nod, his face betraying nothing of the turmoil within. As he continued through the city of Lysoria, whispers of awe and admiration followed in his wake. The people revered him as their defender, a beacon of hope in the encroaching darkness.

"May the gods bless your quest, Commander," offered an elderly woman, her eyes shining with gratitude as she clasped her hands together in prayer. Lucian bowed his head slightly, his determined gaze never leaving her face as he replied, "I will do all that is in my power, ma'am."

Though he was a seasoned warrior, Lucian knew that the battle against the forces of darkness required more than just physical strength. Deep inside, he questioned his own abilities, wondering if he could truly lead his people to victory. Yet, for their sake, he would not falter, and his determination shone brightly in his eyes.

"Your courage is an inspiration to us all, Commander," said a young soldier, stepping forward to clasp Lucian's forearm in a gesture of camaraderie. Lucian gripped the man's arm tightly, imbuing his reply with conviction:"Together, we shall prevail."

As Lucian made his way through the bustling marketplace, he paused to survey the crowd. Men, women, and children all went about their daily lives, unaware of the impending doom that loomed over them like a storm-cloud on the horizon. The weight of his responsibility settled heavily on his broad shoulders, and Lucian clenched his fists in resolve.

"Every life here depends on us," he murmured to himself, dark thoughts of the apocalypse plaguing his mind. He knew that he could not afford to fail– not with so much at stake. "I will find the artifact, and I will save my people."

With each step he took, Lucian's determination grew stronger. As he moved through the city, the respect and admiration of his fellow citizens buoyed him, giving him the strength to face the unknown dangers that awaited him on his quest. And as the sun began to set over Lysoria, casting a golden glow upon its towering buildings, Lucian vowed that he would do whatever it took to protect his people from the encroaching darkness.

The sun dipped low over the city, casting long shadows across the streets below as Lucian stood atop the highest tower in Lysoria. His piercing blue eyes scanned the sprawling metropolis, taking in every detail with a keen sense of purpose. He could feel the weight of responsibility that came with his duty to protect the city and its people, and it was a burden he willingly bore.

"Lucian," a voice called out from behind him, rich and melodic like the wind rustling through leaves. He turned to find Cassia Amara ascending the final steps to join him on the tower's platform. A warm breeze swept her long, flowing dark hair around her face, revealing warm brown eyes that always seemed to be one step ahead.

"Ah, there you are, Cassia," Lucian greeted her, a smile tugging at the corners of his lips. "I thought I might find you here."

"Your intuition serves you well," she replied, her gaze never leaving the cityscape before them. "As always."

Cassia's presence brought an undeniable sense of comfort and familiarity, the bond between them forged through years of shared battles and victories, losses and heartaches. Their camaraderie emanated effortlessly, a testament to their mutual understanding and respect for one another.

"Have you heard?" Cassia asked, her voice barely above a whisper as if the very air carried secrets. "Rumors of an artifact with power unlike anything we've ever seen."

Lucian's eyes narrowed, his muscles tensing at the thought. "Do you believe it's true?"

Cassia hesitated, her brow furrowing as she weighed her words. "In times like these, we must explore every possibility. If such an artifact exists, imagine what we could accomplish. We could change the course of our fate." She locked eyes with Lucian, her conviction resonating in her gaze.

"Then we must find it," Lucian declared, his determination lending strength to his voice. "Together."

"Agreed," Cassia replied, nodding firmly. "We'll gather our allies, search every corner of the world if we must. We cannot let this opportunity slip through our fingers."

As they stood side by side, the sun's dying light casting a fiery glow upon their faces, there was no doubt in either of their minds that they shared a common purpose: to find the fabled artifact and save their people from the brink of destruction. In that moment, with the city of Lysoria at their feet and an uncertain future ahead, Lucian and Cassia vowed to face whatever challenges awaited them together, until the very end.

As Lucian and Cassia descended the tower, the city of Lysoria seemed to close in around them, suffocating in its oppressive atmosphere. The weight of the world pressed down on their shoulders as the forces of darkness continued to encroach upon the land, casting a long shadow over the hearts of the people.

"Can you feel it?" Cassia whispered, her voice barely audible amidst the clamor of the bustling market below. "The fear that grips this city?"

"Every day, it grows stronger," Lucian murmured, his piercing blue eyes scanning the faces of the people around them. They moved through the streets like ghosts, their eyes hollow, faces gaunt, and shoulders slumped with the burden of despair. The malevolent presence had wormed its way into the very fabric of their lives, threatening to snuff out all hope and plunge them into eternal darkness.

"Something must be done," Cassia urged, her warm brown eyes full of determination. "We cannot let the darkness consume us."

"Patience, Cassia," Lucian replied, though he shared her urgency. "We will find a way to overcome this evil. We must."

Their journey took them deeper into the heart of the city, where the whispers grew louder— urgent, desperate voices sharing fragments of hope amidst the despair. It was there that Lucian's keen ears caught the faintest murmur, so soft it would have been lost to most.

"…the artifact power beyond measure could turn the tide…"

Lucian froze in his tracks, his heart pounding in his chest. Could this be the key they sought? He exchanged a quick glance with Cassia, who seemed to understand his thoughts without a word being spoken.

"Let's follow them," she suggested quietly, nodding in the direction of the speakers— two cloaked figures who were hurriedly making their way through the throng of people.

"Stay close," Lucian instructed, his voice low and tense as they shadowed the strangers through the city streets. He could not shake the feeling that this artifact held the key to their salvation— but would it be enough to turn the tide against the forces of darkness?

As they trailed the cloaked figures, Lucian's thoughts raced with possibilities, his determination to find this artifact growing stronger by the second. The fate of his people, of the entire world, hung in the balance— and he knew deep within his soul that he would stop at nothing to save them from the encroaching abyss.

"Whatever it takes," he vowed silently, his eyes locked on the retreating forms of the strangers who carried the whispers of hope. "I will not let the darkness win."

The sun hung low in the sky, casting an eerie red glow over the city of Lysoria as Lucian and Cassia moved through its streets, a sense of urgency driving them on. The ominous light seemed to reflect the weight of the impending doom that threatened to engulf the world, but it only served to strengthen their resolve.

"Over there," Cassia murmured, nodding towards a small group of people huddled together near the entrance to a dimly lit alleyway. "Let's see if they've heard anything."

"Good idea," Lucian agreed, his voice deep and determined. They approached the group cautiously, surveying the scene with keen eyes. "Greetings, friends," he began, his tone warm and inviting despite the danger that loomed over them all. "We seek information on an artifact rumored to hold great power— one that could help us stand against the forces of darkness. Have you heard of such a thing?"

The group exchanged wary glances before one man, his face lined with worry and fatigue, responded hesitantly. "There are whispers, yes about a temple hidden deep within the mountains, guarded by ancient magic and deadly traps."

"Is it true?" Cassia pressed, her eyes searching the faces of those gathered for any sign of deceit or uncertainty.

"Who can say for sure?" another man answered, shrugging his broad shoulders. "But even if the legends are true, who would be brave enough to face such dangers?"

"I am," Lucian declared, his piercing blue eyes burning with determination. "With your help, we can gather the strength needed to take back our world from the clutches of evil."

The group exchanged glances once more, but this time, something stirred in their expressions— a spark of hope, perhaps, or the faintest flicker of defiance. Slowly, one by one, they nodded their agreement.

"Very well," the first man said, his voice steady despite the fear that surely gripped his heart. "We will aid you in your quest, but we must tread carefully– for the forces of darkness are ever watchful, and their reach is long."

"Then let us move swiftly and with purpose," Cassia urged, her warm brown eyes filled with determination. "For every moment we waste, the shadow grows darker and more oppressive."

As they continued to traverse the city streets, gathering allies to their cause, Lucian's thoughts turned to the ancient temple and the deadly trials that awaited them there. He knew that the path before them would be fraught with danger, but he also understood that this was their only hope– their one chance to defy the darkness and save their world from eternal ruin.

"Whatever awaits us within that temple," he vowed silently, his heart full of courage and conviction, "we will face it head-on and emerge victorious. For the sake of our people, and for all those who have suffered at the hands of these malevolent beings, we will not falter. We will stand firm against the tide of darkness, and we will reclaim our world."

The sun dipped low in the sky as Lucian Valerius stood before the gathered crowd, his piercing blue eyes scanning the faces of those who had chosen to join him and Cassia Amara in their perilous quest. The wind tousled his dark hair, casting shadows across his chiseled features. There was a resolve in his gaze that spoke of an unwavering sense of duty, one forged in the fires of countless battles against the encroaching darkness.

"Friends," he began, his voice strong and steady despite the heavy weight of responsibility that lay upon his broad shoulders. "We stand on the precipice of a great struggle– a battle not just for our own lives, but for the very soul of this world."

He paused, allowing the gravity of his words to sink in, then continued, his tone growing more intense. "I cannot promise you that this journey will be without hardship, nor can I guarantee that we will all emerge unscathed. What I can offer you is the chance to fight back against the forces that threaten to consume us all– to reclaim our destiny from the clutches of evil."

"Will you stand with me?" he asked the assembled group, his eyes burning with determination. "Will you face the unknown and walk the path of danger for the sake of our people and our world?"

A murmur of assent rippled through the crowd, and Lucian felt a surge of pride at their shared resolve. He glanced over at Cassia, her warm brown eyes meeting his, reflecting their shared conviction.

"Then let us make haste," Lucian declared, raising a hand in a gesture of unity. "Together, we will retrieve the artifact that has the power to turn the tide of this war, and we will cast these malevolent beings back into the abyss from whence they came."

With that, he turned and strode toward the city gates, Cassia at his side, the wind whipping around them as if urging them onward. The gathered allies fell into step behind them, their expressions resolute and purposeful.

As they passed through the towering archway that marked the boundary between Lysoria and the untamed wilderness beyond, Lucian felt a twinge of sorrow for the bustling metropolis he was leaving behind. But there was no time for regret, not when the fate of all mankind hung in the balance.

"Whatever lies ahead," he thought, his heart swelling with determination, "we will face it together– as one united force against the darkness."

And so, with the sun sinking beneath the horizon and the shadows lengthening before them, Lucian Valerius, Cassia Amara, and their band of courageous companions set forth on their perilous quest, leaving the familiar comforts of Lysoria behind in search of a brighter future for all.

The sun beat down upon the bustling city of Lysoria, its golden rays casting long shadows across the cobblestone streets. The air buzzed with activity as merchants called out their wares, children laughed and played, and the clatter of horse hooves echoed against the towering stone buildings.

Through this vibrant tapestry of life strode a man who seemed to embody the very essence of strength and determination. Lucian Valerius moved with purpose, his tall, broad-shouldered frame cutting a path through the crowd like a ship through choppy waters. His short, dark hair was damp with sweat, but it did nothing to diminish the intensity of his piercing blue eyes.

"Lucian!" a young boy called out, running up to him with a grin. "Can you show us how to do that thing with the sword again?"

"Perhaps later," Lucian replied, his voice firm but kind. "I have important matters to attend to."

As he continued on his way, Lucian's thoughts raced, turning over the grim task that lay before him. He knew all too well the weight of responsibility that rested on his shoulders. The end of the thousand-year captivity of Satan was near, and the world teetered on the brink of darkness. It was up to him and his allies to prevent the apocalypse of mankind.

"Is it true?" a voice whispered, causing Lucian to turn his head. An elderly woman stood beside him, her eyes wide with fear. "Is he really coming back?"

"Have faith," Lucian said softly, placing a reassuring hand on her shoulder. "We will do everything within our power to keep the darkness at bay."

"May the Almighty watch over you," the woman murmured, clutching his hand for a moment before shuffling away.

Despite the dread that gnawed at him, Lucian couldn't help but feel a sense of pride at the trust and faith the people of Lysoria placed in him. It only served to strengthen his resolve.

"Lucian," a familiar voice called out, and he turned to see one of his most trusted allies– Cassia Amara– approaching him. Her flowing auburn hair framed her face, and her sharp green eyes were filled with determination.

"Are you ready?" she asked, her tone urgent.

"Always," Lucian replied, his unwavering resolve shining through in his voice.

"Then let us gather our team," Cassia said, her gaze sweeping across the city's bustling streets. "The time has come for us to stand against the darkness."

And so, with heavy hearts but spirits ignited with hope, Lucian Valerius and Cassia Amara set forth on their dangerous mission, united in their determination to save the world from an unthinkable fate. For they knew that, should they fail, all that they held dear would be lost to the encroaching shadows.

In the dimly lit chamber of an ancient stronghold, Lucian Valerius honed his sword with exacting precision, each stroke of the whetstone against the cold metal echoing through the room. He paused to wipe sweat from his brow, his blue eyes focused and determined. The weight of responsibility bore down on him, but he refused to be crushed beneath it.

"Lucian," a voice called out softly, and he looked up to see Cassia Amara entering the chamber. Her flowing auburn hair cascaded over her shoulders, and her sharp green eyes pierced him with concern. "You've been at this for hours," she said, stepping closer. "We leave at dawn; you need rest."

He shook his head, resuming his methodical sharpening. "There's no time for rest, Cassia. Not when darkness threatens to engulf the world."

"Your dedication is admirable," she replied, "but even the most valiant hero needs sleep."

"Sleep is a luxury we can't afford," Lucian retorted, his frustration mounting. "Every moment wasted brings us closer to the end."

"Is that what you truly believe?" Cassia asked, her voice tinged with sadness.

"Indeed." His voice softened as he locked eyes with her. "If I falter, if we fail, all is lost."

"Have faith, Lucian," Cassia urged, placing a hand on his arm. "We will face this together, as we always have."

"Your unwavering loyalty means more than you know," he whispered, finally setting aside his sword and standing tall before her. "Together, we shall stand against the encroaching darkness."

"Your advisors have gathered valuable information," Cassia offered, her own resolve burning brightly in her eyes. "They await your instructions."

"Then let us not keep them waiting," Lucian replied, his determination surging anew.

Together, they strode from the chamber and into a small council room where a group of advisors huddled over maps and scrolls. Lucian listened intently as they detailed possible routes and strategies, weighing each option with care. As the night wore on, he stood firm in his decisions, unyielding in his commitment to their cause.

"Remember," he told them, his voice resolute, "we fight not only for ourselves but for all mankind. Our mission is paramount."

As the first light of dawn streaked across the sky, Lucian and Cassia stood shoulder to shoulder, their faces etched with determination. They had prepared as best they could, forging ahead with unwavering resolve.

"Let us embark on our journey," Lucian said quietly, his eyes locked on the horizon. "For it is only through our actions that we may stem the tide of darkness and save the world from a fate worse than death."

As Lucian and Cassia stepped out into the courtyard, the sun casting long shadows across the cobblestones, they found themselves in the midst of a chaotic whirlwind of activity. Soldiers and servants hurried to and fro, packing supplies and preparing the horses for their journey. Amidst the commotion, Cassia's keen eyes darted around, assessing the scene with razor-sharp precision.

"Lucian, we need more rope," she said, her voice calm but firm as she flashed him a knowing look. "And make sure everyone has enough water. It's going to be a long journey."

"Of course," he replied, grateful for her unwavering support. With a nod of acknowledgement, he turned to address the bustling crowd. "You heard her! Double-check your supplies!"

As the soldiers scrambled to follow his orders, Cassia gracefully wove her way through the chaos, her agility on full display as she scanned the area for anything they might have missed. Her quick wit and resourcefulness had saved them from disaster countless times, and Lucian knew he could rely on her to ensure that they were fully prepared for the perils ahead.

Soon, the team of determined comrades assembled before them, each one a testament to the diverse skills and backgrounds that would prove invaluable on their treacherous mission. There was stoic Gaius, a seasoned warrior with a steady hand and an unwavering gaze; brilliant Aurelia, whose vast knowledge of ancient lore would guide them through the darkest of paths; stealthy Silvanus, whose lithe frame and nimble fingers made him a master at infiltration and reconnaissance; and spirited Junia, a skilled archer whose fiery spirit burned brighter than any arrowhead.

"Friends," Lucian began, his voice commanding the attention of all present, "we stand on the precipice of a battle unlike any we have ever faced. The enemy we confront is not one of flesh and blood, but of darkness and despair. Our mission is nothing less than the salvation of all mankind."

He paused, allowing his words to sink in as he met each of their eyes in turn. "I have chosen you because I believe in your abilities, your courage, and your dedication to our cause. We may face seemingly insurmountable odds, but together, we shall overcome them and restore light to this world."

A murmur of agreement rippled through the group as they exchanged resolute glances, their faces etched with determination. Cassia stood at Lucian's side, her unwavering loyalty a beacon of hope amidst the gathering storm.

"Are you ready?" Lucian asked, his gaze sweeping over the assembled team.

"We are," came the resounding reply, a chorus of voices united by a common purpose.

"Then let us begin," Lucian declared, his voice ringing out like the clarion call of a trumpet. And with that, they set forth into the unknown, the fate of the world resting on their shoulders.

The sun dipped below the horizon, casting an eerie blood-red glow across the desolate landscape. Once verdant fields now lay scorched and barren, while skeletal remains of once-majestic trees reached skyward like tendrils of despair. A relentless wind howled through the ashen wasteland, carrying with it a pervasive sense of dread.

"Lucian," Cassia called out over the howling wind, her sharp green eyes scanning the horizon for any sign of danger. "We need to find shelter soon. The storm is approaching."

Lucian's piercing blue eyes followed her gaze, his brow furrowing in concern. As if on cue, the first droplets of rain began to fall from the darkening sky- not the gentle, life-giving rain that had once nourished the earth, but a foul, acrid deluge that seared the ground upon contact.

"Agreed," he replied, his voice heavy with the weight of responsibility. "We must protect ourselves and the team."

As they trudged onward, Lucian's thoughts drifted back to their past adventures together. He recalled the many battles they had fought side by side, their tireless efforts to stem the inexorable tide of darkness that sought to engulf the world. Through it all, their bond had only grown stronger, forged in the crucible of adversity.

"Remember when we faced the Serpent of Abaddon?" Cassia asked, her lips curling into a wry smile despite the gravity of their situation. "I never thought we would survive that encounter."

"Nor did I," Lucian admitted, a hint of amusement in his voice. "But we did, because we faced it together. We will overcome this challenge as well."

Cassia nodded, her expression resolute. "We have come too far to fail now."

Their journey continued in silence, punctuated only by the distant rumble of thunder and the hiss of rain as it met the scorched earth. Each step they took brought them closer to the heart of darkness, the epicenter of the malevolent force that threatened to extinguish all hope.

"Lucian," Cassia whispered, her voice barely audible above the wind. "Do you ever fear what lies ahead?"

"Of course," Lucian replied, his gaze never leaving the path before them. "But I know we can face whatever comes our way, because we have each other."

Cassia squeezed his shoulder, her touch a beacon of warmth in the cold, unforgiving night. "Together, we will prevail."

As the storm intensified around them, Lucian and Cassia pressed onward with renewed determination. For they knew that the fate of humanity rested on their shoulders, and they would not- could not- falter in their quest to banish the darkness and restore the light.

Under the ominous sky, the shadows of Lysoria's crumbling buildings stretched across the cobblestone streets. As Lucian and Cassia made their way through the desolate city, a sense of urgency gripped their hearts like an iron vice. They understood that this mission might be the last hope to save mankind from eternal darkness.

"Lucian," Cassia began, her voice tinged with determination, "we both know the sacrifices we've made in the past, but this mission…it feels heavier."

"Indeed," Lucian agreed, his piercing blue eyes scanning the devastated surroundings. "I believe we're on the verge of something monumental. This may be our chance to tip the balance and give humanity a fighting chance against the encroaching darkness."

Cassia's sharp green eyes met his, her unwavering resolve reflecting his own. "Then we must succeed," she declared, "no matter the cost."

As they arrived at their secret headquarters, Lucian found his team waiting for him- each comrade prepared to face the perils that lie ahead. He could see the anxiety etched on their faces. It was time to instill in them the same fiery determination he shared with Cassia.

"Friends," he began, his authoritative voice cutting through the tense atmosphere, "I will not lie to you. The path before us is treacherous, and many of us may not return. But we have come together because we believe in a world where light triumphs over darkness. We fight for those who cannot fight for themselves, and we will face this evil head-on!"

His words seemed to ignite a spark within his comrades as they stood taller, each one ready to confront the looming threat.

"Remember," Lucian continued, "our strength lies in unity. Together, we can overcome any challenge. Our bond and our will to protect humanity shall guide us through the storm that awaits."

As the team listened intently, their eyes burned with newfound resolve. They knew the gravity of their mission and were prepared to follow Lucian into the abyss.

"Let us embark on this journey, not as strangers brought together by fate," Lucian concluded, "but as brothers and sisters united under a common purpose- to save mankind from the darkness that threatens to consume us all!"

With resounding cheers, the team acknowledged their leader's call to arms. As they prepared for the treacherous road ahead, Lucian and Cassia exchanged a glance, their unshakable bond fueling their determination to face the end of days side by side.

The sun dipped low in the sky, casting a warm orange glow and elongating shadows across Lysoria's bustling streets. The air buzzed with anticipation as Lucian surveyed the team, each member attending to their final preparations.

"Alright, everyone," he called out, his voice firm yet reassuring. "Double-check your supplies and ensure your weapons are ready. We leave at dawn."

Determined faces nodded in response, already focused on their tasks. A cacophony of clanking metal and rustling cloth filled the air as they worked.

Lucian approached Cassia, who was meticulously sharpening her twin daggers, sparks flying with each swipe of the whetstone. She glanced up at him and offered a tight smile, betraying her concern.

"Are you certain we're ready for this, Lucian?" she asked, her sharp green eyes searching his.

He hesitated, his mind racing with possible dangers and uncertainties. Yet, he knew the answer lay deep within his heart. "No one can ever be truly ready for a battle like this," he admitted, his piercing blue eyes unwavering. "But I have faith in our team, in our purpose. We've faced the impossible before, and we'll do it again- together."

Cassia nodded, her resolve strengthened by Lucian's conviction. They shared a moment of understanding before returning to their tasks.

As the hours passed, a solemn gravity settled over the group. Though their camaraderie rang strong, the weight of their mission bore down upon them, the sky above darkening like the impending storm to come.

In the predawn light, with their packs laden and weapons gleaming, Lucian and his team assembled before the towering archway that marked the boundary between civilization and the untamed wilderness beyond. The ancient stones seemed to hold their breath, awaiting the fateful moment.

"Remember," Lucian reminded them, "whatever lies ahead, we face it as one. We are the light that will pierce the darkness."

With those words, their final farewell to the comforts of Lysoria, Lucian led his team through the archway and into the unknown. As they crossed the threshold, the weight of a thousand years of prophecy settled upon their shoulders.

Yet, they did not falter, for in their hearts burned the fire of hope, the indomitable will to save mankind from the darkness that threatened to consume them all. Together, they marched forward, determined to confront the end of days with unwavering dedication and courage.

XI

RISING TENSION

As the group ventures deeper into the temple, they face increasingly dangerous challenges and powerful foes. The stakes are raised, and their resolve is tested as they struggle to overcome these obstacles.

The first light of dawn cast a warm glow on the wild tresses of Maya Sterling's dark hair, as she stood at the edge of the dense jungle. Her piercing eyes scanned the treacherous foliage before her, weighing the challenges that lay ahead. Tall and strong, with a build forged through years of daring exploration, the fearless adventurer exuded an air of confidence that was hard to ignore.

Maya's love for uncovering ancient secrets was an insatiable hunger that gnawed at her soul. It was this passion that had led her to chase legends whispered in hushed tones by the superstitious villagers who lived in fear of the unknown. And it was this same passion that now drove her toward the heart of darkness, where both perils and revelations awaited.

"Rumors say there's an ancient temple hidden deep within this jungle," Maya whispered to herself, her voice barely audible above the howls of distant beasts and the rustling of leaves. "A temple that holds a power beyond our wildest dreams—the Heart of the Jungle."

As she stepped cautiously into the underbrush, she could feel the dampness seeping through her sandals, the soil beneath her feet teeming with life. The jungle closed around her, like the jaws of a monstrous beast eager to swallow her whole. Yet, in the face of danger, Maya remained undeterred. Her experiences had molded her into a cautious, yet resilient explorer, slow to trust and vigilant in the presence of peril.

"Stay focused, Maya," she muttered, steeling herself for the journey ahead. The temple was said to be guarded by the Heart of the Jungle itself—a colossal golem whose towering form loomed ominously over the ancient shrine; its intentions shrouded in mystery. This deity was worshipped by a long-lost civilization, and those few who still remembered its name spoke of the immense power it granted to those who proved their worth.

"Is this power a blessing or a curse?" Maya wondered, as she hacked her way through the thick foliage, her machete slicing through vines and branches with ease. The jungle seemed to pulse with energy, as though it were alive and aware of her intrusion. A deep-rooted unease settled in her chest, but her determination remained unshaken. She had come this far, and there was no turning back now.

"Whatever lies hidden within that temple," Maya thought, her heart pounding with anticipation, "I will uncover its secrets and unravel the enigma of the Heart of the Jungle." And with each step further into the depths of the verdant abyss, the weight of prophecy and the whispered promise of apocalypse weighed heavily upon her shoulders, driving her ever onward toward her destiny.

"Curse this infernal heat," Maya Sterling muttered to herself, wiping the sweat from her brow. The relentless sun was bearing down on her like a vengeful god, but she pressed onward, her piercing eyes scanning the bustling marketplace for any sign of the informant who had promised her vital information.

"Maya!" called out a raspy voice from the shadows. Startled, she peered into the darkness to find a wizened old woman hunched over a table, her gnarled fingers clutching an ancient-looking parchment.

"Who are you?" Maya demanded, approaching cautiously.

"An admirer of your work," the crone replied, her eyes glinting with mischief. "I've heard tales of your exploits, and now I have something that might interest you."

"Is that so?" Maya asked, intrigued despite herself. Her heart raced as the woman unfurled the parchment, revealing a detailed map of the uncharted jungle, with an enigmatic temple marked at its center.

"Legend speaks of the Heart of the Jungle, an ancient power hidden within the depths of the temple," the woman whispered, her voice tinged with awe. "Its secrets could change the course of history, or herald the end of days."

"End of days, you say?" Maya's curiosity was piqued, her mind racing with visions of apocalyptic power and world-shattering revelations. "Tell me more."

"Truth be told, no one knows what lies within the temple," the woman admitted, a haunted look in her eyes. "But if you're brave enough to seek it, you may find answers… or doom."

"Then I'll take my chances," Maya declared, her resolve steeled by the prospect of uncovering the truth behind the Heart of the Jungle. She snatched up the parchment and handed the woman a pouch of coins, her mind already racing ahead to the adventure that awaited her.

"May the gods have mercy on your soul, Maya Sterling," the crone whispered as she watched the intrepid adventurer disappear into the crowd. "For you are about to face a darkness beyond imagining."

With each step toward her fateful encounter with the temple and the Heart of the Jungle, Maya's excitement grew. Unbeknownst to her, she was walking a razor's edge between salvation and destruction, and only time would reveal whether she could conquer the secrets hidden within or succumb to the apocalyptic fate that awaited those who dared to unlock the ancient power slumbering beneath the temple's stone facade.

The sun cast an ominous glow on the horizon, painting the sky with hues of blood and fire as Maya stood at the edge of the jungle. The weight of her decision bore down upon her, the knowledge that she alone could not unravel the secrets of the ancient temple nestled within the verdant heart of the wilds. With a deep breath, she resolved to assemble a team of experts who shared her passion for unearthing the lost mysteries of the past.

"Only the worthy shall claim the Heart of the Jungle's power," the words of the crone echoed in her mind, as if carried on the wind's whispers. It was said, in hushed tones, that those who possessed the courage, wisdom, and strength to endure the trials of the temple would be granted abilities beyond imagination. These immense powers held the potential to alter the course of human history– or herald its end.

"Time to find those who can help me uncover the truth," Maya muttered, her piercing eyes scanning the horizon as she began her search. Her resourcefulness and determination would be her guiding star, leading her to those who could traverse the depths of the jungle and face the impending darkness alongside her.

"Hey!" she called out, spotting a lone figure by a campfire. "I'm looking for brave souls willing to embark on an adventure like no other. Are you up for the challenge?"

"Depends on what we're chasing," the stranger replied, his voice cautious yet tinged with curiosity. He rose from his seat, revealing a tall, sinewy frame hardened by years of exploration.

"An ancient temple, hidden deep within the jungle. Its secrets could change the world… or bring about our doom." Maya's words hung heavy in the air, a testament to the gravity of their quest.

"Count me in," the man responded without hesitation, a fierce glint in his eyes. "But only if you're ready to face the unknown, and whatever price we may pay for it."

"Believe me," Maya grinned, her determination shining like a beacon in the darkening twilight. "I've never been more ready."

As they stood at the precipice of the unknown, the last vestiges of daylight fading into indigo night, the weight of their choices bore down upon them. They were the chosen few who would dare to challenge the ancient power slumbering within the heart of the jungle– a power that could either usher in a new age of enlightenment or herald the end of days.

"Let's find the others," Maya said with steely resolve, leading her newfound ally deeper into the tangled wilderness. Together, they would forge a path toward destiny, embracing the trials ahead with unwavering courage and an unquenchable thirst for knowledge.

"May the gods have mercy on us all," she whispered as they ventured forth, bound by their shared quest to unlock the enigmatic secrets of the Heart of the Jungle and face whatever fate awaited them at the temple's threshold.

In the depths of her safe house, surrounded by ancient scrolls and artifacts, Maya Sterling's eyes glowed with determination. Her fingers traced over the worn pages of a dusty tome, its secrets whispering to her the path she must follow. The Heart of the Jungle called to her, its immense power tantalizing her senses. She knew she could not conquer this quest alone– she needed a team of experts, as diverse and skilled as the challenges that awaited them.

"Time to gather my allies," she murmured, her voice low and resolute. Her search began in earnest, reaching out through her network of contacts, delving into the shadowy corners of knowledge where only the most daring dared to tread.

Her heart pounded as she poured over countless profiles and testimonials, each person bearing the potential to shape her destiny. And then, amidst the sea of candidates, one man stood out like a beacon of hope– Jocalon Cal, a brilliant archaeologist whose keen insight into the past was matched only by his thirst for discovery.

"Cal," Maya whispered, her excitement bubbling beneath the surface. "The first piece of my puzzle."

She contacted him, her words laced with urgency and passion. The conversation crackled with intensity, the air thick with anticipation. As Maya shared her vision, painting a vivid picture of the ancient temple and the Heart of the Jungle's power, she felt a connection forming between them, a bond forged in their mutual pursuit of the unknown.

"You must understand, Cal," she implored, her gaze locked onto his bespectacled eyes, the light of conviction burning within them. "This is more than just an archaeological expedition. We are on the precipice of uncovering something that could change the course of human history. We cannot allow this opportunity to fall into the wrong hands."

Cal, hesitated, weighing the gravity of her words. "I… I understand, Ms. Sterling," he finally said, his voice steady and resolute. "You can count on me."

"Excellent," Maya replied, a fierce smile playing at the corners of her mouth. Her heart swelled with pride and purpose as she added, "Together, we will pierce the veil of darkness and bring the truth to light."

As the conversation ended, Maya leaned back against a old dry tree, as a chair, feeling the weight of responsibility settle upon her shoulders. She was assembling an unstoppable force, a team that would stand against the looming apocalypse and usher in a new age for mankind.

Jocalon Cal," she mused, her mind already racing ahead to the next challenge. "Welcome to the end of days."

With renewed vigor, Maya plunged deeper into the shadows, searching for those who would join her in this monumental journey. The temple awaited, shrouded in mystery and danger, but she was undeterred– for she knew that the end of Satan's reign was at hand, and she would be the one to herald its downfall.

The sun dipped low on the horizon, casting a warm glow over the ancient city where Maya and Jocalon Cal sat sipping water along the way. Around them, merchants shouted in foreign tongues, their voices mingling with the hum of the bustling metropolis. Maya's pulse quickened as she observed the meeting place for seekers of knowledge and treasure alike; it was here that her journey would truly begin.

As they conversed, Cal's spectacled eyes sparkled with excitement, mirroring Maya's own enthusiasm for the task ahead. "There's so much we don't know about this temple," he mused, stirring his water jug absently. "It's likely that the civilization who built it possessed secrets long forgotten, buried along with their very existence."

"Exactly," Maya interjected, leaning forward in earnest, her dark hair cascading around her face like a silken waterfall. "We have a chance to unearth those secrets, to bring light to the darkest corners of history. Imagine what we could learn, Cal– the power that awaits us within that temple!"

"Indeed," he replied, a hint of trepidation flickering across his features. "But we must tread carefully, Ms. Sterling. There is a reason these secrets have remained hidden for so long. We are not the first to seek them, nor will we be the last. We cannot allow our discoveries to fall into the wrong hands."

"Agreed," Maya said firmly, her piercing eyes narrowing with determination. "That's why we need a team we can trust, experts in their fields who share our passion for uncovering the truth."

Cal nodded, his expression thoughtful. "Your leadership will be crucial in guiding us through the perils that lie ahead. I have no doubt that you possess the fortitude and vision necessary to see this mission through to its end."

"Thank you, Cal," Maya replied, her heart swelling with pride and renewed conviction. "I won't let you– or the rest of our team– down."

As they continued to discuss their plans, Maya's thoughts churned relentlessly. She knew that assembling a skilled team was paramount to their success, but time was running out. With each passing day, the world crept closer to its prophesied end, and she could feel the weight of fate pressing down on her shoulders.

But she would not falter. She would forge this group of disparate souls into a unified force, a beacon of hope in humanity's darkest hour. Her persuasive abilities and indomitable spirit would see them through the trials ahead, and together, they would face the encroaching apocalypse head-on.

" Cal," she said resolutely, her eyes locked onto his. "Let us begin our search for the others who will join us in this quest. The temple may be shrouded in darkness and danger, but we are the light that will pierce it– and bring about the end of Satan's reign."

"Indeed," he agreed solemnly, raising his water jug in a toast. "To the end of days."

Maya clinked her own jug against his, their resolve fortified by the knowledge that they were embarking on a journey that could change the course of human history. And as the sun dipped below the horizon, casting the city in a foreboding twilight, they set off to gather their allies for the monumental battle that lay ahead.

The scent of oil and metal filled the air as Maya stepped into Lila Reyes' workshop. The room was a labyrinth of scattered blueprints, half-assembled pottery, and arcane devices that seemed to hum with untapped potential. Lila herself stood hunched over a workbench, her short, curly hair providing a dark halo around her intent face as she tinkered with an intricate brass contraption.

"Ms. Reyes," Maya began, her voice echoing through the workshop.

"Call me Lila," he replied without looking up, her fingers nimbly adjusting gears and dials. "Titles are for bureaucrats and stuffed shirts."

"Very well, Lila," Maya said, allowing a smile to touch her lips. "I've come to you because we need your resourceful mind and talents prowess. Legends speak of an ancient temple deep within the jungle, protected by traps and puzzles that no one has ever deciphered. If what I've heard about you is true, then you're the key to unlocking its secrets."

Lila glanced up from her work, curiosity sparking in her eyes as she assessed Maya's earnest expression. "You have my attention. But why should I join you? What's in it for me?"

"Revelation," Maya answered, her gaze unwavering. "And the chance to prove yourself invaluable to a cause greater than any of us. We're on the precipice of the end of days, and this temple may hold the power to tip the scales back in humanity's favor."

"Count me in," Lila agreed, her shoulders straightening with resolve. She extended her hand, which Maya grasped firmly. In Lila, Maya saw a kindred spirit— someone who would not shy away from danger but instead would rise to meet it head-on.

Next, they sought out Ravi Patel, a seasoned explorer whose exploits had become the stuff of legend. They found him perched atop a tree, his muscular form silhouetted by the setting sun as he surveyed the jungle below.

"Ravi," Maya called up to him, her voice laced with urgency. "We need your unparalleled knowledge of the wilds and your instincts to guide us through treacherous terrain. Will you join us in our quest to save humanity?"

"Maya Sterling," Ravi mused as he descended gracefully from the branches, landing before her with a soft thud. "I've heard much about you. Your reputation precedes you, as does the importance of your mission. You have my loyalty."

"Thank you, Ravi," Maya said, feeling a surge of excitement as the last piece of their team clicked into place. "Together, we will journey to the heart of the jungle and face whatever trials lie ahead."

"Then let's not waste any time," Lila chimed in, her face alight with anticipation. "The end is nigh, and there's no telling what challenges await us within that temple."

"Indeed," Cal, agreed solemnly. "But I have faith in our abilities– and in the power of the Heart of the Jungle."

As they stood together on the edge of the encroaching wilderness, Maya felt a thrill of exhilaration race through her veins. At long last, she had assembled her team– a group of individuals who shared her passion for uncovering ancient secrets and her unwavering determination to save humanity from its prophesied doom.

"Let us begin," she declared, her eyes blazing with resolve. "For we are the light that will pierce the darkness and bring about the end of Satan's reign."

With those words, Maya Sterling led her intrepid companions into the heart of the jungle, where untold dangers– and the hope of salvation– awaited them.

Maya Sterling is a woman on a mission. She has assembled a team of fearless explorers to journey deep into the heart of the jungle, seeking to uncover ancient secrets and save humanity from its prophesied doom. Her team includes Lila, a kindred spirit who shares Maya's passion for adventure and danger, as well as Ravi Patel, a seasoned explorer whose exploits have become the stuff of legend.

Together, they stand on the edge of the encroaching wilderness, ready to face whatever trials lie ahead. Maya feels a thrill of exhilaration race through her veins as she looks out into the unknown, knowing that she has finally found a group of individuals who share her unwavering determination to succeed.

As they venture deeper into the jungle, Maya's resolve is tested time and again. They must navigate treacherous terrain, avoid deadly predators, and overcome seemingly insurmountable obstacles. But through it all, Maya remains steadfast in her belief that they will succeed.

Their goal is to find the Heart of the Jungle– an ancient artifact that holds the key to saving humanity from its prophesied doom. But the journey is not without its challenges. They encounter fierce resistance from those who would seek to stop them, and they must draw upon all their skills and instincts to overcome these obstacles.

In the end, Maya and her team are victorious. They find the Heart of the Jungle and use its power to bring about the end of Satan's reign. Along the way, they discover truths about themselves and each other that they never could have imagined.

Maya emerges from the jungle a changed woman– stronger, wiser, and more determined than ever before. She knows that there will be other challenges ahead, but with her team by her side, she is ready to face them head-on.

In a world draped in the shadows of forgotten history, ancient artifacts whispered secrets of unfathomable power. Hidden within the crevices of time, these relics held the key to unlocking mysteries that could shape the course of human destiny. Amongst the silent ruins and beneath the sands of countless lands, lay the remnants of civilizations that had once harnessed these great forces. This was a world on the cusp of revelation, teetering dangerously between the unraveling of age-old prophecies and the abyss of oblivion.

Against this backdrop of wonder and intrigue stood Maya Sterling, a woman forged by her unwavering resolve to uncover the lost secrets of the past. Her dark, wavy hair cascaded down her back, framing the sharp angles of her face. Piercing green eyes bore into the ancient texts before her, as if willing them to divulge their hidden knowledge. Of average height, she carried herself with an air of quiet confidence, her every movement betraying her passion for unearthing the long-buried truths of history.

"Another dead end," she muttered under her breath, frustration tightening her voice. She slammed shut the dusty tome she had been poring over for hours, sending a cloud of particles swirling through the dimly-lit chamber.

"Maya, you can't expect to find all the answers in one night," chided a fellow researcher, attempting to offer some solace.

"Time is running out," Maya replied, her eyes never leaving the now-closed book. Her thoughts wandered to the prophecy she had dedicated her life to understanding– the prophecy that foretold the end of the thousand years of Satan's captivity and the doom it would bring upon mankind.

"Look, I know how important this is to you," the researcher said softly, placing a hand on Maya's shoulder. "But we will find what we're looking for. We have to keep the faith."

"Faith," Maya echoed, a wry smile tugging at her lips. She turned to face her companion, her gaze resolute. "Faith can only take us so far. It's our actions that will determine the fate of humanity."

As she spoke these words, Maya's mind burned with the fire of her conviction, fueled by her relentless pursuit of the ancient relics that held the power to change the course of history. There was no room for doubt in her heart; she would stop at nothing to save mankind from its prophesied doom.

And as Maya Sterling stood amongst the relics of a time long past, she knew that her journey had only just begun.

The air hummed with a mixture of anticipation and dread as Maya methodically laid out her gear, each piece meticulously chosen for the treacherous journey ahead. The ancient texts had warned of the perils that lay within the heart of the jungle– the darkness that clung to its canopy like a shroud, the creatures that slithered and prowled unseen among its shadows, and the unforgiving terrain that threatened to ensnare even the most skilled traveler.

"Are you certain you have everything you need?" asked a worried voice, piercing through Maya's thoughts.

"Nothing is ever certain," she replied, her fingers lingering on the worn hilt of her machete. "But I am prepared to face whatever challenges lie ahead."

In the dimly lit storage room, shelves laden with artifacts and curiosities from bygone eras stood watch over Maya as she carefully secured a coil of rope to her pack. The silence was punctuated only by the distant rumblings of thunder, an ominous reminder of the storm that would soon descend upon the world if she failed in her quest.

"Remember, Maya," the voice continued, tinged with urgency, "the prophecy states that we must retrieve the artifact before the end of the thousand years of Satan's captivity. There isn't much time left."

"I know," she whispered, the weight of her responsibility settling heavily on her shoulders. She glanced at the map spread out on the table, its frayed edges testament to her tireless research. Every possible route into the jungle had been considered, every hidden danger recorded in her mind. She knew the risks all too well, but there was no other choice.

"Promise me you'll be careful," the voice pleaded, the fear palpable.

"Careful won't save us," Maya stated, a steely resolve shining in her green eyes. "Only action will." She paused, allowing herself a moment of vulnerability. "But I promise you this: I will not rest until the artifact is found, and mankind's fate is secured."

With that, she hoisted her pack onto her shoulders and surveyed her surroundings one last time. The ancient relics seemed to whisper their secrets to her, urging her forward on her perilous journey. Danger lurked around every corner, but so too did the tantalizing possibility of salvation.

"Let's go," Maya said, her voice resolute. She turned to face the darkness that lay beyond the storage room, ready to confront the unknown in a desperate bid to save humanity from its prophesied doom.

The sun dipped below the horizon, casting a fiery orange glow over the jungle as it succumbed to twilight. Maya Sterling sat at her makeshift desk in the heart of the camp, poring over ancient texts and maps that seemed to hold the key to humanity's salvation. The flickering light of a lantern illuminated her face as she carefully translated the cryptic symbols etched into the parchment.

"Figure anything out yet?" a voice asked from behind her

"Patience," Maya replied, her green eyes never leaving the page in front of her. "These texts were written centuries ago in a language long forgotten. Decoding them takes time." Her fingers traced the intricate lines of an ancient map, searching for clues hidden within its borders.

"Time is something we don't have much of," the voice reminded her, worry evident in its tone.

"Which is why I'm working tirelessly," Maya said, her determination fueling her through each exhausting day and sleepless night. She tapped on a particular location on the map, scrutinizing it with a focused gaze. "I believe this is where the artifact lies– the Heart of the Jungle."

"Are you sure?"

"Nothing is ever certain in this line of work," she responded, her voice steady despite the pressure mounting upon her shoulders. "But my instincts are rarely wrong."

As she continued deciphering the texts, a worn photograph caught her eye. It depicted a younger Maya standing beside her grandmother, both beaming with pride as they held up a small, recently unearthed artifact. A pang of nostalgia washed over her as she remembered the woman who had ignited her passion for unearthing ancient secrets.

"Your grandmother would be proud," the voice said softly, sensing her thoughts.

"Her spirit guides me every step of the way," Maya murmured, brushing a tear from her cheek. Her grandmother had been a trailblazer in their field, unearthing countless artifacts and uncovering hidden truths. Now, it was Maya's turn to continue her legacy and protect the world from the prophesied doom.

"Her stories of ancient worlds always captivated me," she recalled, a wistful smile playing on her lips. "They filled my dreams with wonder and ignited a fire within me that can never be extinguished."

"Your passion is what will see us through this," the voice said reassuringly. "Now let's find that artifact and save humanity."

"Agreed," Maya replied, her resolve strengthened by the memory of her grandmother. She unfolded another map, studying the complex network of trails that snaked through the perilous jungle ahead. "We have a long journey ahead of us, but if we succeed, the fate of mankind will be forever altered."

As night enveloped the camp, Maya Sterling continued her tireless work– driven by a burning desire to honor her grandmother's memory and secure the future of humanity against the darkness that threatened to consume it all.

The soft glow of the lanterns illuminated the parchment map that lay sprawled across the wooden table. Its edges curled with age, and the ink had faded in places, but to Maya Sterling, it held secrets that could change the course of history. As she traced her finger along a winding path leading into the heart of the jungle, a fleeting memory crossed her mind– one that had shaped her life and fueled her determination.

"Mom, dad, look!" a young Maya exclaimed, holding up a small artifact she had found buried in the dirt. Her parents turned towards her, their faces beaming with pride.

"Careful, sweetheart," her mother cautioned gently as she approached. "You never know what powers these ancient relics might hold."

"Maya, you have a gift," her father said, his voice filled with wonder. "Just like your grandmother."

Tragedy had struck soon after, stealing away both her parents in a sudden accident. The weight of their loss had been unbearable, but it had only served to strengthen her resolve. She would honor their memory by continuing their work, discovering the ancient truths that had long been hidden from the world.

"Maya!" a hushed voice snapped her back to the present. She looked up to see one of her trusted companions rushing towards her, clutching a crumpled envelope in his hand. "This came for you. It's urgent."

"Thank you," she replied, taking the envelope and carefully extracting the letter within. Her eyes widened as she read the words scrawled hastily across the page.

"An anonymous tip," she murmured, her pulse quickening. "They claim to know the exact location of the Heart of the Jungle."

"Is this reliable?" her companion asked, concern etching his features. "It could be a trap."

"Or it could be our only chance to save humanity," Maya countered, her voice laced with determination. "I have to follow this lead, even if it means facing Victor Solis."

"Victor Solis?" her companion's eyes narrowed. "He'll stop at nothing to claim the artifact for himself."

"Which is why we must get there first," Maya declared, her green eyes blazing with resolve. She turned back to the map, plotting their course towards the heart of the jungle. "We cannot let him unleash the darkness that lies within the Heart of the Jungle. If he does, it could mean the end of mankind and the beginning of an age of chaos and suffering."

"Then we shall follow you into the depths of the unknown," her companion pledged, his voice tinged with awe. "For our families, for our world, and for the legacy of your parents and grandmother."

"Thank you," Maya said softly, her heart swelling with gratitude. Together, they would face the perils that lay ahead, guided by a shared purpose and the unshakeable belief that the fate of humanity rested in their hands. The end of the thousand years of captivity of Satan was near, and they would do everything in their power to ensure that the prophecies never came to pass.

Maya stood before the ancient map, feeling the weight of her decision like a stone in her chest. The air in the small, cluttered room was heavy with tension and the scent of dust-covered tomes. She fanned herself with an old notebook, while sweat trickled down her temples. The world outside seemed oblivious to the darkness that loomed.

"Are you sure about this, Maya?" her companion asked, his voice laced with concern. "This journey will be fraught with danger and uncertainty."

"Saving humanity has never been a walk in the park," she replied, her green eyes hardening with resolve. "The Heart of the Jungle is our best hope, and I cannot let Victor Solis get his hands on it. If he does, we're all doomed."

"Very well," her companion sighed, knowing better than to argue with her when she had set her mind on something. "We shall need a team. A group skilled and courageous enough to face whatever challenges await us in the depths of the jungle."

"Agreed," Maya nodded, determination thrumming through her veins. She began mentally assembling the team she would need for such a perilous endeavor.

"First, we'll need a guide who knows the jungle inside out," she said, thinking of the perfect candidate. "Rafael Silva. He's spent years exploring uncharted territories. His expertise will be invaluable."

"Ah, yes," her companion nodded in approval. "I've heard of him. The man can navigate any terrain with his eyes closed."

"Next, we'll need someone proficient in ancient languages and deciphering hidden messages. This is where Lord. Alice Mitchell comes in. Her work on lost civilizations is unparalleled, and she'll help us make sense of the cryptic signs we might encounter."

"Indeed, she's brilliant," her companion agreed, recalling the remarkable woman from a past expedition. "What about defense and survival? The jungle is home to countless dangers, both seen and unseen."

"Tonio Vasquez," Maya declared without hesitation. "A former military man, skilled in combat, tracking, and wilderness survival. He's the best at what he does."

"Excellent choice," her companion nodded, trust evident in his eyes.

"Finally," Maya continued, "we'll need someone who can help us navigate through any potential traps or puzzles guarding the artifact. That's where Lila Chen comes in. She's a mechanical genius and an expert in ancient technologies."

"Ah, yes, I've heard of her intricate work with ancient mechanisms," her companion said, impressed by Maya's selection.

"Then it's decided," Maya stated firmly, clenching her fists in determination. "We must gather our team quickly and embark on this journey. There's no time to waste."

"May the light of hope guide us through the darkness ahead," her companion whispered, placing a hand on her shoulder, offering support and solidarity. And as they began to prepare for their perilous quest into the heart of the jungle, the weight of the world rested on their shoulders, but so too did the unwavering determination to save it from the prophesied doom.

The sun dipped low in the sky, casting a blood-red hue over the dense foliage that marked the beginning of their treacherous journey. Maya stood before her assembled team, their faces a mosaic of determination and apprehension. She knew that each one of them had faced their own demons to be here, but this was a battle unlike any other. This was a battle for the very soul of humanity.

"Friends," she began, her voice steady despite the weight of her words. "I stand before you not as your leader, but as your comrade in arms. We embark on a perilous quest to save our world from an ancient prophecy that threatens to consume us all."

Her eyes blazed with conviction as she continued, "We seek the Heart of the Jungle, an artifact of unimaginable power that holds the key to preventing the apocalypse foretold in the scriptures. I may not know what form the end will take, but I do know that we cannot afford to fail."

Silence hung heavy in the air as they absorbed the gravity of their mission. With a steely resolve, Maya looked at each member of her team, addressing them individually. "Tonio, your strength and survival skills are unmatched. Your expertise will be invaluable in navigating the treacherous terrain."

"Lord. Morgan, your knowledge of the ancient world will guide us through the secrets hidden within the jungle's depths. Lila, your mastery of ancient mechanisms will ensure that no puzzle or trap will stand in our way."

"Each of you brings a unique skill set to this journey, and together, we will overcome the challenges that lie ahead. We are not mere treasure hunters or adventurers; we are the last line of defense for humanity itself."

As her impassioned speech reached its crescendo, Maya clenched her fists at her sides, her green eyes sparking with intensity. "Let us stand together as the darkness encroaches, and fight for the future of our world. We are humanity's hope!"

The team exchanged glances before nodding in unison, their spirits lifted by Maya's unwavering determination. They stood together on the edge of the encroaching wilderness, their hearts pounding with a mix of fear and anticipation.

"Into the heart of darkness," Maya whispered, her breath mingling with the ominous wind that rustled through the trees. "May we emerge victorious or not at all."

And with that, they stepped into the unknown, ready to face the unimaginable horrors that awaited them in the depths of the jungle, united in their mission to save humanity from its prophesied doom.

XII

NEW HAVEN LAY
SHROUDED IN DARKNESS

In the dark and gritty city of New Haven, Raphael "Rafe" Sylvestre is a master of the shadows. With his sharp hazel eyes and messy dark hair, Rafe is a cunning and resourceful rogue who knows how to gather information and strike at his enemies when they least expect it. He has spent his late twenties living a life of danger and deception, always on the run from his troubled past.

Despite his guarded exterior, Rafe is fiercely loyal to those he cares about. When his childhood friend, the beautiful and headstrong Isabella, comes to him for help, Rafe can't resist her plea. Isabella's brother has been kidnapped by a dangerous gang, and she needs Rafe's expertise to rescue him.

But as Rafe delves deeper into the seedy underbelly of New Haven, he uncovers a web of corruption and deceit that threatens to consume him. The inciting incident occurs when Rafe discovers that the kidnapping was not just a random act of violence, but part of a larger conspiracy involving some of the city's most powerful figures.

As the conflict rises, Rafe finds himself in over his head. The more he uncovers about the conspiracy, the more dangerous it becomes. And when Isabella is kidnapped in an attempt to silence him, Rafe realizes that he must risk everything to save her and bring down the corrupt forces that threaten to destroy them both.

With quick wit and a sarcastic sense of humor, Rafe navigates the treacherous waters of New Haven's criminal underworld. He confronts corrupt police officers, ruthless gang leaders, and even his own troubled past as he fights to save Isabella and bring justice to those who have been wronged.

In the climactic scenes, Rafe faces off against the mastermind behind the conspiracy in a tense and thrilling showdown. With Isabella's life hanging in the balance, Rafe must use all of his cunning and resourcefulness to emerge victorious.

New Haven lay shrouded in darkness, a city whose soul teetered on the edge of an abyss. The grimy streets slithered between decaying buildings like twisted veins, their surfaces marred with the scars of neglect and despair. Flickering streetlights cast sallow pools of light amidst the gloom, their feeble glow barely strong enough to ward off the sinister shadows that lurked at every corner. In the distance, the wailing of sirens punctuated the air, a cacophonic dirge that seemed to echo through the ages.

It was here, in this forsaken place, that the dangerous gangs and corrupt officials held dominion over the lives of men. Like ravenous wolves, they prowled the city's underbelly, devouring all who dared to defy their rule. Their influence extended even to the police force, transforming once-honorable men into puppets who danced to the tune of their malevolent masters. Drug trafficking, extortion, and bloodshed were but a few of the criminal activities that flourished under their watchful gaze.

"Did you hear about the latest shipment?" muttered a hooded figure as he leaned against a graffiti-strewn wall, his voice barely audible above the din of the sirens.

"Keep your voice down," hissed another, glancing furtively around. "The Viper doesn't like loose lips."

Giovanni "The Viper" Romano was the embodiment of the dark forces that ruled New Haven. Tall and broad-shouldered, his imposing presence was heightened by the serpent tattoo that slithered up his arm, a testament to the venomous power he wielded. He reveled in the thrill of violence, using it to maintain his iron grip on the city's criminal underworld. Cunning and calculating, The Viper was always two steps ahead, anticipating his rivals' moves and crushing them without mercy.

"Right, right," the first man stammered, his eyes darting nervously around. "I just... I can't believe how much we're bringing in. We're untouchable."

"Remember who made us that way," the second man warned, casting a meaningful glance towards the shadows where The Viper was rumored to be watching. "And don't forget what he'll do if you cross him."

As their conversation faded into silence, the city seemed to hold its breath, waiting for the inevitable clash of titanic powers that would determine the fate of New Haven and its inhabitants. A storm was brewing on the horizon, and only one thing was certain: when it finally broke, there would be no escaping its wrath.

Amidst the squalor of New Haven, a figure moved with purpose through the shadows. Rafe Sylvestre's sharp hazel eyes flickered like sparks in the night, taking in every detail of the decaying city around him. His messy dark hair, wild and untamed as the storm that brewed within his soul, framed his face as he blended seamlessly into the darkness.

"Your payment," muttered Rafe, his voice barely audible as he handed a crumpled stack of bills to a man leaning against a crumbling brick wall. The informant's eyes gleamed greedily, and Rafe knew he had bought the man's loyalty, at least for tonight.

"Word is that The Viper has been preparing for a big move," whispered the informant, his gaze never leaving the money. "A power play that'll solidify his grip on the city."

Rafe's brow furrowed in thought, his mind racing through the possibilities. He knew all too well the devastation that would follow in the wake of The Viper's actions– innocent lives destroyed, families torn apart, and souls cast into the abyss. But he also knew that this information could be the key to dismantling the corrupt empire that held New Haven in its thrall.

"Where? When?" demanded Rafe, his voice tight with urgency.

"Somewhere near the docks," the informant replied hesitantly. "But I don't know when. It'll happen soon, though."

"Keep your ears open," Rafe instructed, his tone hard as steel. "I need specifics."

As he slipped away from the informant, Rafe's thoughts churned like the turbulent seas that bordered the city. The end of days was looming ever closer, and he would do everything in his power to save as many souls as possible from the fires of destruction.

Navigating the underworld with practiced ease, Rafe eavesdropped on hushed conversations, piecing together fragments of information like a master craftsman weaving an intricate tapestry. He observed the movements of rival gangs, the fear in the eyes of those who dared to defy The Viper's rule, and the desperate prayers offered by the innocent as they sought salvation.

"Lord, give me the strength to face this darkness," Rafe whispered, his thoughts turning inward as he grappled with the weight of his mission. "Help me bring justice to this city before it is swallowed whole by the coming apocalypse."

As Rafe continued his quest for knowledge, the storm within him grew ever stronger, fueled by the cries of the suffering and the wicked deeds committed under the cover of New Haven's perpetual night. But he would not falter; he would stand against the forces of darkness until the very end, fighting for the souls trapped in the decaying heart of the city.

Rafe's sharp hazel eyes scanned the dimly lit alley, his gaze intent on a group of shadowy figures huddled together in whispered conversation. His heart raced as he gripped a small, worn photograph tightly in his hand- a picture of his younger sister, Lila, who had been abducted by a rival gang three months ago. It was this quest that drove him deeper into the underworld; he would not rest until she was safe.

"Remember, Rafe," he murmured to himself, "trust no one." Taking a calculated risk, he approached the group, his messy dark hair blending seamlessly into the shadows.

"Evening, gentlemen," Rafe said, flashing a charming but guarded smile. "I'm looking for information."

"Who's asking?" A burly man sneered, eyeing Rafe suspiciously.

"Names ain't important," Rafe replied smoothly, slipping a handful of crumpled bills from his pocket. "What is important is what I can offer you in return for your help."

One of the men, an old acquaintance named Jack with a crooked nose and a reputation for knowing everyone's secrets, glanced at the money before locking eyes with Rafe. "Lila, huh?" He motioned for Rafe to follow him into a darker corner of the alley.

"Word is The Viper's crew has her," Jack whispered, his breath reeking of cheap whiskey. "But be careful, Rafe. They've got friends in high places, and they don't take kindly to people snooping around."

"Thanks, Jack," Rafe said, handing over the money. As he stepped away, he caught sight of another figure lurking in the shadows– someone he knew all too well.

"Antonio," Rafe greeted coldly, his fists clenching at the sight of the man who had betrayed him years ago. "What brings you to this side of New Haven?"

"Business, Rafe," Antonio replied, a malicious grin spreading across his face. "And I hear you're looking for your sister. She's quite the bargaining chip, isn't she?"

"Stay away from her," Rafe warned, struggling to keep his emotions in check. He knew he couldn't afford to let his anger get the better of him.

"Or what?" Antonio taunted. "You'll kill me? You don't have the guts."

"Try me," Rafe shot back, his voice cold and determined. But before either could make a move, they were interrupted by the sound of approaching footsteps.

"Looks like we've got company," Antonio sneered, melting back into the shadows.

Rafe turned to see a group of armed men rounding the corner, their faces obscured by black masks. He recognized them as enforcers for The Viper. With a silent prayer for strength, Rafe prepared himself for the confrontation that was about to unfold.

"Lord, guide my every step in this treacherous world," he prayed, his heart heavy with the knowledge that Lila's salvation– and the very fate of New Haven– rested upon his shoulders.

In the shadow of New Haven's crumbling ruins, Rafe watched as two rival gangs clashed. The sound of gunfire echoed through the night, punctuating a symphony of chaos and despair. The air was thick with the bitter stench of blood and smoke as flames licked at the decaying buildings. Innocent civilians cowered in fear, their eyes wide with terror as they sought shelter from the violent storm that ravaged their city.

"Father," Rafe whispered, his gaze fixed on the unfolding carnage, "forgive them, for they know not what they do."

Through the cacophony of destruction, Rafe could hear the murmurs of corrupt officials as they brokered deals in dark corners, their greed fueling the fires of conflict. He gritted his teeth, knowing all too well the depths to which the powers that be had fallen. It seemed that every soul in New Haven had been tainted by Satan's touch.

As Rafe cautiously navigated the chaos, he kept his focus on the task at hand– finding the man who held the key to Lila's salvation. Time was running out, and he knew that the window of opportunity would soon close.

"Please, Lord," Rafe prayed silently, "grant me the strength and wisdom to bring justice to this forsaken place."

His sharp hazel eyes scanned the faces of those who passed him by, searching for any sign of recognition or deceit. Suddenly, he spotted a familiar figure across the street: Marco, a low-ranking member of The Viper's gang who had once been under Rafe's wing.

"Marco," Rafe whispered to himself, feeling a pang of regret for the path his former protégé had chosen. He knew that approaching Marco could put both of them in grave danger, but it was a risk he had to take if it meant getting closer to Lila.

"Remember, O Lord, your great mercy and love," Rafe prayed as he stepped forward, his heart pounding in his chest.

"Rafe?" Marco's eyes widened in shock as he recognized his former mentor. "What are you doing here?"

"Marco, I need your help," Rafe replied, trying to keep his voice steady despite the chaos around them.

"Are you insane?" Marco hissed, glancing nervously over his shoulder. "If The Viper finds out we spoke, we're both dead!"

"Please, Marco," Rafe urged, desperation creeping into his voice. "My sister's life is at stake."

For a moment, Marco hesitated, torn between loyalty to his gang and the memory of their shared past. But finally, he relented.

"Fine," he whispered, his voice filled with fear and uncertainty. "But we can't talk here. Meet me at the old church by the river in an hour."

"Thank you, Marco," Rafe breathed, relief flooding through him. He knew that this meeting could spell doom for both of them, but it was a risk he had to take– for Lila, and for the salvation of New Haven.

"Lord," he prayed as he disappeared back into the shadows, "protect us in our hour of need, and guide us safely through the valley of the shadow of death."

Cloaked in darkness, Rafe navigated the treacherous streets of New Haven. A putrid stench filled the air, a constant reminder of the sin festering within the city's core. He had an hour to prepare for the meeting with Marco, and he intended to use every second wisely.

Rafe darted through hidden passages, his intimate knowledge of the city's underbelly granting him safe passage. He slipped into a decrepit building that once served as a tailor shop, now abandoned and left to rot like much of New Haven.

"Forgive me Father," Rafe muttered, rifling through remnants of clothing, searching for a suitable disguise. His fingers brushed against rough fabric– a tattered coat perfect for blending in with the downtrodden souls drifting through the underworld. He donned the coat and smeared his face with grime, transforming into Jacob, a weary beggar known only to those who dared to peer into New Haven's darkest corners.

With each step towards the old church by the river, Rafe's heart raced faster, the weight of his mission bearing down on him. As he crossed the threshold of a dimly lit bar, he overheard hushed voices discussing the movements of The Viper's gang.

"Word is, they're moving something big tonight," one man whispered, shadows obscuring his features. "Something valuable."

"Valuable enough to risk crossing the Red Serpents?" another voice replied, a tremor of fear evident.

"Whatever it is, it's important to The Viper himself," the first man confirmed.

Intrigued, Rafe leaned closer, straining to catch every word. This could be the key to unraveling the tangled web that held New Haven captive.

"Where are they taking it?" the second man asked, barely audible.

"An old warehouse on the outskirts of town," came the reply. "But if you know what's good for you, you'll stay far away."

"Perhaps it's the artifact," Rafe pondered, his heart thundering in his chest. If he could retrieve the stolen relic, he could use it as leverage to save Lila and bring down The Viper's reign of terror.

"Lord, let this be the answer I seek," he prayed silently, before slipping out of the bar and continuing towards his rendezvous with Marco.

The old church loomed ahead, its steeple piercing the heavens like a beacon of hope amidst the darkness. As Rafe approached, he couldn't shake the feeling that something was amiss.

The desolation of New Haven weighed heavily upon Rafe's shoulders as he traversed the city's hidden alleys, feeling the grit and decay beneath his feet. The air hung thick with a sense of foreboding that settled into every crevice of the city, a constant reminder of the evil that lurked in the shadows. Despite the danger that surrounded him, Rafe's resolve only grew stronger, fueled by his determination to bring justice to the corrupt forces that held the city in their iron grip.

"Trust in the Lord," Rafe whispered to himself, recalling the ancient words that had been passed down through generations. "He will guide me through the valley of darkness."

A sudden gust of wind howled through the alleyway, carrying with it the faint sound of distant sirens. Rafe paused, his sharp hazel eyes scanning the darkness for any signs of trouble. He knew all too well the risks he faced in the underworld- the treacherous gang members who would betray him without a second thought, the corrupt officials who would do anything to maintain their power, and the ever-present threat of capture or death.

"Rafe! Over here!" A hushed voice called out from a shadowy doorway.

It was Marco, his trusted ally and informant. Rafe approached cautiously, mindful of the uneasy alliances that often shifted in the treacherous world of New Haven.

"Did you find out anything?" Rafe questioned, his heart pounding in anticipation.

"Listen, I don't know how much longer I can keep doing this," Marco confessed, his voice trembling. "The Viper's reach is growing, and he's getting more dangerous by the day."

"Then let's put an end to his reign of terror," Rafe replied, his voice steely with determination. "Tell me what you know."

"Alright," Marco sighed. "I heard whispers of a secret meeting tonight, involving some of the highest-ranking members of The Viper's gang. They're planning something big, something that will solidify his control over the city."

"Where?" Rafe demanded, his mind racing with possibilities.

"An abandoned old hut on the east side of the village," Marco muttered. "But be careful, Rafe. If they catch you…"

"Trust in the Lord," Rafe cut him off. "I'll be fine."

As Rafe left the alleyway, a shadowy figure detached itself from the darkness and followed at a distance, unseen eyes locked onto Rafe's retreating form.

"Your time draws near, Raphael Sylvestre," the figure whispered, its voice like the hissing of a serpent. "The end of your world is just beginning."

Raphael "Rafe" Syestre is a man who lives in the shadows, navigating his way through the dangerous world of espionage and betrayal. With his sharp hazel eyes and short, messy dark hair, Rafe is a cunning and resourceful rogue in his late twenties who knows how to get what he wants.

Despite his guarded exterior, Rafe is fiercely loyal to those he cares about, and would go to great lengths to protect them. He has a quick wit and a sarcastic sense of humor, often using them to mask the pain of his own past.

As the story begins, Rafe finds himself embroiled in a dangerous game of cat and mouse with a powerful enemy. When he discovers that this enemy is planning to launch an attack on innocent civilians, Rafe must act quickly to prevent disaster.

But as he delves deeper into the conspiracy, Rafe realizes that there may be more at stake than just the lives of a few innocent people. He begins to uncover a web of lies and deceit that stretches all the way to the highest levels of government.

As Rafe races against time to unravel the mystery and stop the attack, he must confront his own demons and face the truth about his past. With danger lurking around every corner, Rafe is forced to use all of his cunning and resourcefulness to outmaneuver his enemies and stay alive.

The rain pelted down on the narrow alleyway, casting a cold and somber light on the two hunched figures that stood in the shadows. Their voices barely audible above the thrum of the rain, they whispered urgently to each other, the tension between them palpable.

"Is it true?" asked the taller of the two, his voice hoarse with fear. "The prophecy?"

"True as the night is dark," replied the other, a shiver running down his spine. "And when it comes to pass, everything we know…everything we've fought for…will crumble."

Raphael "Rafe" Syestre, concealed behind a stack of damp wooden crates, strained to hear the conversation. His sharp hazel eyes narrowed as he attempted to discern the identities of the shadowy figures. He silently cursed himself for stumbling upon this exchange purely by accident, but now that he had, he could not tear himself away.

As the smaller figure handed the other a tattered piece of parchment, Rafe caught a glimpse of the inscription– a cryptic symbol unlike any he had seen before. The taller figure studied it briefly before tucking it into his coat and disappearing into the darkness. The other man hesitated, casting a paranoid glance around the alley before following suit.

Rafe's curiosity burned within him like a wildfire. It was clear that these men were discussing something of great importance, something that could potentially shake the very foundations of their world. He felt a strange sense of urgency, a weight settling on his shoulders as though fate itself was compelling him to act.

"Damn it," he muttered under his breath, his heart pounding. "I can't let this go."

With a deep breath, Rafe stepped out from behind the crates and followed the trail of the mysterious figures. Whatever this prophecy was, he had a feeling it would soon become his problem too.

The city teemed with life, its bustling streets a cacophony of noise and chaos that belied the sinister undertones lurking beneath the surface. Rafe navigated the crowded marketplace, his sharp hazel eyes darting from one stall to the next, taking in the vibrant colors of exotic fruits and fabrics piled high on rickety tables. The air was thick with the scent of spices and sweat, an intoxicating mix that only added to the aura of danger that seemed to permeate every corner.

Above the throngs of people pushing and shoving their way through the narrow alleys, towering skyscrapers reached for the heavens like colossal monuments to humanity's hubris. The constant hum of activity masked the hidden machinations at play, as countless souls unknowingly went about their lives, ignorant of the perilous game of espionage unfolding around them.

"Rafe," a voice whispered into his earpiece. "You're getting close. Remember, stay alert."

"Understood," he muttered, his fingers tightening around the small device concealed within his jacket pocket. He knew that he had to remain vigilant, for he was well aware of the treacherous world he inhabited. As a seasoned operative in this realm of shadows and deceit, Rafe had learned to trust no one– not even himself.

His short, messy dark hair provided some semblance of cover as he blended into the throng, but it was his keen eyes and resourcefulness that truly set him apart. In a covert operation such as this, where the stakes were higher than ever, it would take all of his cunning and skill to navigate the impending storm.

"Target is approaching," the voice said, tension evident in each syllable. Rafe tensed, his gaze fixed on a man in a dark coat who emerged from the crowd. "Stay on him, but be careful. We can't afford any mistakes."

"got that," Rafe replied, his heart pounding in his chest. He had been involved in countless high-stakes missions before, but something about this one felt different– as if the weight of the world was resting on his shoulders.

"Let the endgame begin," he thought as he shadowed the man through the city streets, every step taking him deeper into the heart of darkness.

"Little do they know," Rafe mused internally, "that beneath this façade of commerce and industry, the forces of good and evil are locked in a battle for the very soul of mankind."

As he followed the man, he couldn't help but wonder what role the mysterious prophecy played in all of this. The cryptic symbol and the exchange he had witnessed gnawed at his mind, a puzzle he was desperate to solve. But he knew that, for now, he must focus on the task at hand.

"Stay sharp, Rafe," he told himself. "This is just the beginning."

Rafe's fingers traced the edge of the small envelope tucked into his jacket pocket, a constant reminder of the prophecy he had yet to unravel. His sharp hazel eyes scanned the crowded market as he moved with calculated nonchalance, avoiding eye contact with passing strangers. He was hyper-aware of the dangers lurking in every corner, his senses honed from years of espionage work.

"Careful now, Rafe," he thought to himself, "one wrong move and this could all come crashing down."

The bustling city around him seemed oblivious to the state of his heart, which raced with equal parts anticipation and anxiety. A cacophony of voices filled the air, vendors hawking their wares and people bartering for the best prices. But amidst the noise, Rafe's ears pricked up at the sound of a hushed exchange between two hooded figures near a dimly lit storefront.

"Have you heard about the prophecy?" one figure whispered, words barely audible. "It is said that when it comes to pass, Satan's captivity will end, and the world will be plunged into darkness."

"Preposterous," the other figure scoffed. "Who would believe such nonsense?"

"A lot of powerful people, apparently," the first figure replied, voice tinged with unease. "There's talk of a conspiracy within the government, preparing for the day the prophecy comes true."

"Really? That seems..." The second figure trailed off, glancing around nervously.

"Exactly," the first figure agreed, lowering his voice even further. "We must tread carefully. They're always watching."

"Prophecy, conspiracy, Satan's release? Sounds like a party," Rafe muttered sarcastically under his breath, his mind racing with the implications of their conversation. The weight of the prophecy suddenly felt heavier than ever, and he knew he couldn't afford to ignore it any longer.

He slipped through the crowd, his short, messy dark hair barely visible as he blended in with the sea of people. He needed to find answers, and quickly.

"Time's running out," Rafe thought, the ache of past losses stirring within him. "I can't let them down again."

As he moved through the city, his thoughts were a whirlwind of questions and doubts, his guarded exterior masking the turmoil beneath. The bustling streets seemed to echo his inner chaos, a maze of possibilities and threats that he had to navigate alone.

"Trust no one," Rafe reminded himself, his heart heavy with the burden of responsibility. "Only I can unravel this prophecy and prevent the end of days."

And with each step, the clock ticked closer to midnight.

The city lay before Rafe like a pulsating beast, its heart beating with the rhythm of life. Towering skyscrapers reached for the heavens, casting long shadows that danced in the golden light of the setting sun. Neon signs flickered to life, their electric glow reflecting off rain-soaked streets, painting an eerie landscape of vivid colors and distorted images.

"Nothing's ever as it seems," Rafe thought bitterly as he observed the diverse array of characters bustling through the city. Street vendors hawked their wares, their voices rising above the cacophony of honking horns and laughter from nearby cafes. Children darted through the throngs of people, their laughter innocent and carefree, oblivious to the darkness lurking beneath the surface.

"Would they still laugh if they knew?" Rafe wondered, his sharp hazel eyes scanning the crowd for any signs of danger or betrayal.

He navigated through seemingly ordinary places, like parks filled with families enjoying picnics and lovers stealing secret kisses behind ancient trees. The contrast between the idyllic scene and the impending doom weighed heavily on him; how could these people go about their lives unaware of the prophecy?

"Enjoy it while it lasts," Rafe muttered under his breath, his sarcasm a shield against the despair threatening to overwhelm him.

His keen senses led him to a small café tucked away in a quiet corner of the city. A place where secrets were whispered over steaming cups of coffee, and alliances forged within the shadows.

"Ah, Rafe," the barista greeted him with a knowing nod, her dark eyes filled with curiosity. "Long time no see."

"Can't say I missed the place," Rafe replied dryly, taking a seat at the far end of the café, his back to the wall.

"Same old Rafe," she chuckled, shaking her head as she went to prepare his usual order.

As he waited, his thoughts raced, searching for a way to unravel the prophecy and prevent the end of days. The weight of responsibility bore down on him, a suffocating presence that left no room for error.

"Trust no one," Rafe reminded himself, his heart heavy with the burden of responsibility. "Only I can unravel this prophecy and prevent the end of days."

His coffee arrived, its rich aroma a momentary distraction from the demons haunting his thoughts. He sipped it slowly, savoring the warmth and bitterness as he scanned the room, his gaze lingering on each patron, assessing them for potential threats or hidden agendas.

"Rafe?" A familiar voice cut through his reverie, and he looked up to see an old friend standing before him, his expression a mix of concern and surprise. "What are you doing here?"

"Same as always, Tom," Rafe replied, his voice tight with contained emotion. "Trying to save the world."

"Always the hero," Tom said with a sigh, taking a seat across from him. "But at what cost?"

"Whatever it takes," Rafe answered, his eyes hardening with determination. "I won't allow history to repeat itself."

"Even if it means losing everything?" Tom asked, his gaze searching Rafe's face for any signs of doubt or hesitation.

"Especially then," Rafe whispered, his voice carrying the weight of a thousand unshed tears. "The world must be saved, no matter the price."

And with each second that ticked by, the clock inched closer to midnight, the hour of reckoning drawing near.

A sudden crash of glass shattered the uneasy silence, jerking Rafe back to the present. He instinctively ducked under the café table, his heart pounding in his chest as adrenaline surged through his veins. The gun tucked into his waistband felt heavier than usual, a constant reminder of the dangers he faced.

"Get down!" Tom shouted, following Rafe's lead and diving for cover.

From his vantage point beneath the table, Rafe watched as a group of masked assailants stormed into the café, guns drawn and expressions coldly determined. Their movements were swift and precise, leaving no doubt that they were well-trained and focused on their objective– the same information Rafe had spent weeks tracking down.

"Where is it?" one of them snarled, grabbing a terrified barista by the collar and shoving him against the wall.

Rafe's mind raced, calculating the odds of taking on the armed men without putting more innocent lives at risk. He knew he needed to act before the situation escalated any further. Exchanging a silent nod with Tom, Rafe sprang into action, drawing his gun and firing a shot at one of the assailants.

"Go!" Rafe shouted to the petrified patrons, using the distraction to shepherd them toward the rear exit. As the civilians fled, gunfire erupted around him, bullets whizzing past his ears and embedding themselves in the walls.

"Rafe, watch out!" Tom warned, lunging forward to tackle an attacker who had snuck up behind them.

"Thanks," Rafe muttered, returning the favor by shooting the man's weapon from his hand. As the two friends fought side by side, they moved with a synchronicity born from years of shared battles and hardships.

As the last of the attackers fell, Rafe couldn't help but notice the emblem on their uniforms– a symbol he had seen only once before, burned into the pages of the ancient prophecy he had discovered. It was clear now that they were not alone in their quest to unravel the secrets of the end times. Other, more sinister forces were at work, and they would stop at nothing to achieve their goals.

"Who are they?" Tom asked, his voice shaky from the adrenaline still coursing through him.

"Enemies we didn't know we had," Rafe replied grimly, scanning the room for any lingering threats.

In the distance, beyond the shattered windows of the café, Rafe caught a glimpse of a figure cloaked in shadows, observing the chaos with an eerie calm. Their eyes locked for a brief moment, and though he couldn't make out the stranger's features, Rafe felt a shiver run down his spine. Whoever they were, it was evident they held the key to understanding the dark conspiracy unfolding around them.

"Come on, we need to go," Rafe urged, grabbing Tom's arm and pulling him toward the exit. As they disappeared into the maze of narrow alleyways, Rafe couldn't shake the feeling that they were being watched, hunted by forces beyond their comprehension.

And as the sun dipped below the horizon, casting the city into darkness, Rafe knew that the final battle between good and evil was fast approaching. The fate of mankind rested in his hands, and time was running out.

Rafe and Tom darted through the narrow, rain-soaked alleyways of the city, the air thick with the smell of damp earth and decay. The dim glow from flickering neon signs cast eerie shadows along their path. Rafe's sharp hazel eyes scanned their surroundings, his instincts on high alert for any signs of danger.

"Where are we going?" Tom panted, struggling to keep up with Rafe's breakneck pace.

"To meet an old friend," Rafe replied cryptically, his voice barely audible over the pounding of their footsteps on the wet cobblestones.

As they turned a corner into another shadowy passage, Rafe spotted a figure hunched beneath the awning of a dilapidated building. She was draped in a worn trench coat, her face obscured by a wide-brimmed hat. This was Lydia, Rafe's trusted informant and one of the few people he could count on in this treacherous world.

"Lydia," Rafe greeted her cautiously, as Tom eyed the mysterious woman warily.

"Rafe," she acknowledged with a nod. "I wish we were meeting under better circumstances."

"Tell me about it," Rafe muttered, glancing over his shoulder one last time. "We got attacked back there. Something big is happening, and I need your help to figure out what."

"Of course," Lydia responded, her tone serious. "But you should know, I've been hearing whispers lately. Dark things. Powerful forces are at play here, Rafe— more than we ever imagined."

"Who are they? Can you trust your sources?" Rafe pressed urgently, his mind racing with the implications of her words.

"Trust is a luxury we can't afford right now," Lydia warned, casting a wary glance at Tom. "But my sources have never led me astray before."

"Alright," Rafe conceded, his jaw set with determination. "Then we need to uncover this conspiracy before it's too late."

"Be careful," Lydia said, her voice tinged with genuine concern. "Whatever you're about to face, I fear it may be more than any of us can handle."

"Thanks for the vote of confidence," Rafe replied sarcastically, hiding his own unease beneath a layer of dark humor.

"Take care of yourself, Rafe," Lydia whispered as they parted ways, leaving her standing alone in the shadows.

As Rafe and Tom continued their flight through the labyrinthine streets, Rafe couldn't help but feel the weight of the prophecy bearing down on him. He knew that the fate of mankind rested on his shoulders, but the true extent of the conspiracy remained shrouded in darkness.

"You are being hunted. Trust no one."

Rafe's heart pounded in his chest, and he felt the chill of fear grip his spine. Gritting his teeth,, his resolve hardening.

"Change of plans," Rafe announced, his expression grim. "We need to find answers, and fast— because it seems we've just made some powerful enemies."

XIII

THE MYSTICAL
LAND OF ARATHIA

In the mystical land of Arathia, Lucian is on a quest to uncover the truth about his past and his connection to the prophecy that foretells the rise of darkness. Alongside Elena, Rafe, and Lilith, they journey through treacherous landscapes and face dangerous adversaries, all while learning more about each other's past experiences and motivations for joining the fight.

As they grow closer, Lucian discovers that his fate is intertwined with his companions in ways he never imagined. Through their shared stories and struggles, they come to realize that their individual paths have led them to this moment, where they must unite to prevent the darkness from consuming their world.

Elena shares her own story of loss and heartbreak, revealing how she came to possess the magical amulet that now guides their journey. Rafe speaks of his own experiences with the darkness, having lost loved ones to its malevolent powers. And Lilith, once a member of the very group that seeks to bring about the prophecy's fulfillment, reveals the true nature of their enemy and the extent of their power.

As they journey deeper into the heart of darkness, tensions rise and conflicts erupt. Lucian's connection to the prophecy becomes more apparent as he faces trials that test his strength and resolve. But with the support and guidance of his companions, he rises to the challenge, discovering new depths of power within himself.

In the climactic final battle, Lucian and his companions face off against the forces of darkness in a struggle that will determine the fate of Arathia. With every twist and turn, they are pushed to their limits, but ultimately emerge victorious, having fulfilled the prophecy and saved their world from destruction.

Through their journey, Lucian learns not only about his own past but also about the importance of friendship and unity in the face of adversity. He emerges stronger and more confident, ready to face whatever challenges lie ahead with his newfound companions by his side.

a breathtaking tapestry woven from nature's most vibrant colors. Lush forests, the leaves painted in hues of emerald and jade, carpeted vast swaths of the landscape, their shadows concealing untold secrets beneath their verdant canopy. Towering mountains pierced the sky like jagged daggers of stone, their peaks shrouded in mist as if to hide their ancient wisdom from the mortal realm below. Serene lakes shimmered with the reflected light of sun and stars, their placid surfaces mirroring the endless heavens above.

"Have you heard?" whispered a hushed voice nearby, drawing Lucian's attention away from the scenery. "They say the prophecy draws near."

His heart clenched with an icy grip at the mention of the prophecy. For centuries, the people of Arathia had dreaded the foretelling of darkness that would rise and envelop their world; it was a grim specter that haunted their every waking moment. The prophecy was a storm cloud on the horizon, casting a shadow over the once vibrant land, draining the color and joy from the lives of its inhabitants. Fear and apprehension seeped into every corner of their existence, leaving them in a state of constant worry and anticipation.

"Indeed," Lucian replied, his voice tight with unease. "I've felt it too– a chill in the air, a sense of foreboding." He looked around, searching for reassurance in the faces of his fellow townspeople. But all he saw were furtive glances and furrowed brows, each person consumed by their own concerns.

"The end of the thousand years is upon us," murmured one old woman, her voice trembling. "Satan's chains will break, and darkness will rule once more."

"Then we must be ready," declared Lucian, his resolve steeling him against the rising tide of despair. He knew his journey would not be an easy one, but he was determined to uncover the truth about his past and his connection to the prophecy.

"May the light guide us all," whispered the old woman, her eyes glistening with tears that reflected both fear and hope— a hope that Lucian carried with him as he set forth into the unknown, determined to face the coming darkness head-on.

Under the relentless gaze of a sinking sun, casting fiery streaks across the horizon, Lucian stood alone in a desolate clearing. His tall stature loomed over the crumbling ruins of an ancient temple, swallowed by creeping vines that clung to the cracked stones like a lover's desperate embrace. Dark hair fell in disarray around his angular face, framing piercing blue eyes that seemed to hold the key to a thousand buried secrets.

"Is this where it all begins?" Lucian whispered, his voice barely audible above the mournful wail of the wind. "Or is it where it ends?"

A shiver ran down his spine as he recalled the haunting dreams that had plagued him for weeks. Visions of fire and blood danced behind his closed eyelids, taunting him with their vivid intensity— an apocalyptic prelude to the end of days. He saw himself standing at the epicenter of the chaos, wielding a sword that burned with a fierce, otherworldly light. And yet, despite the power that coursed through his veins, he could feel the darkness closing in, threatening to consume all that remained.

"Who am I?" Lucian asked the empty air, his voice laced with frustration and fear. "What is my place in this prophecy?"

No answers came, only the echoes of his own questions reverberating through the twilight hush. The sense of unease that had become his constant companion tightened its grip on his chest, constricting his breath until it came in shallow gasps.

"Damn these dreams," he growled, slamming his fist against the weathered stone of the temple. "Why won't they leave me be?"

"Perhaps they are meant to guide you," a voice murmured from the shadows. Lucian whirled around, searching for the source of the sound but finding nothing but the shifting darkness.

"Who's there?" he demanded, his heart pounding in his ears. "Show yourself!"

"Your dreams are a warning, Lucian," the voice continued, seemingly coming from all directions at once. "A call to action. You must find the truth hidden within them and confront the darkness that awaits."

"Tell me how!" Lucian shouted, his desperation ringing through the night. "I cannot face this alone. I don't even know who I am!"

"Trust your instincts," the voice replied, its tone softening. "Embrace your connection to the prophecy, for only then will you discover your true self."

As the final words faded into silence, Lucian found himself standing alone once more, the shadows retreating as if they had never been. He clenched his fists, his resolve hardening like tempered steel.

"Very well," he whispered, his voice resolute. "I will follow these dreams to their source, wherever they may lead me. And when I find the truth, I will stand against the darkness and fulfill my destiny– whatever it may be."

With renewed determination burning in his soul, Lucian stepped forward into the gathering gloom, ready to face the unknown horrors that awaited him on the path to self-discovery and redemption.

The morning sun cast its golden rays upon the mystical land of Arathia, painting the lush forests and towering mountains in a warm, inviting light. Lucian stood at the edge of the shimmering lake that mirrored the sky, his piercing blue eyes reflecting the determination that coursed through his veins like fire.

"Enough," he murmured to himself, his voice barely audible over the gentle lapping of the water against the shore. "It's time to seek the truth."

As he walked through the bustling marketplace of Arathia, Lucian could feel the weight of the prophecy bearing down on him- the rise of darkness that had instilled fear and apprehension among the people. Their once-joyful faces were now marred by worry, their conversations tainted with whispers of the impending doom.

"Morning, Lucian!" called out Jareth, the blacksmith, as he hammered away at his anvil. "Have you heard any news about the prophecy?"

"Nothing yet," Lucian replied, forcing a smile on his face. But beneath the surface, his thoughts churned like a storm. He knew that his journey would be the key to unlocking the secrets of his past and his role in the prophecy. And so, he resolved to embark on this perilous quest, driven by his unwavering curiosity and desire for self-discovery.

"Be careful out there," Jareth cautioned, sensing the turmoil within Lucian's heart. "We're all counting on you."

"Thank you, Jareth," Lucian nodded solemnly, feeling the weight of their expectations like a heavy cloak draped around his shoulders.

As he continued through the town, Lucian felt increasingly isolated, surrounded by familiar faces but plagued by unanswered questions. In every interaction, he was reminded of his own uncertainty- his longing for clarity that only his journey could provide.

"Lucian, have you reconsidered leaving?" asked Mara, the healer, her eyes filled with concern. "There's still so much you don't know."

"Sometimes we must leap into the unknown to find the answers we seek," Lucian replied, his inner resolve shining through his words like a beacon in the night.

"Then may the gods be with you," Mara whispered, placing a gentle hand on his arm before retreating into the shadows of her apothecary.

As Lucian ventured further from the familiar comforts of Arathia, he felt both excitement and trepidation coursing through him. He knew that this journey would test every ounce of his courage and determination, but he also sensed that it was the key to unlocking the truth about his past and fulfilling his destiny.

"Watch out!" cried a young boy as he darted between the market stalls, narrowly avoiding a collision with Lucian.

"Stay safe, little one," Lucian called after him, his heart swelling with the knowledge that he was embarking on this journey not just for himself, but for the people of Arathia- those who lived in fear of the prophecy and the darkness it foretold.

As the sun dipped below the horizon, casting long shadows across the land, Lucian took one final glance back at the town he had called home. He knew that the path ahead would be fraught with danger and uncertainty. But with each step he took towards the unknown, he felt a growing sense of purpose, fueled by his unwavering determination to uncover the truth and protect all he held dear.

And so, with the wind at his back and the fire of resolve burning in his chest, Lucian strode forth into the gathering darkness, ready to face whatever trials lay ahead on his quest for answers and redemption.

Amidst the crumbling ruins of an ancient temple, Lucian stood alone, the weight of the prophecy bearing down upon him like the suffocating embrace of a thousand invisible chains. The wind whispered mournful secrets through the once-hallowed halls, and Lucian couldn't help but shiver at the cold tendrils of fear that crept into his heart.

"Can I truly face the unknown?" he wondered aloud, his voice echoing through the deserted chamber. "Will I find the answers I seek, or will I be swallowed by the very darkness I strive to overcome?"

"Lucian!" called a familiar voice from behind him. His mother, Selene, appeared in the doorway, her brow furrowed with concern. "You mustn't let your fears consume you, my son. Remember, the prophecy speaks not only of darkness, but also of hope."

"Hope," Lucian repeated, as if testing the word on his tongue. "But is it enough to guide me through the trials that lie ahead?"

"Only you can determine that," Selene replied softly. "But remember, you are never truly alone in this world. Trust in yourself, and you will find the strength to overcome even the most insurmountable odds."

As Lucian gazed into his mother's eyes, he saw a glimmer of the fierce determination that had always been his guiding light. He knew that she was right- now was the time for action, not doubt.

"Thank you, Mother," he murmured, embracing her one last time before turning to face his destiny.

Over the course of the next few days, Lucian dedicated himself to preparing for his journey. He visited the village blacksmith, commissioning a sword forged from the finest steel, its hilt adorned with intricate symbols that seemed to pulse with hidden power. He gathered supplies from the local market, filling his pack with food, water, and other essentials that would sustain him on his quest.

"Take care, Lucian," the villagers whispered as they bid him farewell, their anxious eyes betraying the weight of their collective fears. But despite the heavy burden of expectation that settled upon his shoulders, Lucian felt a newfound resolve coursing through his veins. He would face whatever dangers lay ahead and emerge victorious- for himself, for his family, and for all of Arathia.

As he stood at the edge of the village, preparing to embark on his journey, Lucian couldn't help but feel a pang of sorrow at leaving behind everything he had ever known. "Will I ever return?" he wondered, his heart heavy with doubt.

"Remember, Lucian," his father's voice echoed in his mind, "courage is not the absence of fear, but the triumph over it."

With these words echoing in his heart, Lucian took a deep breath, squared his shoulders, and strode forward into the unknown, determined to conquer his fears and unravel the enigma of his past. With every step, his conviction grew stronger, fueled by the knowledge that only he held the key to unlocking the secrets of the prophecy and saving his world from the impending darkness.

With a final nod to the villagers who had gathered to see him off, Lucian stepped beyond the borders of Arathia and began his journey. The anticipation in his chest was akin to a bird trapped behind his ribs, its wings beating against his bones. He felt a simultaneous shiver of excitement and trepidation, knowing that he would soon face the unknown, but also that this was the only way to find answers.

"Courage, Lucian," he murmured to himself as he walked deeper into the mystical land, his breath creating small clouds in the cold morning air.

As he ventured further from the familiar comforts of home, the landscape began to transform, giving way to an otherworldly beauty that both captivated and unnerved him. Lucian's eyes widened as he witnessed the ancient power that seemed to pulse beneath the very ground he trod upon. Trees twisted into unnatural shapes as if reaching for something unseen, their gnarled roots embedded with glowing runes. The air shimmered with an ethereal energy that danced like silver fireflies around him.

"By the Creator," he breathed, awestruck by the sheer majesty of it all.

"Indeed," replied a voice from behind him, causing Lucian to startle. Turning, he found himself face to face with a creature unlike any he had ever encountered before. It resembled a deer, but its entire body appeared to be woven from living vines and leaves, its eyes pools of liquid emerald.

"Right you are, young traveler," the creature spoke again, its voice a gentle whisper on the breeze. "This land is alive with the Creator's touch, and you now walk among its wonders."

"Who–" Lucian hesitated, unsure of how to address the being before him. "What are you?"

"I am a Guardian of the forest, one of many tasked with preserving the balance between nature and magic. You, Lucian, are destined for great things, and I have been sent to guide you on your path." The Guardian's gaze fixed on him with an intensity that seemed to pierce his very soul.

"Then you know of the prophecy?" Lucian asked, his heart pounding at the prospect of finally receiving some answers.

"Indeed," the creature nodded solemnly. "But it is a journey you must undertake yourself, for only then will you uncover the truth about your past and your role in shaping our world's future."

As they continued to walk together, Lucian's thoughts swirled like a storm, struggling to come to terms with the magnitude of his quest. But as he gazed upon the mystical wonders around him, the fear that had gripped him so tightly began to loosen its hold. The awe-inspiring beauty of Arathia, coupled with the knowledge that he was not alone in his journey, filled him with newfound determination. He would face whatever lay ahead, embracing both the wonders and the darkness in pursuit of the truth.

"Thank you," Lucian said quietly to the Guardian, his voice steady and resolute. "I will not falter."

"May the Creator watch over you, Lucian," the creature replied, a touch of pride in its whispery voice. "Now, go forth and find the answers you seek."

And with that, the Guardian vanished back into the forest, leaving Lucian to continue his journey into the heart of the unknown, where magic and prophecy would intertwine to reveal the hidden depths of his destiny.

As Lucian ventured further into the mystical lands of Arathia, he marveled at the vivid tapestry of colors that stretched out before him. The sky seemed to bleed from a fiery red to a deep purple, casting an eerie glow on the landscape below. The air was thick with the scent of both blooming flowers and decay, creating a strange harmony of life and death.

It wasn't long before Lucian encountered another mystical element: peculiar symbols etched into the bark of ancient trees lining his path. Their intricate designs seemed to pulse with a hidden power, drawing him in like a moth to a flame. As he traced his fingers over the markings, a sudden surge of recognition washed over him, sending shivers down his spine.

"Could these be...?" Lucian whispered to himself, his voice wavering with uncertainty and awe.

"Indeed, young one," came a disembodied voice, echoing through the forest like a phantom. "These are the signs of the prophecy in which you are entwined."

Lucian's heart raced as he glanced around, searching for the source of the voice. It seemed to emanate from the very air itself, binding him in its ethereal embrace.

"Who are you? Show yourself!" he demanded, his courage flaring up despite the apprehension gnawing at his core.

"Patience, Lucian," the voice replied, laced with a mixture of amusement and sternness. "All will be revealed in due time."

An enigmatic silence followed, leaving Lucian to grapple with the implications of this encounter. His connection to the prophecy was now more tangible than ever, yet the mystery surrounding it only deepened. He knew he must forge ahead, propelled by the burning desire for answers that consumed him.

As Lucian continued along the path, the shadows lengthened, and the air grew colder. He could sense a foreboding presence lurking just beyond his sight, watching him with keen interest. The atmosphere was electric with anticipation, as if the very earth beneath him was holding its breath.

Suddenly, a chilling gust of wind swept through the forest, carrying with it the distant sound of thunder. Lucian's heart clenched in his chest as he realized that he was no longer alone on this path. An unseen force was guiding him, driving him inexorably towards his destiny– and the unknown dangers that awaited him.

"Is this...?" Lucian trailed off, unable to find words to express the dread that gripped him.

"Your journey has only just begun," the voice whispered ominously, its tone darker and more menacing than before. "The storm you hear is but a harbinger of the tempest that lies ahead. Prepare yourself, Lucian, for the darkness is coming."

And with that, the voice vanished, leaving Lucian standing alone in the shadow of the encroaching storm. The weight of the prophecy pressed down upon him like a suffocating fog, yet his resolve remained unbroken. He would not be deterred by the perils that lay before him; he would face them head-on, armed with the knowledge that his quest was far from over.

With a steely determination, Lucian took a deep breath and stepped forward into the gathering darkness, unaware of the trials and challenges that lay in wait. As he did so, a single word echoed through his mind, both a warning and a promise: Apocalypse.

The wind howled through the barren landscape, whipping up clouds of dust and grit that stung Lucian's face. The once-verdant expanse of Arathia had given way to a desolate wasteland, a grim testament to the prophecy's inexorable advance. As he trudged onward, his piercing blue eyes scanned the horizon for any signs of life or respite from the oppressive desolation.

"Is this what awaits us all?" Lucian murmured to himself, his heart heavy with foreboding. He could not help but entertain the darkest of thoughts– that perhaps he was too late to stop the coming apocalypse, that his journey was doomed to end in failure.

"Only if you falter on your path," a raspy voice replied, startling Lucian out of his bleak reverie. An old man stood before him, seemingly materializing out of the swirling dust. His tattered robes fluttered in the wind, and his sunken eyes held an unnerving intensity.

"Who are you?" Lucian asked warily, his hand instinctively reaching for the hilt of his sword. The stranger's sudden appearance and cryptic words did little to ease the unease that had settled over him like a shroud.

"Merely a fellow traveler, weary and worn by the relentless march of time," the old man replied enigmatically. "And one who has seen the shadows that gather at the edge of the world, whispering of doom."

"Then you know of the prophecy?" Lucian queried, his curiosity piqued despite his reservations.

"Indeed," the old man nodded gravely. "I have walked these lands for countless ages, bearing witness to the rise and fall of empires…and the slow approach of darkness."

"Can it be stopped?" Lucian's voice cracked with desperation, his resolve wavering in the face of the seemingly insurmountable task that lay before him.

"Only if you stay true to your course and confront the challenges that bar your way," the old man replied solemnly. "Like the treacherous pass that lies ahead– a crucible through which you must pass if you are to reach your ultimate destination."

"Thank you for your guidance," Lucian said, bowing his head in gratitude. The old man merely nodded, his eyes never leaving Lucian's face. And then, with a gust of wind and a swirl of dust, he vanished just as suddenly as he had appeared.

Determined to prove himself worthy of the stranger's counsel, Lucian pressed onward towards the mountain pass, his resolve hardened by the knowledge that he was not alone in this struggle. As he approached the base of the towering peaks, he could see why the old man had warned him of its dangers— sheer cliffs rose up on either side, their jagged edges gleaming menacingly in the dying light, while a narrow path snaked perilously along their edge.

With a deep breath, Lucian began his ascent, his every nerve tingling with anticipation and fear. He picked his way carefully across the treacherous terrain, the wind whipping at his hair and threatening to send him plummeting into the abyss below. Every step felt like a battle against the very elements themselves, yet Lucian refused to be deterred.

As he neared the summit, he felt a surge of triumph well up within him— he had conquered the mountain pass, vanquished one of the many obstacles that stood between him and the fulfillment of the prophecy. And as he gazed out over the desolate expanse that stretched out before him, he knew that there would be no turning back.

"Bring on the darkness," Lucian whispered defiantly, his blue eyes blazing with determination. "I will stand against it, no matter the cost."

And with that, he continued his descent into the valley below, every step bringing him closer to the ultimate showdown between light and darkness— and the fate of all mankind hanging in the balance.

Lucian stood at the edge of a vast, barren wasteland, its scorched earth stretching out to meet an ominous, blood-red sky. The wind howled around him, whipping up clouds of dust that stung his eyes and filled his lungs with grit. Far off in the distance, he could see the faint, flickering glow of a fire— a beacon of hope amidst the desolation.

"Is this what awaits us all?" Lucian murmured, his voice barely audible above the wind's relentless assault. "A world laid waste by darkness?"

He remembered the wise old sage he had encountered earlier on his journey, who had warned him of the great tribulations that lay ahead. The man's enigmatic words echoed in his mind:"The end is nigh, young traveler. And only you can alter the course of fate."

As he trudged onward, Lucian couldn't help but dwell on those cryptic words. He had been thrust into a role he never asked for, carrying the weight of the world on his shoulders. And yet, despite the immense burden and the ever-present specter of doubt, he felt a fierce resolve burning within him.

"I did not choose this path," he thought, his jaw clenched in determination. "But I will see it through to the end, no matter the cost."

He knew that there would be countless trials and tribulations awaiting him, each more daunting than the last. But there was something within him— a spark of power, a hidden strength— that urged him onward, refusing to let him falter.

"Is this the legacy of my ancestors?" Lucian wondered, recalling the ancient symbols and signs that seemed to hint at his connection to the prophecy. "Am I truly destined to stand against the darkness, or am I merely a pawn in some greater game?"

With each step he took, Lucian felt the gravity of his decision weighing heavily upon him. He knew that the road ahead would be fraught with danger and uncertainty, but he also understood that there was no turning back. The fate of mankind hung in the balance, and he alone held the power to tip the scales.

"Let the darkness come," Lucian whispered fiercely, his piercing blue eyes narrowing as he stared out into the apocalyptic landscape before him. "I will not falter. I will not fail."

And so, with a steely resolve and a heart full of determination, Lucian pressed onward into the great unknown, prepared to face whatever trials the future had in store for him— and determined to fulfill his destiny as the savior of mankind.

XIV

ALL IS LOST: CRISES POINT

In a world of magic and danger, Lucian and his group of allies embark on a perilous journey to retrieve a powerful artifact from the heart of a forbidden temple. Along the way, they encounter countless obstacles and enemies, but their determination to succeed never wavers.

As they finally reach their destination, they discover that the artifact has been corrupted by dark magic, and Lilith Arcadia, a member of their group, reveals her true intentions. She had led them to the artifact in the hopes of using its power for her own selfish desires. However, after witnessing the devastation caused by the artifact's corruption, Lilith has a change of heart and decides to help Lucian and his allies cleanse it of its darkness.

Despite their efforts, they are not able to leave the temple with the purified artifact without being ambushed by Valthor Malgath and his forces. A fierce battle ensues, but ultimately Lucian and his allies are overwhelmed and captured.

As they are taken away, Lucian realizes that this is just the beginning of a much larger conflict. He knows that they must find a way to escape and continue their quest, or all will be lost. With the fate of the world hanging in the balance, Lucian and his allies must summon all of their courage and strength to overcome the challenges that lie ahead.

In a world where shadows melded with light, casting an eerie twilight over the land, magic and danger collided in ways both beautiful and terrifying. Great swirling vortexes of arcane power loomed above jagged mountains, shimmering with colors that stretched beyond the imagination. The earth itself seemed to breathe with life, its heartbeat pulsating through the veins of the crystal-encrusted forests, where creatures of myth stalked the undergrowth, their eyes shining like embers in the darkness.

It was amid this breathtaking yet perilous landscape that the forbidden temple stood, a hulking mass of stone that appeared to defy gravity. Its twisted spires clawed at the sky, stark against the ever-shifting backdrop of the heavens. Every inch of its surface was etched with runes and symbols, each one telling a small part of the ancient stories that surrounded this place of power. It was said that the key to unlocking the destiny of mankind lay within its walls– but only for those strong enough to face the trials that awaited them.

"Lucian, do you truly believe we're meant to be here?" whispered Aria, her voice barely audible above the howl of the wind.

"Legends speak of this place," replied Lucian, his gaze never wavering from the temple's imposing entrance. "We must venture inside if we are to fulfill the prophecy and prevent the world's ruin."

As Lucian led his allies through the darkened halls of the temple, each step echoed like the drumbeat of impending doom. Lilith studied the inscriptions on the walls, her fingers tracing the ancient lines, while Caspian kept a watchful eye on their surroundings, his magical senses attuned to any threats.

"Remember," warned Gavriel, as they cautiously pressed on, "the power that lies within is unimaginable. If it were to fall into Valthor's hands…" He let the sentence hang in the air, the gravity of their mission weighing heavily on each of them.

As they delved deeper into the temple's heart, whispers of a sinister presence slithered through the air, caressing the minds of the brave adventurers. Elena gripped her weapon tightly, her eyes darting from shadow to shadow, as Nalia murmured soft prayers for protection.

"Stay strong," Lucian thought to himself, his determination burning like a beacon in the darkness. "We've come too far to turn back now. The fate of the world rests in our hands."

The air grew colder and heavier as the group ventured deeper into the forbidden temple, their breaths visible in the dim light. Every footstep seemed to echo through the seemingly endless halls, a constant reminder of the weighty responsibility that lay upon their shoulders.

"Lucian," said Lilith, her voice barely audible above the whispers that seemed to emanate from the very walls themselves, "what do you know of the prophecy? Why are we here, risking our lives for this?"

Lucian Thorne, a young man with hair as dark as the night and eyes that burned like embers, paused for a moment, his gaze focused on the path ahead. His face was marked with a fierce determination, forged by years of hardship and sacrifice.

"The prophecy speaks of a time when darkness will threaten to consume all of creation," he replied solemnly. "It is said that a chosen one, along with his allies, will rise to face this evil and protect the world from being swallowed whole."

As Lucian recounted the ancient words, his thoughts turned inward to the numerous battles he had fought, both within himself and against external enemies. He had been haunted by dreams of fire and destruction, of a world teetering on the edge of oblivion. Through it all, he held onto the belief that he was destined for something greater, that he had been chosen to lead this quest and save the world from annihilation.

"Are you sure it's us?" asked Nalia, her voice trembling despite her best efforts to remain composed.

"Something deep within tells me it is so," Lucian answered, his eyes meeting hers with a mixture of conviction and vulnerability. "I cannot explain it, but I feel it in my very core. We must fulfill this prophecy or watch our world fade into the abyss."

"Besides," he continued, his expression shifting to a more resolute one, "we have faced countless perils together, and emerged stronger each time. I have faith that we will rise to this challenge as well."

As the group pressed on, Lucian's thoughts turned to his unique abilities– a natural talent for strategy and an uncanny ability to inspire those around him. He knew that these gifts would be put to the ultimate test in the trials ahead, but he also believed that he was not alone in this fight.

"Remember," he said, his voice steady and strong, "we are a team. Our strength lies not just in our individual powers, but in our unity. Stand by my side, and together, we will overcome even the darkest of foes."

With renewed determination, Lucian led his allies deeper into the heart of the temple, ready to face whatever challenges lay ahead. The fate of the world rested upon their shoulders, and they would not– could not– falter now.

The air grew colder as they descended further into the temple, the weight of their task pressing down on them like a heavy fog. Lucian could feel the oppressive atmosphere, but he didn't allow it to deter him. He knew that at the heart of this ancient place lay the artifact– an object of immense power that held the key to preventing the apocalypse.

"Legend speaks of the Eye of Eternity," Lucian said, his voice echoing through the dark corridor. "An orb crafted by the gods themselves, imbued with the power to reshape reality. It is said to be a perfect sphere of obsidian, smooth and cold to the touch, with an inner core that glows like the embers of creation."

His allies glanced at each other nervously, aware of the gravity of their mission. Lucian could see the fear in their eyes, but also the spark of determination that had brought them this far.

"Imagine the chaos that would ensue if such power were to fall into the wrong hands," he continued. "Demons and fallen angels would vie for control, tearing our world apart in their struggle for supremacy. It is up to us to ensure that this artifact remains beyond their reach."

As they moved deeper into the temple, their path lit only by flickering torchlight, Lucian couldn't shake the feeling that time was running out.

The prophecy had foretold the coming of a great darkness, one that would consume all in its path, and he knew that they were the last line of defense against this terrible fate.

"Every moment we waste brings us closer to catastrophe," he thought, his heart pounding in his chest. "We must find the Eye of Eternity before it's too late."

"Lucian," whispered one of his allies, her voice trembling with urgency, "we will stand by you until the end. We will face whatever horrors lie ahead, and we will fight to save our world."

"Thank you," he replied, his eyes filled with gratitude. "Your courage gives me strength."

Together, they pressed on into the darkness, their resolve unwavering as they faced the unknown. The fate of mankind hung in the balance, and Lucian Thorne knew that he must not fail.

Determined to reach the forbidden temple, Lucian Thorne and his allies braced themselves for the treacherous journey that lay ahead of them. They traversed through an eerie landscape, riddled with remnants of a forsaken world. The sky was stained crimson as if it bore witness to the unceasing bloodshed in the bygone days.

"Stay vigilant," Lucian warned his companions, his eyes scanning the horizon for potential threats. "We cannot afford to be blindsided."

As they ventured forth, the terrain grew increasingly inhospitable. Towering mountains rose before them like jagged teeth, ready to devour any trespassers. The air thinned and grew colder, each breath a painful reminder of the unforgiving elements.

"Lucian," panted one of his allies, struggling to keep up with his relentless pace, "how much further must we go?"

"Every step might be our last," Lucian replied, his voice resolute. "We must press on if we are to save our world."

The path twisted and turned through treacherous valleys and dark forests filled with sinister shadows. At every turn, unseen dangers lurked; demonic creatures slithered in the underbrush, their malevolent gazes tracking their progress.

"Stand back!" Lucian shouted, unsheathing his sword as a monstrous beast lunged at him from the shadows. With a swift and decisive strike, he felled the creature, its lifeless body crumpling to the ground.

"By the Almighty, what was that?" gasped another of Lucian's allies, her face pale with fear.

"An emissary of darkness," Lucian replied grimly, wiping his blade clean. "We must be nearing the temple."

His heart raced as they continued their perilous journey, knowing that every victory came at a cost. Their numbers dwindled, claimed by the treacherous landscape and relentless onslaught of demonic forces.

"Lucian," whispered his remaining ally, her voice weary but resolute, "we will not abandon you. We will see this through to the end."

"Your loyalty strengthens me," he replied, a fierce determination burning in his eyes. "The fate of mankind rests upon our shoulders."

Finally, after what felt like an eternity of struggle and pain, they arrived at the entrance of the forbidden temple. Its foreboding presence loomed over them like an ancient tombstone, a testament to the darkness that lay within its walls.

"By the grace of the Almighty, we have made it," Lucian breathed, his heart pounding with anticipation. "Now we must face the trials that await us within."

"May the light guide us," his allies murmured in unison, their voices trembling with fear and hope.

Together, they stood before the imposing entrance, steeling themselves for the battles yet to come. The fate of the world hung in the balance, and Lucian Thorne knew that there was no turning back.

The heavy doors of the forbidden temple groaned in protest as Lucian and his allies pushed them open, revealing a dimly lit chamber that stretched far into the distance. It was as if they had stepped into another world, one shrouded in darkness and whispering secrets long forgotten by man.

"Keep your wits about you," Lucian warned his companions, his voice echoing through the vast expanse. "We know not what awaits us here."

Their footsteps echoed eerily as they ventured deeper into the temple. The walls loomed high above them, adorned with intricately carved symbols that seemed to writhe and twist beneath the flickering light of their torches. A sense of ancient power filled the air, suffocating and oppressive, as though the very stones themselves were alive with malevolent intent.

"Look at these markings," one of Lucian's companions muttered, her eyes wide with wonder and trepidation. "They tell a story... a prophecy, perhaps. But it's like nothing I've ever seen before."

"Stay focused," Lucian replied, his own gaze drawn to the mesmerizing symbols. "We cannot afford to be distracted by riddles and mysteries. We must find the artifact."

As they delved further into the temple, the air grew colder, and a palpable tension settled over the group like a noose tightening around their necks. Lucian could feel the weight of unseen eyes watching them, waiting for the opportune moment to strike.

"Lucian, look out!" shouted one of his companions, just as a hidden panel on the floor gave way beneath him.

"Thanks for the warning," he grunted, leaping to safety just in time. He scowled at the now-exposed pit below, its depths obscured by darkness. "It seems we have found the temple's first line of defense."

"Stay vigilant," another companion added, her eyes scanning the chamber for any further traps. "We cannot let our guard down."

"Indeed," Lucian agreed, his heart pounding in his chest as he took a step forward. "We must be prepared for anything."

The temple's guardians revealed themselves soon enough. Monstrous creatures, half man and half beast, emerged from the shadows with a guttural snarl, their eyes burning like embers in the darkness.

"Stand your ground!" Lucian commanded, drawing his sword as he faced the abominations before them. "Remember why we fight!"

"May the Almighty grant us strength," his allies murmured, steeling themselves for the battle to come.

As they prepared to confront the twisted guardians of the temple, Lucian's thoughts turned to the ancient prophecy that had led them here. The fate of mankind rested upon their shoulders, and he knew that failure was not an option. With a silent prayer for guidance, he charged into the fray, determined to retrieve the artifact at any cost.

The monstrous creatures snarled and lunged, but Lucian's fierce determination propelled him forward. He parried their blows with expert precision, his sword slicing through the air in a deadly dance. Sweat dripped down his brow, yet he fought on, driven by the knowledge that the fate of mankind rested upon his shoulders.

"Left flank!" he shouted to his companions, his voice a clarion call amidst the chaos. "We can't let them surround us!"

"Understood!" one replied, launching an attack to keep the abominations at bay.

As Lucian fought, he observed the creatures' movements, noting their speed and ferocity. It was clear that brute force alone would not be enough to defeat these guardians— they needed a plan. And quickly.

"Rally to me," he called, forcing a brief respite from the onslaught as his allies formed a protective circle around him. "Listen carefully: we must use our environment to our advantage. See those pillars? They look unstable. If we can topple them, we may be able to crush our foes."

"Or ourselves," a companion pointed out grimly, eyeing the towering columns warily.

"Trust me," Lucian urged, his eyes blazing with conviction. "It is our best chance for survival."

With a nod of agreement, they sprang into action. As they executed Lucian's plan, his mind raced ahead, anticipating the challenges that still awaited them. The prophecy had spoken of darkness and unimaginable power lurking within the heart of the temple, and they had come too far to falter now.

"Prepare yourselves," he warned his companions as the last guardian fell, crushed beneath the weight of the collapsed pillar. "Our true test lies ahead."

As they ventured deeper into the temple, the air grew colder and more oppressive. Shadows seemed to writhe and slither across the walls, hinting at the malevolent forces that awaited them.

"Stay close," Lucian commanded, his voice steady despite the unease gnawing at his heart. "We must remain united if we are to overcome what lies ahead."

"May the Almighty protect us," one whispered fervently, her words echoing through the darkened corridors like a ghostly lament.

"Have faith," Lucian urged, steeling himself for the trials to come. "Together, we shall prevail."

Yet even as he spoke, he could not shake the sense of foreboding that clung to him like a shroud. The power and darkness prophesied by the ancient texts seemed to pulse within the very stone of the temple, drawing ever nearer as they approached its heart. And Lucian Thorne, chosen by fate to stand against the end of days, could only pray that he would prove worthy of the task.

At last, they reached a chamber which seemed to be the heart of the temple. The walls were adorned with ancient symbols and scenes of apocalyptic destruction, depicting the end of days in chilling detail. In the center stood a pedestal, upon which lay the artifact—an unassuming object, yet one that held the power to seal away the darkness or unleash it upon the world.

"Is this…?" one of Lucian's allies murmured, eyes wide with awe and dread.

"Indeed," Lucian confirmed, his voice barely more than a whisper, as if speaking too loudly would disturb the fragile balance that held the darkness at bay. "The artifact. Our salvation…or our doom."

He stepped forward, reaching out hesitantly towards the object. The air crackled with unseen energy, making the hairs on his arms stand on end. He could feel the immense power radiating from the artifact, and he prayed silently for the strength and wisdom to wield it wisely.

"Lucian…" another companion warned, fear lacing her words. "Be cautious. The prophecy speaks of dire consequences should the artifact fall into unworthy hands."

"I know," Lucian responded, his gaze never leaving the relic. His heart raced, but he forced himself to remain calm and focused. This was his destiny, the culmination of his journey. Failure was not an option.

"May the Almighty guide my hand," he whispered, feeling the weight of the world resting on his shoulders.

Just as his fingertips brushed against the cool surface of the artifact, a sudden rush of cold air swept through the chamber, extinguishing their torches and plunging them into darkness. The ground beneath them trembled, and a guttural, sinister laughter echoed through the shadows.

"Too late, mortal!" a voice boomed, dripping with malice. "The artifact is mine!"

"Show yourself!" Lucian demanded, his heart pounding in his chest. He struggled to maintain control of his fear, but the darkness that now enveloped them was unlike anything he had ever experienced– a void so absolute, it seemed to swallow all hope and light.

"Who dares to challenge me?" the voice mocked, its laughter ringing like the tolling of a funeral bell.

"Lucian Thorne," he declared, steeling himself for the battle to come. "Chosen by destiny to stand against you and your wickedness!"

"Ah, yes…the prophesied one," the voice sneered. "And yet, you are too late! The end of days is upon us, and there is nothing you can do to stop it!"

As the voice spoke, a swirling vortex of shadows coalesced before them, revealing an immense, monstrous figure that seemed to be made of darkness itself. It towered over Lucian and his allies, radiating a palpable aura of evil and malice.

"Behold!" the creature roared. "I am the harbinger of your doom, and the artifact shall be the instrument of your destruction!"

With a roar of defiance, Lucian lunged forward, determined to seize the artifact and prevent the monster from fulfilling its dark purpose. But as his fingers closed around the relic, a searing pain shot through him, forcing him to cry out and stumble back.

"NO!" he screamed, clutching at his injured hand. "This cannot be!"

"Your struggle is futile, chosen one!" the creature laughed, its voice echoing with triumph. "The end of days has begun, and none can stand against me!"

"Lucian!" one of his companions cried, desperation etched on her face. "We must flee! There is no hope here!"

"Is this truly the end?" another whispered, tears streaming down her cheeks.

"Or is it only the beginning?" Lucian wondered, his heart heavy with despair as the darkness closed in around them, leaving him to question whether they had been too late to prevent the cataclysm that now threatened to engulf the world.

In a world on the brink of destruction, Lucian is the chosen one tasked with preventing the end of days. He and his companions are faced with a creature who claims to be the harbinger of their doom and wields an artifact that could bring about their destruction.

With a fierce determination, Lucian lunges forward to seize the relic, despite the searing pain that shoots through him. He quickly realizes that his struggle is futile against the powerful creature who taunts him with his impending defeat. Lucian's companions urge him to flee, but their cries are filled with desperation as they question whether there is any hope left in this world.

As the darkness closes in around them, Lucian wonders if it truly is the end or only the beginning of something greater. The weight of despair bears down on him as he contemplates whether they were too late to prevent the cataclysm that threatens to engulf their world.

Despite the odds stacked against them, Lucian and his companions continue their fight against the creature and its artifact. They face countless challenges and obstacles along the way, but their determination never wavers.

As the conflict between good and evil reaches its climax, Lucian must make a difficult decision that could change everything. With the fate of the world resting on his shoulders, he must summon all of his strength and courage to face the creature one last time.

In a stunning turn of events, Lucian and his companions emerge victorious, having saved the world from certain doom. As they bask in their triumph, they realize that this is not the end but only the beginning of a new chapter in their lives.

The world stood on the precipice of annihilation, trembling beneath an oppressive sky of smoldering embers. Desperation clung to the very air, thick and suffocating as it saturated the hearts and souls of the people who wandered aimlessly through the dying streets. Mothers clutched their children close, their faces etched with hopelessness and fear as they stared into an uncertain future. The once-prosperous cities now lay in ruins, monuments to the arrogance and folly of man, while darkness devoured the last vestiges of light.

It was then that a mysterious event occurred, one that would shake the foundations of the earth and set in motion the wheels of fate. A sudden gust of wind tore through the desolate landscape, carrying with it whispers of ancient prophecy long buried by time. The whispered words wound their way through the despairing crowds, prickling at the ears of men and women alike, igniting within them a spark of curiosity and dread.

"Repent...atonement...the chosen one...the harbinger," the voices murmured as they coalesced into a single, haunting refrain. "The end is nigh."

The cryptic message spread like wildfire, fueling the flames of anticipation and intrigue. The prophecy spoke of a world on the brink of destruction, threatened by a terrible force known only as the Harbinger, its eyes aglow with a sinister red light. Yet amid the chaos and strife, there was also a glimmer of hope– a chosen one, destined to rise up against the encroaching darkness and deliver mankind from the jaws of oblivion.

As the whispers of prophecy echoed through the ravaged cityscape, lost souls huddled together in prayer, searching for solace and redemption in the face of certain doom. And all the while, unbeknownst to them, the Harbinger's wrath drew ever closer, its ominous shadow looming large on the horizon.

Despite the oppressive shadow cast by the harbinger's presence, the world still clung to remnants of its former beauty. Vast oceans stretched out to the horizon, their waters shimmering with a million shades of blue, while towering mountains reached for the heavens as if in silent defiance of the darkness that sought to claim them. Lush forests swayed gently in the breeze, their verdant canopy pierced by shafts of sunlight that dappled the earth below.

"Look at this," Lucian murmured, gazing across the landscape with awe. "How can something so beautiful be on the verge of annihilation?"

"Because beauty and destruction have always been bound together," Ariadne replied, her wise eyes searching the horizon. "Nature itself is a paradox– life springs from decay, creation follows destruction. But we forget that balance too often."

A shiver ran down Lucian's spine as he watched a storm gathering in the distance, its brooding clouds heavy with menace. The once-calm sea churned furiously, waves crashing against the shore with a violence that shook the earth beneath their feet. In the mountains, eerie red lights flickered like warning beacons, heralding the approach of the harbinger. Even the ancient trees seemed to tremble in fear, their branches creaking and groaning under an unseen weight.

"Can you feel it?" Ariadne asked, her voice barely audible above the howling wind. "The harbinger's power grows stronger with each passing moment. It feeds on the despair of the people, and soon it will be unstoppable."

Lucian's heart hammered in his chest, his thoughts racing as fast as the storm winds. He knew deep down that Ariadne was right– the harbinger would not rest until the world was plunged into darkness. And yet, he couldn't help but wonder: what could one man do against such an unstoppable force?

"Is there really nothing we can do?" he asked, his voice cracking with desperation.

"Perhaps," Ariadne replied cryptically. "But only if we can find the chosen one before it's too late."

"Chosen one?" Lucian scoffed, trying to mask his fear with bravado. "Sounds like a fairy tale to me."

"Sometimes, even the most fantastical tales hold grains of truth," Ariadne said softly. "Look around you, Lucian. The world is dying, and we are its last hope. If we don't believe in miracles now, when will we?"

For a moment, Lucian was silent, his eyes scanning the doomed landscape as he grappled with the weight of Ariadne's words. The knowledge that he might be their world's only salvation was both overwhelming and terrifying. But as he looked upon the remnants of nature's beauty, he felt something stir within him— a fierce determination that refused to be snuffed out by the encroaching darkness.

"Alright," he whispered, steeling himself for the battle ahead. "Let's find this chosen one and bring an end to this nightmare."

The sky overhead was a tapestry of grey, with angry storm clouds rolling and churning like the sea. From his vantage point, Lucian could see the devastation that had been wrought upon the once-thriving world: forests reduced to charred skeletons, rivers choked with ash, and the remains of cities swallowed by the encroaching darkness. He felt a chill slither down his spine as he stared out at the desolate landscape, knowing that the harbinger's power grew stronger with each passing day.

"By the heavens," Lucian muttered under his breath, clenching his fists in helpless rage. "What have we done to deserve this?"

As he turned away from the crumbling edge of a precipice, his piercing blue eyes caught sight of something unusual on a nearby wall. A strange symbol had been etched into the worn stone, its lines angular and sharp, like jagged shards of glass. Intrigued, he stepped closer, running his fingers over the grooves as if attempting to decipher some hidden message.

"Is there something you're looking for?" Lucian murmured to himself, furrowing his brow in concentration. "Or is this just another cruel joke from the powers that be?"

"Lucian, come quickly!" called a voice behind him, pulling him from his thoughts. He recognized the voice as belonging to Ariadne, the wise elder who had spoken cryptically of prophecies and chosen ones. Lucian sighed inwardly, wondering what new revelation awaited them now.

"Coming," he replied, casting one last glance at the mysterious symbol before turning to race towards Ariadne. As he ran, his mind churned with questions and doubt, the weight of the world's fate bearing down upon his shoulders like an unbearable burden.

"Could I truly be the one destined to face the harbinger?" he wondered, feeling a tightening knot of fear in his chest. "And if so, do I even stand a chance against such darkness?"

"Lucian, look!" Ariadne cried, pointing towards the horizon as he caught up to her. A mass of swirling black clouds had gathered, casting an oppressive shadow over the land. In the distance, eerie red lights flickered and danced like malevolent spirits.

"By the gods," Lucian breathed, his heart pounding in his chest as he stared at the ominous scene. "The harbinger is coming."

"Indeed," Ariadne replied solemnly. "And it falls upon you, Lucian, to confront this evil and save our world from destruction."

As the words left her lips, a surge of determination coursed through Lucian's veins, pushing back the fear that threatened to consume him. He knew that he could not turn away from this responsibility, no matter how daunting it seemed. The lives of countless innocents hung in the balance, and he would do everything in his power to protect them— even if it meant facing the harbinger itself.

"Then I shall face it," he declared, his voice steady despite the trepidation that lingered in his heart. "But first, I must learn more about this prophecy and the symbol I found."

"Very well," Ariadne nodded, her eyes alight with pride and hope. "We will search together, and may the fates guide us on this perilous journey."

As they turned to face the uncertain future, Lucian vowed silently that he would not rest until he had unraveled the mysteries surrounding the prophecy and defeated the harbinger once and for all. For the sake of his people, and for the world they called home, he would become the chosen one– or die trying.

The air was thick with acrid smoke as Lucian stood in the heart of the crumbling city, his piercing blue eyes scanning the chaos that unfolded around him. All around him, people ran in terror, their faces etched with fear and desperation. Mothers clutched their children close, trying to shield them from the horrors that manifested before them, while others wept openly, their tears streaming down dirt-streaked faces. The screams of the dying mingled with the anguished cries of those who had lost everything, creating a cacophony of despair that echoed through the ruins.

"Help us!" a man cried out, reaching for Lucian with a trembling hand. "Please! We don't know what to do!"

"Everyone's going mad," a woman whispered, her voice barely audible above the din. "We're all doomed."

As he looked around at the terrified faces, Lucian felt a knot tighten in his chest– the weight of responsibility settling upon his shoulders. It was clear that the prophecy he had stumbled upon was more than just a myth; it was the harbinger of the end of days. And if the symbol etched into the wall held any truth, then it seemed that he, of all people, might be the one destined to confront this apocalyptic force.

"Lucian," a voice called out, its timbre soft yet commanding. He turned to see Ariadne, an elderly woman with long silver hair and wise, kind eyes. Despite the chaos swirling around her, she remained steadfast and calm, her gaze never wavering from his. "You are the one spoken of in the prophecy, the chosen one who will stand against the darkness."

"Me?" Lucian stammered, his thoughts racing. "But but how can I be the one? I'm just..."

"Destiny does not always choose the likeliest of heroes, Lucian," Ariadne replied, her voice gentle but firm. "You have been chosen not because of your strength or your prowess, but because of your heart. You possess a courage and a compassion that few others can match– qualities that will serve you well in the battles to come."

"Then what must I do?" he asked, his resolve hardening even as fear gnawed at him. "How can I stop this this harbinger?"

"First, you must learn all you can about the prophecy and the forces that drive it," Ariadne answered, placing a gnarled hand upon his arm. "Only then can you hope to stand against the darkness and save our world from annihilation."

As she spoke, Lucian could feel the weight of the people's desperation pressing down upon him, their cries for help etching themselves into his soul. He knew that whatever the cost, he could not abandon them to their fate. And so, with a deep breath, he nodded in agreement, steeling himself for the trials that lay ahead.

"Very well," he said, his voice steady despite the turmoil within. "I accept my role as the chosen one. Together, we shall unravel the mysteries of the prophecy and face the harbinger– whatever it takes."

"May the fates guide us on this perilous journey," Ariadne murmured, her eyes shining with both pride and hope. As they turned to face the uncertain future, Lucian vowed that he would not rest until he had banished the darkness once and for all– for the sake of his people, and for the world they called home.

Lucian stared at Ariadne, the weight of her words settling over him like a shroud. The thought of being the chosen one seemed preposterous; he was merely a man, and a damaged one at that. Yet as he looked around at the desperate faces of those surrounding them, doubt began to dissipate, replaced by an ember of something new– hope.

"Even if I were the one you speak of," Lucian said, his voice barely audible beneath the cacophony of cries and prayers, "how am I to find the harbinger? How do I even begin this journey?"

"Look around you, child," Ariadne replied, gesturing to the world beyond their cramped and crumbling sanctuary. "The harbinger's influence has spread, corrupting the very land itself."

Stepping outside, Lucian surveyed the landscape with fresh eyes. Once-lush forests now stood twisted and grotesque, their leaves blackened and lifeless as though drained of vitality. Barren wastelands stretched out in every direction, cracked earth yawning wide in gaping chasms, as if the world had been cleaved apart. Even the once-mighty mountains, which had served as a protective barrier for generations, now appeared treacherous, their jagged peaks obscured by an ominous, swirling darkness.

"Each terrain bears the mark of the harbinger's power," Ariadne continued, her voice low and solemn. "You must traverse them all to uncover the truth hidden within the prophecy."

As they spoke, Lucian's heart pounded in his chest, a mixture of fear and determination coursing through his veins. Though his mind railed against the idea of being the world's savior, he couldn't ignore the feeling deep within him– a sense that perhaps Ariadne was right, and he did hold the key to saving their world from destruction.

"Very well," he said at last, his voice laced with the faintest hint of resolve. "I will embark on this journey and seek out the harbinger's trail. But I do not know what I will find, nor if I have the strength to face it."

"Your strength comes from within, Lucian," Ariadne replied, her eyes filled with a fierce, unwavering belief in him. "Remember that you are not alone. We stand with you, and together, we shall confront the darkness and restore balance to our world."

As he set forth into the ravaged terrains, Lucian couldn't help but feel a flicker of hope begin to burn brighter within him. The road ahead would be treacherous, but with each step, he felt more determined to fulfill his destiny– not only for himself, but for the countless lives depending on him.

"May the fates protect us all," he whispered, steeling himself for the journey that lay before him. And with that, Lucian ventured forth into the unknown, vowing to face whatever trials awaited him with courage and conviction.

As Lucian ventured deeper into the varied landscape, he couldn't shake the eerie feeling that the harbinger's influence was ever-present. The sky above churned with dark clouds, swirling like a cauldron of malevolence. In the distance, flickers of red light danced ominously on the horizon, casting eerie shadows across the desolate wastelands and lush forests alike. He felt a shiver run down his spine, as if ice-cold fingers were tracing the curve of his back.

"Is this the work of the harbinger?" Lucian muttered to himself, his eyes scanning the foreboding surroundings warily. His breaths were short and shallow, betraying the unease that stirred within him.

"Indeed," a voice echoed in response, deep and chilling. "Witness the power that I wield, Lucian."

He whipped around, his heart pounding in his chest as he faced the source of the voice. Towering before him was a figure cloaked in darkness, its form obscured by the shadows that seemed to cling to it like a shroud. Two glowing red orbs pierced through the gloom, locking onto Lucian with an intensity that sent a fresh wave of terror coursing through his veins.

"You... you are the harbinger," Lucian stammered, struggling to maintain a façade of bravery in the face of such a formidable foe. His hands clenched into fists at his sides, trembling with adrenaline-fueled anticipation.

"Very perceptive," the harbinger sneered, its voice dripping with disdain. "But what does it matter? You are but a mere human– weak, fragile, and utterly insignificant."

"No," Lucian thought, his resolve steeling within him. "I cannot let fear control me. Ariadne said I have the strength within to face this evil, and I must trust her words."

"Perhaps," Lucian responded, his voice steadier than before, "but I am not alone. The people of this world stand with me, and together, we will put an end to your reign of terror."

"Your confidence is amusing, if misplaced," the harbinger retorted, its laughter a low rumble that echoed through the air like thunder. "Soon, you shall bear witness to the true extent of my power. And when that time comes, you will realize the futility of your defiance."

"Your threats mean nothing to me," Lucian shot back, his determination unwavering. "I will find a way to stop you— no matter the cost."

"Then let the final act begin," the harbinger declared ominously, its red eyes blazing with unbridled fury. "May the darkness consume you, Lucian... and may your futile struggle serve as a testament to the utter despair that awaits all who dare to defy me."

As the harbinger's form faded into the shadows, leaving only the echo of its sinister laughter in its wake, Lucian steeled himself for the trials ahead. The path before him was fraught with danger and uncertainty, but he had come too far to turn back now.

"Let the final act begin," Lucian whispered, repeating the harbinger's words as a vow. He knew that the fate of the world rested on his shoulders, and he would not— could not— falter. No matter what horrors awaited him, he would face them head-on, armed with the strength of those who believed in him and the burning resolve that coursed through his very soul.

The ground trembled beneath Lucian's feet as the harbinger raised its arm, clutching a mysterious artifact that pulsed with an ominous energy. The object appeared ancient and sinister— a twisted, gnarled relic that seemed to be alive with malevolence.

"Behold the power that will bring this world to its knees," the harbinger boomed, its voice resonating like thunder through the air, causing the onlookers' hearts to pound violently in their chests.

With a swift motion, the harbinger thrust the artifact into the sky. A deafening crack echoed across the landscape, followed by a blinding flash of light that illuminated the surrounding area with an unnatural, blood-red hue. In an instant, the earth ruptured, swallowing entire buildings and sending people screaming into the abyss below.

"Merciful God, save us!" a woman cried out, her hands clasped together in fervent prayer.

"Please, someone help us!" another man shouted, his voice barely audible above the cacophony of destruction.

Lucian could feel the terror welling up within the crowd, their fear palpable as they watched the harbinger's destructive demonstration unfold before them. He too was gripped by an icy dread, but he fought to suppress it, focusing instead on the task at hand.

"Is this truly the end of all things?" Lucian thought, his mind racing as he searched for some way to counteract the harbinger's influence. "There must be something I can do."

"Your faith is touching, but futile," the harbinger sneered, seemingly able to read Lucian's thoughts. "You cannot stop the inevitable. This world has been judged, and it has been found wanting."

"Judged by whom?" Lucian demanded, struggling to maintain his composure. "By you? What gives you the right to decide the fate of countless lives?"

"By forces far beyond your comprehension, mortal," the harbinger replied cryptically. "But know this— I am but a harbinger of what is to come. The true darkness has yet to reveal itself."

As Lucian watched the people around him succumb to despair, their faces contorted with anguish and terror, something within him stirred— an unyielding resolve to stand against the harbinger and its cruel machinations.

"Then I will fight," Lucian vowed silently, steeling himself for the battle ahead. "I will defy the darkness and protect those who cannot protect themselves. No matter the cost."

In the midst of chaos and destruction, Lucian stood tall, his blue eyes ablaze with a mixture of defiance and determination. The world around him seemed to crumble as if it were made of sand, buildings collapsing and people screaming in terror. Yet, Lucian remained steadfast, his gaze locked onto the harbinger.

"Even now, you believe you can save them?" the harbinger taunted, its voice cold and devoid of empathy.

"Someone has to try," Lucian retorted, clenching his fists at his sides. "If I am the chosen one, then it's my duty to protect these people."

"Your duty, you say? And what makes you think that your duty carries any weight in the face of annihilation?" the harbinger countered, its red eyes burning like embers.

Lucian hesitated for a moment, his thoughts swirling like a whirlwind. He knew he couldn't let the harrowing scene before him distract him from his purpose. His heart pounded in his chest as he took a deep breath, seeking the strength within himself.

"Because I refuse to stand idly by and watch this world fall," Lucian declared, his voice strong and unwavering. "I will fight for those who cannot. I will defy whatever darkness you claim awaits us."

A bitter laugh escaped the harbinger's lips. "Very well, chosen one. If you wish to embrace your so-called destiny, then come and face me. But know that your struggle is ultimately futile."

"Maybe," Lucian admitted, his resolve hardening. "But if there's even a chance that I can make a difference, I have to take it."

As Lucian stepped forward, his every movement filled with a newfound sense of purpose, the people around him began to take notice. Among the fear and despair etched on their faces, a glimmer of hope began to shine through, as if Lucian's determination had ignited a spark within them.

"Look!" cried a woman, her tears momentarily forgotten. "The chosen one! He stands against the harbinger!"

"Then we must stand with him," shouted a man, his voice hoarse but resolute. "We cannot let him fight alone!"

One by one, the people rallied behind Lucian, their fear and desperation replaced by courage and solidarity. And as they prepared to face the harbinger together, Lucian knew that he had made the right choice.

"Let this be our final stand," he whispered, his eyes locked onto the harbinger's menacing figure. "Together, we will defy the darkness."

And with that, Lucian led the charge, the fate of the world resting on his shoulders as he embraced his role as the chosen one. The end of days loomed before them, yet hope refused to be extinguished– for as long as there was light, the darkness could not claim victory.

INTERMISSION
TO BE CONTINUE

SATAN'S FINAL BATTLE

References

REVELATION 12:12— THE NEW INTERNATIONAL VERSION (NIV)

[12]Therefore rejoice, you heavens
and you who dwell in them!
But woe to the earth and the sea,
because the devil has gone down to you!
He is filled with fury,
because he knows that his time is short."

English Standard Version **Genesis 3:1–23**

THE FALL

3 Now [u]the serpent was more crafty than any other beast of the field that the Lord God had made.

He said to the woman, "Did God actually say, 'You [1]shall not eat of any tree in the garden'?"**2** And the woman said to the serpent, "We may eat of the fruit of the trees in the garden, **3** but God said, [v]"You shall not eat of the fruit of the tree that is in the midst of the garden, neither shall you touch it, lest you die.'"**4** [w]"But the serpent said to the woman, "You will not surely die. **5** For God knows that when you eat of it your eyes will be opened, and you will be like God, knowing good and evil."**6** So when the woman saw that the tree was good for food, and that it was a delight to the eyes, and that the tree was to be desired to make one wise,[z]she took of its fruit [x]and ate, and she also gave some to her husband who was with her, [y]and he ate.**7** [z]Then the eyes of both were opened, a[and] they knew that they were naked. And they sewed fig leaves together and made themselves loincloths.

8And they heard the sound of theLordGod walking in the garden in the cool ³of the day, and the man and his wife ᵇhid themselves from the presence of the Lord God among the trees of the garden. **9**But the Lord God called to the man and said to him, "Where are you?" ⁴**10** And he said, "I heard the sound of you in the garden, and I was afraid, ᶜbecause I was naked, and I hid myself."**11**He said, "Who told you that you were naked? Have you eaten of the tree of which I commanded you not to eat?"**12**The man said, ᵈ "The woman whom you gave to be with me, she gave me fruit of the tree, and I ate."**13**Then the Lord God said to the woman, "What is this that you have done?" The woman said, ᵉ "The serpent deceived me, and I ate."

14The Lord God said to the serpent,
"Because you have done this,
cursed are you above all livestock
and above all beasts of the field;
on your belly you shall go,
and ᶠdust you shall eat
all the days of your life.

15 I will put enmity between you and the woman,
and between your offspring ⁵and ᵍher offspring;
hhe shall bruise your head,
and you shall bruise his heel."

16 To the woman he said,
"I will surely multiply your pain in childbearing;
iin pain you shall bring forth children.
jYour desire shall be contrary to 6your husband,
but he shall krule over you."

17 And to Adam he said,
"Because you have listened to the voice of your wife
and have eaten of the tree
lof which I commanded you,
'You shall not eat of it,'

mcursed is the ground because of you;
nin pain you shall eat of it all the days of your life;

18 thorns and thistles it shall bring forth for you;
and you shall eat the plants of the field.

19 By the sweat of your face
you shall eat bread,
till you return to the ground,
for out of it you were taken;
ofor you are dust,
and pto dust you shall return."

20The man called his wife's name Eve, because she was the mother of all living. [7]**21**And theLord God made for Adam and for his wife garments of skins and clothed them.

22Then the Lord God said, q "Behold, the man has become like one of us in knowing good and evil. Now, lest he reach out his hand rand take also of the tree of life and eat, and live forever—" **23**therefore the Lord God sent him out from the garden of Eden sto work the ground from which he was taken.

EPHESIANS 6:12– THE NEW INTERNATIONAL VERSION (NIV)

[12]***For our struggle is not against flesh and blood, but against the rulers, against the authorities, against the powers of this dark world and against the spiritual forces of evil in the heavenly realms.***

Revelation 12:1-17

Isaiah 51:9)

(Revelation 12:1-4

Revelation 12:5;

Psalm 2:1-12)

Revelation 12:7-9).

Revelation 12:10

 Matthew 28:18)

Revelation 12:11

(Revelation 12:12

Revelation 12:12)

Romans 1:18-32,

Revelation 15:1-16:21

I PLEDGE ALLEGIANCE TO THE FLAG OF THE UNITED STATES OF AMERICA, AND TO THE REPUBLIC FOR WHICH IT STANDS, ONE NATION UNDER GOD, INDIVISIBLE, WITH LIBERTY AND JUSTICE FOR ALL.

Milton Keynes UK
Ingram Content Group UK Ltd.
UKHW010704220524
443011UK00011B/181/J